He
fou
cree

She
she
out
Go

Wi
sw
kn
obe

"He
voi

"Th
fol
mi

...ast beside her, still holding her hand." Willy was ...hind an hour ago," he said. "By a canoeist, in the ...ek, half a mile below the Alibi."

...he didn't understand. Found? She felt guilty that ...was half-relieved. That it wasn't Emily, who was ...out with Widar. Or Vic, or Sharon and the baby. Oh,...

..."Willy?" "What was he doing in the creek? He can't ...swim. Tim never could teach him to swim. He ...knows enough to stay away from there. Willy always ...always. He won't go near the creek unless—"

..."He wasn't trying to swim, Ruth," Colm said, his ...voice gritty as dust. "He was dropped there."

...

..."This is fine storytelling, mixing some rural ...plainness with both big-time and small-time ...misdeeds."

—Publishers Weekly

Mad Season

Nancy Means Wright

TORONTO • NEW YORK • LONDON
AMSTERDAM • PARIS • SYDNEY • HAMBURG
STOCKHOLM • ATHENS • TOKYO • MILAN
MADRID • WARSAW • BUDAPEST • AUCKLAND

For my extended family—Vermonters all
and for Dennie Hannan

MAD SEASON

A Worldwide Mystery/April 1998

First published by St. Martin's Press, Incorporated.

ISBN 0-373-26270-1

Printed in U.S.A.

Spring at last, and all Hell's afire!
                    —author unknown

ONE

IT WASN'T USUAL, Lucien thought, this knocking in the middle of the night, and when it came, it meant an emergency of some kind. There was the trucker had run out of gas at two in the morning and come pounding on his door. The high school kids, drunk and run the car into the broad side of the barn. And he and Belle up most of the night trying to calm the cows.

The problem was they'd built the damned road too close to the house, and tricky the way the shoulder sloped down into the limestone ditch. How many he'd hauled out of that ditch he couldn't count. Big rain, and the mud slid off the road, taking the cars with it. Just yesterday a woman with red fingernails, car too big for the road, wanting more than help—wanting to buy his land, turn it into a hundred houses. Mother of God! "I'm not selling," he told Belle. "My grandpapa he didn't break his back on this land for nothing. I don't part with one goddamn foot of it, I'm telling you."

"They offered ten thousand dollars an acre over to Benoit's," Belle said, "and they took it."

But he said, "I got over half that right here, don't I?" and patted his inside pocket.

And Belle saying, "Only fools carry cash. The world's not the same's it was."

But he knew who were the fools. His own papa, for

one, God rest his soul. He trusted it all to that bank, and come the crash what'd he have but a caved-in barn and ninety-five acres of clay?

No, he'd keep his where it was safe. If they took the money, they'd take him. And who'd want him? Tough as an old mule he was, sure. Veins like rope, Belle said, skin like bull leather. She threatened to take the polish to it instead of soap. Hard weather and hard work, that's what it was. Up at four milking, planting, haying—jobs never ended. Now middle of the night hauling some poor fool, probably, out of the ditch. Mary and Joseph!

The knock came again, a man's voice, his name. "Lucien? Open the door, Lucien!"

Hey, door's unlocked, they didn't have to wait on him. He never locked it, though Belle starting to complain. But hell, if he didn't go, Belle would, and moan about the cold. Woodstove's not enough, she wants oil heat.

Here she was already awake, gray-black braid across her breast frizzing out under the elastic, but the breasts still firm. Only the one child, that's why. And that one a girl, with a ten-thumbed asshole of a husband. Who was to carry on?

"They're calling you," Belle said, like he couldn't hear. She heaved her thick body up on an elbow. "It's someone we know. Maybe next door. They been having trouble with that girl. She goes with the wrong kind, Ruth says so, stays out late."

"Lucien? Answer the door. I need help, Lucien!"

The voice unfamiliar. But it don't mean nothing. More folks in town knew him than he knew them.

They knew him because he ran for selectman that time, shook hands a lot. It was that Ruth Willmarth next door put him up to it. School budget up and getting so only flatlanders could afford to live here. So he stuck out his neck and lost to a flatlander by fifteen votes.

"Will you go or I go?" Belle said, "so's we can get back to sleep." He saw how wrinkly and puffed the skin was in the crease of her elbow, and her just sixty-three. It used to be soft when he married her. She was the prettiest thing he ever seen, down from a border town. Quebec roots like him, but a quarter Abenaki Indian in her. You saw it in the snap of the black eyes, way she walked, quiet, feet splayed a little. Then the farm took it out on her, slaving all day.

"I'll go," he said. He planted his feet on the splintery floor, then winced. It was only after a long sleep he felt the pain. Some days he thought he'd never walk again.

"Lucien? Come down," the voice said. "We run out of gas, Lucien." The kitchen door slammed.

The old dog, Raoul, barking—took a hurricane to get him to bark, he was that old. The men, for there was more than one sounded like, already inside.

Was it Halloween? Why were they here? Not gas they wanted. Stockings over their heads and faces, blue jeans, boots. It was the boots on the big one that startled him, the sharp smell of new leather, the hard pointed toes, some fancy silverwork. It was how fear smelled. He hadn't smelled it so bad for years, not since the war. The Fascist boots, kicking him.

He picked up the maple stick he prodded the cows

with. "You shouldn't be here," he said. He only meant to threaten them. One of them turning back already, the taller thinner one, calling back the other, he heard a muffled voice. But the big one, like a bull in heat, coming at him. Then there was Belle. He turned to warn her off.

"Get back," he said.

Something exploded in the side of his head. He wheeled about, was struck in the belly. The dog barked and went still. "Go, Belle," he groaned, doubled with pain, but she was bent over him, screaming. And then a thump like the sound of an overripe apple hitting the ground and Belle pitching across his foot, the big one standing over her.

He swung at the head with his stick, his fists. He was flung against the old Kelvinator, heard it squeal, knocked into the iron sink. He couldn't feel the pain now, just a numbness, the outrage. There was a tug-of-war for the stick, and he lost. Then it came: the stockinged head arched back, the boot lifted. It was the hurricane again, but now he was the porch, knocked off his props and flung in the air, crashing down on the other side of the house, the boards shrieking as they wrenched apart, fell in one on top of the other....

THERE WAS SOMETHING about this morning that made Ruth Willmarth uneasy—she didn't know what. Usually she enjoyed a morning like this, mist on the mountains, hugging the ground like shredded paper. "Shredded paper," she liked that. She'd had a poem in the high school lit magazine once. How did it go?

"The sun is a golden poppy—da-da da-da..." Was it almost twenty-four years ago? Her mind was foggy. Like all those years had never been, and there'd been nothing, ever, but this farm, and three children, and a grandchild already. And the husband who'd left for New York one morning after milking and hadn't come back.

She was so stunned she just kept running the farm. Took over the milking on top of the syruping, the records, dairy meetings, vet checks. It was unending, but she'd always liked a routine. What else could she do? Where else would she live?

She put the uneasiness down to worries about family: her son Vic, her daughter Emily coming in late last night—that city boyfriend! It was work that relieved the stress. She swept in the mangers, shoved back the bits of hay, grain, corn the cows had dropped in their stampede to eat. Another week or two and they'd be out in the field, in only for milking, which made it easier. Black-and-white Holsteins, thirty head. Used to be fifty but when Pete left she had to sell some. Kept the hired man, Tim, though. She couldn't do it alone!

Here was Tim now, coming up from the sugar house, the foster boy tagging behind. "Fields still too wet to plow," Tim said. "Maybe next week. So Willy and me gonna plant trees. Your husband ordered 'em last spring."

Scotch pine, for Christmas trees—Pete's plan for making use of a rocky area. He was always jumping on new money-making schemes: pigs, turkeys, soybeans. He'd abandon them when they got to be a hassle.

"If you think there's time. Not a thousand again?"

He grinned, nodded. He had on that cowboy hat he got out West one year, it looked ridiculous on him. He was still the hippie he'd been back in the sixties. But he gave a hard day's work, did half the milking, most of the syruping. "I thought Vic might help. We can get 'em in in a week and still finish up the sugaring."

"He'd rather do that," she agreed, "than help in the barn."

Lately her son Vic had refused barn chores altogether, wouldn't even feed his pet calf, didn't want the smell on him. Kids teasing him, that was why. "Farmer boy," they said, the city kids moving up here with their city ways.

Actually, she liked the idea of Vic working with Tim. Vic had taken Pete's leaving hard. She knew he needed him, especially with this trouble in the school. Though Pete wouldn't have done much about it. "Had to fight my own battles as a kid," was the cliché on his latest postcard.

"Can you hold the fort till noon?" she asked Tim. "I have errands in town."

"Consider it done. Hey, Willy? We'll hold the fort till the lady gets back?"

"Who's a lady?" she said, and smiling, held out her palms, red and mottled from barn chores and tough as winter gloves.

Tough lady, sure, but why this feeling deep in her bowels that something was going to happen, was already happening, to her family maybe? She ran, ran back to the house and took the porch steps in two jumps.

And inside found the fire had gone out in the wood-stove.

THE SUNLIGHT SWIPED at Lucien's face like a knife blade. Instinctively he threw up his hands. But then the light softened with the passing clouds, and he let them fall back across his chest. The window above him was crooked, a shiny diagonal. He squinted, and it sharpened into a blade of color.

It came over him that it wasn't the window that was wrong but himself. "Mother of God," he groaned. "What happened?"

When he tried to move, the joints screamed, like he was rusted out. He turned his neck to look for Belle. It was like twisting the top of an old bottle.

God, she was still there, crumpled like a piece of paper, braid across her eyes. He crawled to her, fumbled for her pulse, felt nothing, panicked, grasped her shoulders. "Belle, Belle!" Threw himself on her chest, his cheek against hers.

Then felt the barest breath. Or was it from the half-open door—they never closed that behind, fire out in the woodstove. And the dog, old Raoul, lying at a queer angle, front paws not matched up with the rear. Afraid to explore further, not wanting to in case the breath he felt was from outdoors; wanting, needing to hope, he dragged his body toward the phone. His arms hauled the belly behind like a hay rake. It bumped along with painful scrapes and grinds, a sharpness in an elbow where an elbow wasn't touching. The smell of leather boots still in the room, the smell of blood—his blood, Belle's. He cranked his head about; a red ring haloed her head where the blood sank into the floor. He was glad now he didn't get the linoleum in the kitchen though she wanted it, the living room was enough. Then she went and covered that with a rag rug. You never knew about women.

The phone wire was cut, they done that too. Outraged, he dragged himself to the door, hoisted his body over the sill. The porch needed sanding, painting, the old boards drove splinters into his hands, his knees, bare toes. He saw with surprise he was in his nightshirt and the sun up already—he was always dressed by sunup. And then he was down the steps, rolling, he couldn't walk: he'd get in a crouch and fall over, like the boot got him again—where? His cheek was bloody and full of holes, like he was Jesus nailed to the cross. Close his eyes and that was all he knew: the boot in the face, the smell of fear. And vomit up in his throat now.

He vomited into the mud, again and again, then just dry heaves. He wanted to let go right now, right here, collapse in the mud. He could die this minute, it'd be easy.

But there was Belle.

He hauled himself to the road. Someone would find him, pull him out of the mud like he done the others. Get to a phone. He lay down along the sloping shoulder of the road. He could only hope they wouldn't come around the bend too fast, mostly they did, town wouldn't put up a sign. He couldn't keep a lookout, he was that bad. He let his head drop in the mud. His body like trash you'd throw out a window.

When the car came, finally, he couldn't lift his head to see who.

IT WASN'T TILL she got Lucien to the hospital that Ruth thought of Belle. If Belle had been all right she'd have phoned, wouldn't she? "Where's Belle?" she asked as they loaded Lucien onto a stretcher. But his eyes were scrunched up in his head like he didn't want to know the answer, was driven deep into his bones. She almost hadn't stopped, was headed into the Larocque drive to get Lucien to help when she realized it was Lucien himself hurt. The ambulance was out when she phoned from home, so she and Tim got him in the car. Now if it was Pete, well, Pete had a way of never hurrying, even in emergency: He "had to think," he'd say. "I hope we never have a fire," she'd told him. "We'd be ashes before you decided to call the firemen."

But she wasn't thinking straight herself, was she? Halfway out to her car and she still hadn't called the police. Though it could have been some other kind of accident, farm accident. How many nights she'd lain awake worrying about fingers in the machinery, tractors overturning. It was in God's hands, her fundamentalist sister-in-law would say when the kids got pumping too high on the tire swing. And Pete would laugh, too, say God was the only way, though there was nothing spiritual about Pete.

So afterward she raced back to the Larocques'. Belle would be frantic, wondering where he was. She could phone the police from there. He must have been struck by a car, a hit and run. She balled her fists—irresponsible inhumans!

Was it true he kept money in his pockets? She'd heard that but couldn't imagine it. Lucien was different, but not dumb. Anyway, Belle wouldn't stand for it, Belle had smarts. Not classroom smarts, she never went past ninth grade, maybe tenth, but she could have, that was what counted.

Up on the porch Ruth saw where Lucien had come from, the blood stains on the old boards, the door cracking on its hinges where someone had banged it. It wasn't a car that struck him, then, but something else. She entered slowly, afraid of what she'd see.

And she saw.

TWO

IT WAS CRAZY, she told her older daughter Sharon afterward, after the police arrived, after the ambulance came back for Belle, her old friend Colm Hanna leaping into the rear. They were in the Larocque house: Ruth was puttering, though she'd been told not to touch anything. A policeman, Mert was his name, was in the parlor, snooping around—Belle would have hated that. Belle was neat, things were always in order. Ruth picked up a fry pan off the floor, though the officer yelled at her, straightened Lucien's overturned rocker.

"I thought, what a pretty nightgown," she told Sharon. "It doesn't suit Belle, I never see her in anything but ripped overalls, it's like she turns into someone else at night. A sleeping beauty."

"Lucien's the prince?" Sharon said, and smiled, opened her shirt to nurse her baby.

Ruth couldn't smile. "And then I saw the blood, it'd leaked out of her head, into the floorboards. And the dog, they killed the dog. That dog went everywhere with Lucien. It was all—"

"Don't say anymore," Sharon warned and held up her free arm. Sharon was like her father, Pete would pass out when you talked about blood; he fell once when she was bandaging Vic's knee, pitched into the TV. And Ruth had two patients on her hands.

"You're a woman, you're a mother, you have to hear these things," Ruth told Sharon, and Sharon looked secretive, bent to her child. "Belle would have gone out at once. It must have been a terrible blow to the head."

"She'll be all right." Sharon rubbed her chin on the child's fuzzy head. "She'll come through." She wouldn't hear otherwise.

"You go home with the baby," Ruth said. "Emily'll be back from school. I have Tim."

"Are you sure? You don't need moral support?"

"Go home," Ruth ordered, taking charge, though it was hard with Sharon. She waved them off. Her children underestimated her. She was shocked, yes, but charged with energy now—crazy! "Go, go! I'll call if I need you."

"I should get this child home for a nap."

"Yes, that's what I'm saying. Go." And Sharon went, appeased, the child bouncing in the backpack. "Bye-bye," said Ruth, distracted, "bye," though the boy was too young to wave.

With the door shut, the reality of it, the horror, leaped back on her. She couldn't stay in this house a minute longer. She gave the policeman her number and ran back next door. She had work to do, didn't she? A fire siren was sounding outdoors, but she only half heard it, like it was buzzing inside her head. She threw another log in the woodstove.

Stay calm, she told herself as she heated up pea soup for the men's lunch. Move slowly or things will collapse. What things, she wasn't sure, but she knew about the collapse. It came when least expected.

Like that old couple half dead in the hospital. Belle was in a coma, in intensive care, her friend Colm phoned back. Who knew when—if—she'd waken? And how awful to wake alone, a prisoner of tubes, and Lucien a corridor away, in a male ward.

The money was gone, of course. The police had searched the mattress, the closets, loose floorboards—there was only a handful of change in Lucien's coat, all bloodied as it was, the pockets ripped inside out; matches for the woodstove, bits of hay, bent nails, receipts the detective examined and pocketed. And no fingerprints anywhere, except Lucien's and Belle's. Not a single one. The assailants were prepared.

"That's what they were after, the money," said Colm Hanna, the volunteer medic, when he materialized again on his way back from the hospital. It was a double trip for him: first Belle, and then the Charlebois barn up in flames, he said, the hired man burned getting the calves out. She'd have to send over a pie, she thought, even while the Larocques were still on her mind.

They didn't have to know Lucien to have him open the door, she reminded Colm. "Lucien opens for everyone."

"They knew he had money hidden in the house," Colm said, looking foolish, his glasses on crooked, coat smudged with charcoal, his face black as his hair used to be when they went out together in high school—it was starting to gray now. He'd turned ambulance volunteer after he flunked out of med school, lived in the local funeral parlor with his undertaker

father. But earned his "bread," he told people, in real
estate.

"They had to be local," Colm said, "or heard from
someone local."

She nodded, watched him wolf down two sugar
doughnuts. His face was rounder than when she first
knew him, but you could still see the bluish hollows
in the cheeks, hunger lines she called them. The family
was poor, the grandfather a policeman who got shot
on the job. At least the father could count on the mortuary—people kept on dying. He was wise, Colm,
nothing pretentious about him. She just hadn't wanted
to marry him, was all. She was looking for the wrong
things in a man in those days.

But when Colm asked her now who could have
done it, how they'd know about the money, she had
no answer.

"Rumors," she said, spreading her long fingers.
"That bar, the Alibi, the fire shed. Gossip gets around.
Men can be worse than women."

She smiled, saying that, and he grinned back, took
off his glasses and wiped them on his sleeve. Everyone
knew after a family burial you got all the local gossip
from Colm's father.

"I'll think about it," she told him. "I'll talk to the
other neighbors. I'll talk to hus—Pete. I'll talk to Lucien. They said we could go in tonight to see him. I'll
talk to Belle, when..."

He looked sympathetic, chewed on his doughnut,
his jaw working hard. He chewed everything twenty
times, even ice cream. He looked ridiculous doing it,
frankly.

"What right did they have," she said, "breaking into an elderly couple's home, abusing their persons!" She jammed a fist into the palm of her hand.

The red flushed up into his neck, his cheeks. He liked Lucien too, he got his milk there, his spring corn from Belle's stand. He'd drop in for a toddy now and then. Colm liked his toddies—too much, maybe.

"I'll do everything I can to find out who did it," she said fiercely. "I want them caught. I want them prosecuted."

He nodded, coughed. "I'm with you." He pocketed a doughnut as he got up to leave, gave a sly grin. It was good to have an old friend, she thought. She felt safer somehow, no one would violate her house. Would they? She felt a stiffness in her neck.

"They think it was set, no problem with the electrical," he called back, on his way out. "The Charlebois barn."

"Oh my God," she yelled after. "How many bad things can happen in this town?"

But he spread his hands, like he'd just dropped something.

A farm wife was never alone. Now it was Pete's unmarried sister Bertha barging through the back door, the pink beret that matched her pink lips pulled down over her permed hair, the skirt discreet below her plump knees, the shiny black pumps she wore through snow and mud.

The "disappointed woman," Ruth called her. Disappointed in love, in school, in career—she'd wanted to be a teacher but couldn't get into the university. So

Bertha stayed home, turned to the church, was an eldress or something.

She didn't wait for Ruth to speak, just whirled up behind like a motorbike: "You ought to keep your doors locked, Ruth. Anyone could get in." Not bad advice, Ruth thought, for certain people. "I want you to send Vic down with Pete. Now, don't wait! For Vic's sake. Pete's lonely without the children."

"Lonely?" said Ruth, her head in the refrigerator. The men would be in for lunch, she had to concentrate on that.

"And Emily. A young girl! Horrible things can happen. The world's full of sin. All those Hebrews moving in, attracted by the college. I read in the paper..."

"We're all right," muttered Ruth, her blood rising with her sister-in-law's prejudice. "I need my children here. I have a farm to run. And I bank my money, what money there is."

"He sends a check every month, he told me that. Though he doesn't get that much in sales. I told him years ago to get the MBA, but Father had him take over the farm. Though he was never cut out... Oh, he'll be back. Mother brought us up in the church. Of course it was just the Congregational. Thanks to the Lord I've seen the light. But Pete, well, he's forty-two, that's the problem, I read this book—the seven-year "scratch" or something? He can't help himself, he'll come 'round."

She made a little face, straightened her frilly shoulders. The fingers, yellowy with nicotine, though she'd quit smoking she said, combed through the frizzy hair.

Ruth didn't remind her that Pete hadn't seen the

inside of a church since their wedding. As for the "scratch," well, maybe Bertha had a point. Pete was just forty-two when they saw him in the post office nine months ago and lured him into that film. He had a bit part, a farmer fighting the gas pipeline—some need to show off, maybe. And afterward he took off with that woman, that so-called actress. It was like he'd gone mad, Ruth was struck dumb with it.

"Look up antidotes in that home remedy book of yours," she told Bertha.

"What?"

"For 'scratches.'"

Ruth was relieved to see the hired man Tim coming through the door, turned her back to end the conversation. Bertha blew her nose into a pink handkerchief. She didn't approve of Tim's Willy, one never knew what a retarded boy would do. There was the time she'd had a boy from the group home to Thanksgiving dinner, and he'd swept the turkey right off the table, lickety split, down the street! When she told Ruth, when Ruth giggled, Bertha wept with fury.

"You hear about that fire up to Charlebois'?" Bertha said as she prepared to leave, not waiting for an answer. "The whole barn, gone, in a flash!" Her eyes gleamed red.

"They still won't let you in the fire department?" Ruth remembered how Bertha had tried once, years ago it was. Ruth rather admired Bertha for wanting to get into that patriarchal fraternity, odd as it seemed in the face of the woman's antifeminism. She got to some of the fires, anyway—something to do with her belief in hell, Pete said once. But he tolerated his sister the way Ruth couldn't.

"They would if I'd really pushed it. They'd've let me." And patting her permed hair, Bertha trotted off in her black pumps.

Tim had the state forester with him, come to advise on the trees. Of course the forester would stay to lunch—Tim looked sympathetic, but what could he do? She nodded, took a deep breath. A farmer's wife was always changing gears, moods: think of the world's wrongs and then smile, give out with the small talk. Trees, the weather—"We'll discuss it at lunch," Pete would say, while he invited tractor salesmen, artificial inseminators, town auditors, to "discuss it over lunch." Her lunch.

And here they were, talking fertilizers and tree blights like it was an ordinary day and not the aftermath of a brutal assault.

"More soup?" she invited. But it was Willy who held out his bowl.

"He's hungry," Tim said. "He had a night on the town, hey, Willy? Worked up a thirst?"

"Girlfriend?" the forester said, winking at Tim.

"Nah, nah, no girlfriend," Willy bawled, "no girlfriend. Girls are dumb," and the men laughed again.

"He was down at the Alibi," Tim explained, "with his friend Joey, one who lives at the group home. Till they got kicked out. Right, Willy? You made too much noise, got kicked out?"

"Sure," Willy said, enjoying the attention. "Too much noise. Got kick out."

He drained the chicken soup with a slurping noise,

jammed a hunk of buttered bread in his mouth. "Got kick out." He laughed loudly, and so did the two men.

Ruth served the Jell-O and cookies, and Tim said, "Not having any yourself?" She shook her head. Food didn't tempt her today: her mind was a grinding machine. Someone would have to milk the Larocque animals tonight; the daughter and her husband weren't much help—Marie too flighty and Harold an out-of-work accountant who trembled in the presence of cows. How they'd managed that farm alone, the Larocques, no pipeline or milking parlor, all the time discing with that one rickety tractor! It was a miracle, really, they'd hung onto it when so many had sold—herd buyout or developers—or just shot themselves like the Mason brothers down in Rutland. And now when they should be slowing up, enjoying the fruits of their years of labor . . .

"It's not fair!" she cried. "It's not fair!"

And Willy, bringing in plates to the kitchen, glancing at her out of his wide gray eyes, intimidated by her mood, said, "I help clean up. Tim says so."

She waved him off, put on a smile. "You go help the others."

But the boy hung around, wanting to talk, his big fuzzy head waggling. She called him a boy though he'd turned twenty-one, with a body bigger and clumsier than he knew what to do with. Couldn't swim, turn a somersault. Poor Willy! He'd lived in nineteen foster homes, almost one for each year of his life.

"I was plantin' trees," he said. "Tim say I find my, my 'calling.'" It was a funny word. He smiled, showing his bad teeth. "What's that mean, 'calling'? Who's calling? Yoo-hoo.'' He cupped his hands about his mouth. "Who-ooo.''

"It means you've found what you're good at. Like someone called you to it. Up there, so they say.'' She pointed at the ceiling and his eyes followed obediently.

"Though some of us never get called,'' Ruth said, bemused.

"It's okay. Tim, he say his muscles turn to Jell-O, but I like it. I like it with the whip cream.''

"Well, here now. Finish the bowl.'' She dabbed a scoop of cream on it. "You want another chocolate cookie, do you?''

After the afternoon milking, Ruth went to the hospital. They wouldn't let her see Belle, only relatives, and the daughter, Marie, was with her. Belle was still in a coma. The nurse couldn't tell her any more, nor the son-in-law Harold, who stood in the lobby turning and turning his red checkered cap in his hands. Drops of sweat shone on his brow. He could tell her only that the police had come and were sent away.

"A bad business,'' he said in his high-pitched voice. "I never imagined something like this. It shouldn't've happened.'' Ruth nodded and went on down to Lucien's room.

"Help me,'' an old woman squealed. "Help me!''

"I'm sorry. Ruth brushed past the wheelchair, feeling guilty; there was a dampness in her underarms, in the creases of her neck.

She met Colm Hanna in the doorway of Lucien's room. He was dressed in an open-necked blue shirt, olive corduroys—nothing matched, nothing hung right on that thin body. He was holding a blue cotton cap in his hand. Colm was crazy about hats, it was rumored he had a hundred in his closet.

"There's a concussion, multiple lacerations," he said. "He's still confused. So I didn't stay. But I found out one thing: they called him by name. Whoever it was, called 'Lucien,' like they knew him."

He'd seen Belle's daughter and her husband when he came in. Marie was distraught about her parents but couldn't shed any light. The husband, Harold, had little to add—as inarticulate a man as he'd known. "Marie mentioned your boy, Willy. In a funny way, you know, like he might be—"

"Implying what? That Willy's involved?" The blood swelled in her cheeks. "That's absurd. We all know that!"

"Hey, I'm just reporting. We have to think of everyone. Anyone who knew Lucien well, his habits. Your man Tim as well?"

Her dander was up now. "He's a good man, Tim! He never takes a nickel from Lucien, just helps out in his spare time. He's there now." She felt her neck stiffen.

"He might have seen something, Ruth, that's all." He held up his arms in truce.

"Oh, yes, yes, okay, I suppose you're right."

"Maybe I could drop over in the morning, we could both talk to them. Kids'll be in school, I suppose."

"They wouldn't suspect my children!" She took a step back into the corridor, knocked into a door, rubbed her shoulder.

"They might have seen something. You said Emily

came in late, with the boyfriend. Who knows? Hey!''
He dropped his hands at his sides, like the criminal
mind was beyond his ken.

"They get home around four. But Vic, he's only in
fifth grade. I don't want him upset. He's had troubles
enough in school."

"Troubles?"

"He and a couple of other kids. Because they're
farm kids, they smell of the farm. They call him...
look, Colm, I came to see Lucien. I have to get home
to get Vic in bed, help Emily with her paper. I studied
history, remember? Before I turned into a farm wife?''

He looked serious. He'd wanted to marry her, she
kept forgetting that. He couldn't seem to forget,
though. The way he looked at her sometimes, like the
sun hanging over Bread Loaf Mountain, not wanting
to go down.

He waved his cap at her, smiling now, stuck it on
his head at a jaunty angle. He was really quite attractive, with his cheeks filled out. She watched him go
down the hall. He sort of bowled along, like his legs
wanted to go in a different direction from his body,
but shoulders back. You wondered if he'd make the
door all right.

He turned to doff the hat again. And whoa! He was
walking into a supply closet. He looked back, grinned
at his error.

She was smiling herself when she went in to see
Lucien.

The man was too confused to identify the assailants
in any way, and she dropped the subject. It was shock
enough to see him: bruises, odd swellings, the broken

nose she hadn't seen when she picked him up that first time. But then she'd been in shock to find him like that: he'd looked so small in that ditch, like a shrunken potato, and behind him, his meadows swelling up to the foot of the Green Mountains. In the hospital bed now he seemed larger, or maybe it was the bandages that bound his limbs, his forehead.

"Belle?" He reached out his arms.

"Belle's here, Lucien. In another room. She's going to be all right." The wet oozed up under her arms as she spoke. "How are you? Pretty early to be going to bed, isn't it?" She looked at her watch. "Seven-eighteen?"

He didn't smile. He couldn't, of course, there was a nasty cut at the corner of his mouth, red pit marks on his cheek like a machine of some kind had stamped it; some teeth seemed to be missing. He didn't take care of his teeth, Belle said, didn't want to spend the money. "You want them all pulled out, do you?" she'd say. "You want to spend a thousand dollars on false ones?" Ruth had heard the complaint more than once.

"Look in my pocket there." He tried to get up on an elbow but fell back down on the pillow.

"Closet," he said, pointing.

She smelled the coat before she saw it. Funny how she could work with the smell of barn all day and yet it was a surprise when she came on it elsewhere. She reached deep in the seams, where the pocket had ripped, pulled out a stubby pencil, a couple of nails, a handkerchief, some crumpled paper, a pouch of Beechwood tobacco.

"No bills?" Panic spread across his face. "Down in the lining?"

"The police would have it," she lied.

"Police! Mary and Joe, what business they got. Gemme out of this bed. Who's milking? Belle can't do it all, she's getting old, Belle."

"My hired man's over there now," she promised. "The farm's in good hands."

"Help me out of this bed," Lucien repeated. "I can't spend the night here. Belle, she don't like to be alone at night. I say not to worry, but she say you never know who. Look, tell her she can lock the door she wants to."

He fell back again from exhaustion and shut his eyes; the lids were the color of scratched pewter. She sat on the edge of the bed, feeling helpless.

"Belle," he murmured, opening his eyes a crack, holding out a hand. "Get that Tim over to help with the cows. You can't do it alone, Belle. You hear me now? I be down in the morning. Belle?" The eyes shut again, the voice was a whisper.

"Belle? You hear me?"

"I hear you," Ruth whispered back.

EMILY WAS ON the phone when Ruth got home. Ruth removed her shoes before she entered the kitchen— she hated scrubbing floors. It had begun to rain outside, and though it was good for the sapling trees, the mud would put off plowing till May. The old John Deere was problem enough on hard ground. And the barbed wire on the north pasture fence, where she wanted to send the cows, needed mending, the cows would have a heyday. It was one thing after the other!

And now the boyfriend, Wilder, that city boy, on the line, she could tell from her daughter's voice. Ought to have the decency to leave her alone on a night like this. Though Emily didn't seem to think so. She was lying back on the sofa, the wire stretched across the room and over the sofa back. Another quarter inch, it would strangle the iron lamp. They talked this way every night: anyone else who called in would get a busy signal. It didn't bother his parents, of course. Wilder and the older Unsworth boy had their own phones, Emily said. Nice to have that kind of money, Ruth thought.

She nodded meaningfully at Emily as she passed.

"Mom's home," she heard Emily tell Wilder. "I've got to do my history paper. I was helping next door—the Larocques got hurt, you hear that? I didn't know till I got home from school. Somebody in the middle of the night. Must have been after you left. Huh? Yeah, they were hurt bad. Mrs. Larocque's in intensive. Wilder? You there? She'll be okay—we hope so! Wilder, there's still a full moon. Remember? I saw you there in the car, watching. I saw you from my window. You were still there when I pulled the shade. I was with you." Emily's voice was almost a whisper, but Ruth could hear. She'd had keen ears since the births of her children. "I mean, I spoke to you, from my room. Didja hear me? Yeah. Well then, see you in class. I miss you. You get there tomorrow, hear?"

She made a kissing sound into the receiver, and Ruth winced where she stood on the top step.

"Wilder wasn't in school today?" she asked when Emily came upstairs.

"He was starting a cold," Emily said.

"That was a reason to miss school?"

"He had a science test. He didn't study for it."

"Oh." And the subject was closed.

Vic was in his room playing with the G.I. Joes his father had given him. They'd belonged to Pete as a child, and he'd kept them, along with a Mobil Oil truck and a red wagon. When Vic saw Ruth, he put the dolls away. He knew she was uncomfortable with them—because they wore combat fatigues, not because they were dolls. No one could accuse her of being sexist. She hated women forced into roles. Maybe it was why she rather liked being a farmer now—not a farmer's wife, but a farmer.

She said, "After what happened next door I'd think you wouldn't want to play war."

"I'm not playing war."

"Then what do you call it?"

"It's defense. I'm defending our country. Against—" He blushed.

"Against what, Vic?"

"Against the invaders. If I don't, they'll take over."

She sat on his bed. It felt bumpy, like something was stuffed under the blanket. She left it there, maybe she was the invader he was talking about. Though she suspected the invasions had to do with school.

"How was it today?" she asked.

"Okay."

"Just okay? Things were all right at recess?"

He shrugged, changed the subject. "What happened

at the Larocques'? Sharon wouldn't let me go over. She said you'd want me here. Then you went out.''

He looked accusingly at her. His ankles were stick-thin below the khaki pants. The bones stuck out in his hands where he'd clasped them around his knees. He'd have big hands, Doc Collier promised. But it seemed forever for Vic to wait, she knew that. He was one of the smaller ones in his class.

She told him what she knew, which wasn't much. She knew only that the pair had been attacked, she didn't know what time, how hard, by what instrument, though they'd found the maple stick on the floor. But it didn't look thick enough to do them in that way.

Vic gazed down at the floor as she spoke, clasping and unclasping his hands. His face was pale for all the freckles. She sensed he was empathizing. She wanted to go to him, hug him, say it was all right: Mom was here, no one could harm him.

But he was ten years old. Pete was right, she had to let him grow up. Though it was hard not to interfere, hard!

He licked his lips. Finally he said, "He kept his money in that coat. Lot of it, anyway. I know, I saw once. He sent me for a pipe and it wasn't where he said, so I looked in his coat. It was hanging up. And there was all that money, way down. A wad of it. A big huge wad.''

His eyes opened wide like he was seeing it for the first time. He looked worried, and she remembered the time he'd been robbed himself, some junior high kids jumping on him, taking fifty cents, a pack of gum—they were local kids that time.

"I found his pipe in there too, but I didn't tell him where I found it. I didn't want him to think I saw all that money. There were safety pins, the coat was heavy, like he kept more than showed. Then, then I was afraid—"

"Afraid of what?" She clasped her knees. She saw how thin Vic was. He'd been losing weight and she was only just aware of it. She was too busy, she was a terrible mother, she couldn't keep up with farm and family. The fear of losing her children crept over her again and she held out a finger to touch Vic. But he shrank away.

"Afraid he'd remember he put the pipe in there. Did they take the money?"

"I'm afraid so. I'm afraid that's what they were after. The police didn't find any money in the house, or the barn. The thieves must have looked there. Unless he banked it. Colm Hanna says he'll find out tomorrow, though I doubt it."

She remembered Lucien's anxiety about the coat. "And Vic, Mr. Hanna is coming here in the morning. He wants to help us find out who hurt the Larocques. Maybe we could have a talk."

"Me, too?" said Vic, locking his fingers together till the knuckles turned to bone.

"You should tell him what you just told me."

"Why?" The word was almost a shriek. "He'll think I was the one took it. I was in Cub Scouts last night. Down to the town hall. I'd never take his money, you know that!"

She put out a hand and squeezed his shoulder. The child was getting paranoid. "Of course he wouldn't think you did. We just want you to try and remember if you might have seen anyone around his house. Anyone who didn't belong."

Vic frowned. "I don't know if I did. I'll try and think."

"If you know anything, it will help, Vic. We want to find who did it. It's important we find out. We don't want any more victims. The Charlebois barn—"

He glanced up at the urgency in her voice, blinked. He'd been blinking a lot lately, she'd noticed. She stroked his hair, pulled him close, and this time he let her. "Now get in your pj's. We'll need you for extra chores in the morning. We all have to pitch in."

"I remember thinking," he said, yanking his pajamas from under his pillow, "I wouldn't want money like that in my pocket. All smelling of cows. They'd never let me in the games, ever, Billy Marsh, Garth Unsworth, that gang. They don't have cows where they come from."

"Garth Unsworth's mother has sheep, Emily told me so."

"They don't smell like cows. Not as bad."

"They do, you get a barn full of them. You tell that to Garth Unsworth."

She sighed, patted the boy's shaggy head, went to the door. Vic liked to undress in privacy.

"All reeking of cows?" she said aloud as she shut the door.

"That money? Reeking of cows?" she repeated as she went down the hall to her room.

THREE

IT WAS AN average farm, for these parts anyway, the farmhouse in need of paint, the two cement-block stave silos with WILLMARTH SONS in peeling letters, the barn sturdy, painted red. Farmers kept up their barns before their houses, Colm knew that from his work in real estate. The land had a bluish cast, like it was about to grass. Decent soil, he supposed. Not the rich loamy black soil the settlers found when they walked up into the Republic of Vermont, but good earth nonetheless.

He put his father's black wagon in park—the Body Wagon, his father called it, making a joke of everything, you had to do that in the mortuary profession. The old Horizon refused to start, clutch or something—Colm wasn't a machine man, more of a random-abstract, he called himself, frankly. And here was Ruth now, coming out of the barn: handsome woman, wide hipped, in mud-spattered jeans, baggy sweater that couldn't hide her heavy breasts, chestnut hair in a flyaway bun. He was early, she'd want to change probably before breakfast. He knew barns: a cow slaps its tail and you're hit with a sloppy joe sandwich, urine and dung.

He hunched down in the seat to wait.

When he knocked on the door fifteen minutes later she was ready for him, made a face at the car. "Are you lugging a body? Why were you just sitting out there? Think I didn't recognize the town hearse?"

He looked at her, sheepish: a clean pink shirt open at the neck, hair around her face, skin lightly freckled and perspiring, though he could still catch the scent of barn. There was an air of excitement about her, of hurry, nervousness maybe. The doughnuts were offered on a cracked blue willow plate, warm and shiny with sugar.

She sat there, stirring her coffee, waiting for him to speak. She was never one for small talk, even when they went together in high school. They'd dance, just holding on to each other, not saying a word. What happened, anyway? Well, sure. Pete. Pete cutting in on them one day; Pete on the football team; a frat man at the university. How could a scrawny guy in glasses, on the short side, with an out-of-style crewcut, compete? Com-Pete, the irony of the pun.

"You're done in the barn?" he asked, hearing his words hollow against the noise in his chest. "You're doing the milking yourself with, uh, Pete gone? Jeez, I'm sorry about that, Ruth." He was embarrassed now that he hadn't at least called her before this. Not that he hadn't thought about it a hundred times, just never got up the nerve. The Larocque assault gave the excuse.

Her face went through a dozen changes, came out bright as sun on a tin roof. "Well, how gone is gone? We don't know yet. We're in limbo here. Working our arses off. Tim helps with the milking, though. But Pete wants me to sell. Got any clients want a farm? I heard about some developer..."

Her face was flushed after the long speech, the mug trembled in her fingers. They were long fingers. He supposed they'd play a sensitive tune on the cows, he'd read that women got more milk out of a cow than men, there was that affinity.

Jeez, the feel of a woman's fingers came on him nights. Horny nights: jerking off and then remembering the bodies down in the basement. He'd never really get used to those bodies—dead, he sometimes felt, like his middle-aged libido. But he couldn't leave his father alone, a man in his seventies.

"Farm's a lot of work," he said, "with a family, too." He felt the old outrage. He'd never been crazy about Pete, too full of himself. The kind that never grew up.

"I didn't mean to sound off," she said. "It's all right, really, things are working out—were till yesterday. Colm, I want to find who did it to them, Lucien and Belle. I can't wait around for the police. I feel violated myself. Will you help?"

She took a breath. He smiled at her passion.

"The police haven't a clue yet. No witnesses except Lucien and Belle, and Belle unconscious. What can we do, Colm? Who can we talk to?"

She saw him looking at the window. "Finish your coffee and we'll go out and find them. Tim's a madman. Has to get in three hundred trees before it rains, he says. And we're not done with the sugaring."

"Tell about the Larocques," he said. "Tell me what you know about who worked there, came there, knew them well."

She didn't speak for a minute, bit into a doughnut,

stared out the window. The men were stretching a line across the field, attaching it to markers. They were good workers, he saw that. Good workers weren't usually criminals. Though you never knew.

"One thing I've got to tell you," she said finally. "It's Vic's discovery, I should let him tell you, he'd like that. But you won't see him till later."

He waited, took a swallow of coffee. It was good coffee, strong and flavorful. He was feeling comfortable now.

"The money," she explained. "The money they stole, it smelled of barn. Strongly I mean, hand to pocket, fragrant with cow. Kept it down in the seams. I gather it was his bank. I suppose he liked to feel it there, safe."

"Hand-y bank," he said, and she grimaced. "You haven't changed, Colm. That's supposed to be a pun? Anyway, Lucien sent Vic after a pipe once, and he saw. And smelled. Oh, and just this morning Tim said the police found a small stash—five hundred dollars—in the barn, up on a beam! So the assailants didn't look there. Though they might have found something elsewhere, Lucien hinted at that. No wonder Belle complained."

"Or they were in a hurry, afraid to look further."

"Yes, well, anyway, Marie—his daughter—banked it for them, for when Lucien gets home."

"In her account?"

"I don't know. Certainly not Lucien's! But she'll surely give it back. Well, I don't suppose that's the only money in town smelling of cows, but most men bank their money, they don't take it to the barn or stuff it in pocket linings."

"How long does a smell like that hang on?"

"Pretty long. Smell these?" She brought out a pair of boots from the pantry.

He pretended to be knocked out.

"I haven't worn them in two months, they need new soles."

"That helps. Well, good for Vic. Tell him that."

"You tell him. He was afraid the police would think he took the money because he knew where it was. They're due here late morning, you know, to ask questions. I'm not looking forward. That Mert who was there yesterday, I don't want him questioning Vic."

"Wasn't Vic in bed?"

"Sound asleep. And snoring—he has a touch of asthma, on top of his other troubles."

"What else?" he asked. "About the Larocques?"

It wasn't an unusual story: French Canadian couple, married late with one child, practicing Catholics like his own parents, which meant Sunday Mass and forget the rest of the week except for a holy oath or two. Marginal farm with maybe twenty head, no milking parlor, no pipe line, outmoded stump fence, a single tractor to do the jobs—practically nineteenth century, Colm thought. Hand to mouth. Or hand to pocket, for the milk money anyway. There were friends, but not many. Ruth supposed she was Belle's closest friend; a neighbor, she should get over there more often, she felt guilty for not going. Belle lived for the farm and Lucien. For the granddaughter, Michelle.

"Though Marie doesn't visit all that often. She's more sensitive than Belle about the Indian blood."

"The husband?" Colm asked. "I see him at fires."

"Harold? He's a piece of cake. Plump, shy, worships Marie. But out of work and hates it, walks around like an ostrich, head in the dirt. He's a tinkerer, has a toy train in his basement. Marie gripes. She says he's a kid about fires. Loves to hang around them. Like you, Colm?"

"I only go when I'm fired up," he said (he tried too hard for that one). "And it's not because of Bertha."

He saw her smile. They both knew how Pete's sister Bertha came on to Colm in high school, though she was two years ahead. He'd felt like the dog his mother had once that was adopted by a goose. Everywhere the dog went, the goose went. Until one day, in a fury, the dog bit off its head.

Well, he wouldn't do that to Bertha. She was harmless enough. Just annoying, "frustrated" was the word. He'd run into her in the pharmacy once, she'd hid from him. Then he found her in the front seat of his car. Had to talk her out of there.

"Anyhow, Harold's a trained accountant. But who in this town's got enough money to have him add up the wealth?"

"No Grange for Belle and Lucien, no community functions?"

"Grange no, there's a pecking hierarchy there like everyplace else. I got Lucien to run for selectman, and he lost. As for travel—they went to Alberg once, to see her cousin. Belle identified with the Abenaki, it surprised even her. They were trying to get their fishing rights back, had a problem with gambling. Of course Belle has no sympathy with that. She's a no-nonsense, get-your-work-done-and-go-to-bed woman. Well, there's a tiny TV—Marie gave it to them. As far as I know they seldom watch it. They're in bed by eight, up before dawn. They're farmers, for godsake!''

"No enemies."

"You asked that before, I don't know of any. Tim and Willy have helped over there on occasion. Pete and I took over when Lucien went in for a hernia operation last fall. The milk truck comes every third day. There's the mailman, the gas man, salesmen—I can't think of anyone else. He might have had a high school boy help out during harvest, I think I saw one this fall. I couldn't help, I needed Tim here."

"You don't know who this boy was?"

"No, but maybe Emily does. Or—"

"Or?"

"Her boyfriend, Wilder, Wilder Unsworth. Family came up from Long Island last year. Something about the oldest getting into drugs, Emily says. Like it hasn't hit Vermont too! It's the youngest, Garth, who's been tormenting Vic. He's not the only one. There's another—Marsh—father's a prof at the college. Well, Wilder's all right, I guess, at least Emily thinks so, and she's a sensible girl, as adolescent girls go! He's smart in school, pleasant enough when Emily brings him in here. But distant. He's attracted to Emily—but not to the farm. I worry about it, that he's using her."

"How do you know?"

She gave him a fierce look. "How does one know

anything? He—he has a kind of wrinkle in his nose. Doesn't look me in the eye, like I'm one of the cows, dressed up in boots.''

She bit hard into a doughnut. "I'm sorry, Colm, I'm all caught up in Vic's trouble. You can imagine what it's like to be a sensitive fifth grader living on land you lived on all your life, grandfather before that, and some kid comes up and says you're dirt. You should know that. You're Irish.''

"My grandfather knew.''

She looked sympathetic. She knew the story. How he was a town cop, killed by a booze runner up in Burlington—they had his picture on the wall down at the station. Colm was ten years old then, Vic's age. It was good to talk to someone who knew one's story. Comforting. "Do they say that to you, Ruthie?''

"I'm an adult. They don't dare. But I see how it is in town meeting. They sit together, the flatlanders— well, not all, I shouldn't stereotype, there's a lot of well-meaning ones—but asking questions, criticizing. Like how could we run things the way we do? How could we vote down the school budget, this agency, that agency, like we don't care about the poor, the disabled? It's just that we don't have the money, we're trying to survive ourselves. My God, they're driving us off our land! And you're helping, Colm Hanna, you're in real estate.''

He threw up his hands to ward her off. She didn't smile, she was too wound up. "That farm, other side of Larocque's, goes for five hundred thousand dollars. Five hundred thousand! Midwesterner put a couple thousand into it, now he's reselling it for a windfall. No local can afford to buy it.''

He sighed. He knew. That farm broker up here now, panting after the realtors, they'd all had her out looking—all but him, he made sure Ruth knew that. Someone, some developer behind her, he didn't know. He wouldn't be tainted with that brush. One day he'd explain it to Ruth, why he was in real estate.

Maybe he just liked to walk the land, that was all. How else could he walk on other people's property? And how was it their property anyhow, he asked himself: they took it from the Indians. From Belle's forebears.

Or was it anybody's property—ever?

Her nose was shiny with indignation. She laid her hands on the table, the long hard fingers gripped together; she looked toward the window like she hoped someone might come to interrupt their conversation. Was he boring her? He worried about that. He wasn't some gregarious Pete.

He followed her gaze, saw the men outside, progressing slowly along their line, their bodies jerking up and down like oil rigs. As he watched, one of them broke the pattern to do a somersault.

Suddenly she laughed. It was a spontaneous, merry laugh that made him smile. ''That crazy Willy,'' she said. ''He never could do a somersault.''

He smiled, too. She was always laughing back in school when they went together. She was so full of it then, she even laughed at his puns—his English teacher graded him down, the old fart.

"Great doughnuts," he said. "Can I have the recipe?"

She lifted an eyebrow, still smiling.

"I do the cooking. Dad never learned. Though I admit, food doesn't mix with formaldehyde."

"I'll write it out for you. Though I don't use a recipe." Her smile squeezed a dimple into her cheek. It was nice to see it. He supposed she'd gotten out of the habit with Pete.

Jeez, how could that guy walk out on this woman!

They went out to the muddy fields together—he should have worn his rubber boots. She introduced him to the men, then left. She had accounts to do, she said, then she was going to the hospital to see about Belle and Lucien. There was still a little time to make up for neglect, wasn't there? They could compare notes later?

Ruth had a way of looking directly at a man, holding his gaze. It was disconcerting, but exciting. He wondered if she'd fight for her husband the way she fought for this boy. Or was she too proud for that?

"I can do a somersault," Willy told him. "You wanna see? Tim been teachin' me how. I can do it. Mostly I can."

"I saw you," Colm said, "out the window."

Tim laughed. "He can do bettern' that if he wants. He don't always remember to tuck his head under, right, Willy? Right? Now get that pail of trees over here, huh?"

Tim didn't stop work. He thrust his shovel in the earth, then Willy dropped a thready tree root in the hole. The shovel slid out and Tim thumped it down with his boot heel.

"You don't mind if I ask a few questions," Colm said. He picked up the pail and moved it for Tim. He felt like a realtor now, no, a detective. He read stuff at night: Dobyns, Mayer, Gill, that Irish detective. He'd learned one thing: the nicest guys can have secrets, rotten things in the core. The one you least suspected did it. Who could that be in this case?

Tim said, "Terrible thing. Nice old couple. They don't deserve that." He seemed genuinely grieved, but then, what did Colm know? He could only have faith in intuition, his great-gran's second sight. His mother had told him about that, he used to laugh. Now he wanted to believe in it.

He went through a list of dumb questions he'd thought up. The replies yielded little that was surprising. Timothy Junkins, born in Long Island of upward-bound parents. College dropout in the early sixties, joined "the cause," carted off to jail a dozen times for protests. The police would make something of that. The worst was in Chicago—something about a bomb exploding in some lawyer's garage.

"The bastard was supporting the corrupt mayor," Tim explained. "He was establishment with a capital *E*. I don't know how many he swindled. I think he was hooked up with the Mafia."

Colm nodded. He was a sixties man himself, even had a motorcycle—till he ran it into an oak tree. He'd got into one or two sit-ins, protesting the war. A cousin was taken prisoner by the Vietcong, still hadn't surfaced, one of the MIA—undoubtedly dead, though his aunt never gave up hope. A reason, he guessed, for his own anger at injustice. He couldn't sit around and let one human being exploit another.

He'd settled down, Tim said, only in the last dozen years or so. Doing farm work, respite work, helping the mentally retarded—eight states he'd worked in. Married once, and when she wanted to leave he gave her "the works: house, furniture, dog, fifteen birds, the old Ford. Hell, I didn't want it. I didn't need all that. There was another woman, but then she took off. Well, you know how it is. You single?"

Colm nodded. Had Ruth told him that? What more had she told him? But Tim was moving forward with his story.

"So two years ago I came here. Pete hired me. I said could I bring along Willy, he's developmentally disabled, happens to be epileptic, too. I had him on meds by then, though there's still seizures—when he's stressed out. I got a brother with epilepsy—it's tough, he's an artist. Got nothing to do with brains, epilepsy. I learned that early on." Tim's voice rose and fell with the rhythm of the planting.

"How was it working with Pete?" Colm didn't know why he asked, it had nothing to do with the assault. Pete was in New York.

Tim jammed his spade into the ground, leaned on it. "He left her, that tells you somethin'. But he's not a bad guy, he left me alone with my work. But I could tell his heart wasn't in farmin'." He thought a minute and gazed off at the mountains. "Maybe that was part of it. He has an unfocused side to him, prob'ly never will know what he wants. Even if he comes back."

"You think he'll come back?" Colm felt a pull in the groin.

"He's got kids, all this—he's got to settle somethin'. But who knows? Maybe he'll dump the whole thing on her."

"She seems to be dealing with it."

"Yeah. I'll stick around awhile. The two of us, right, Willy?"

"Right," said Willy. "You and me. You wanna pass me them trees, Mister?"

Tim said, "*Those* trees, Willy, *those* trees!" And Colm hefted the pail over.

"Gotta get 'em in right," said Willy. "Gotta get 'em deep in so they live. We wan'm to live, right, Tim?"

"Right," said Tim. "We want 'em to live."

LUCIEN LOOKED UP when Belle entered the room. She was wearing something pink. That was new, Belle never wore pink. Green was her color, like the grass, like the trees. It was because she was Indian he told her, and she laughed. Her mother, though, was ashamed. Indians are dirt, her mother said, people walk on them. Indian color is brown. Marie's worse even, wants nothing to do with Indians. She hit Lucien once—her own dad!—when he called her a squaw. Nine years old at the time. Mother of God!

"I married you, didn't I?" he said aloud. "I married *you*," he repeated. He didn't have to give reasons.

"Lucien?" she said, coming closer to the bed.

What was he doing in bed at this hour? What time was it?

"What time is it?" he shouted. He tried to get up, but Belle pushed him back. "What in hell you doing?" he growled. "The milking don't wait."

"Lucien, it's not Belle."

He rubbed his eyes. What was he doing in bed? "Help me out of this bed, Belle, this damn arthritis. Put some wood in the stove, Belle. I need heat."

"Lucien, it's Ruth. Ruth from next door. You're in the hospital, Lucien. You were hurt, someone hurt you. But you're going to be all right."

Lucien squinted at the pink shirt, at the white face. He recognized her now. She'd been coming in all night, waking him up like he don't have to be up anyway at four-thirty for milking. To stick something in his mouth, his arm, his bum. He turned his head away, closed his eyes. He felt her fussing over him.

"Tell me what you remember, Lucien. Who was it hit you? Were there two of them? What hit you? Where did those marks come from, on your face?"

Too much talk, too many questions. He opened his eyes. He couldn't see her for the fear. It rose between them, thick and white, like lightning hitting all over the farm at once and nowhere to hide. He shielded his face with his arms.

"Where's Belle?" His eyes squeezed shut. "What'd they do with her? Belle!"

BELLE WAS SWIMMING, long lusty strokes that took her out in the stormy lake and then, whiplashed by a wave, back toward shore again. It was out and back, out and back, her hair floating on the weedy water, then sucked under suddenly and down down, into the green, into the glade, shapes spinning around her: cows, fry pans, loose rock, chickens—that man, who was he? Waving his arms. She saw his face on the watery surface, calling Belle, Belle, come back. Come back. Then mother, her face filled with sun, her hair a dark ring, like the Virgin, calling, Belle, Belle, come back, Belle.

"Trying," she cried, algae clogging her throat. Something she had to do up there on the stony shore. "But can't. Can't can't can't..."

Each "can't" swallowing her down and down...

FOUR

COLM SAT IN HIS Horizon in the Willmarth driveway, pushed his glasses back up on his nose. New clutch. Old klutz, he thought. He should take a course in mechanics, save himself money, but he probably never would. The shadow of a silo fell across the blue hood. The air was sweet and fresh, he'd brought in new grass on his feet, and mud. He'd never seen such mud, worse than any April he remembered. Mud season. "Poor sledding" they called it. Or should he say "blood season"? He smiled grimly, thinking of the Larocques.

He was taking notes. It was his habit from real estate: if he didn't write his impressions at once, he'd forget. He switched to his reading glasses. It was a pain, this putting on and taking off of glasses and then misplacing them. His father said why didn't he get bifocals, but he wouldn't give in, not yet.

"Tim Junkins," he wrote, partly for himself, partly to share with Ruth: "Seems honest, industrious. Jail record (political idealism). Worked for Larocques a week before the assault, mending fence, etc. (he'd know the barn, its hiding places). Calls Belle a 'workhorse,' Lucien slowing with arthritis. Saw only the milk tanker, fellow never got out, Lucien and Tim loaded. One other: young fellow selling raffle tickets—some furniture business, win a chair or something. Couldn't see who it was, just the shape, bouncing along like an adolescent. Belle let him in. How to contact Belle?''

An afterthought: Did he approach the Willmarths too? Ask Ruth.

He gazed out the window, imagined her coming across the field, out of the barn, in that pink shirt...

Nope, he admonished himself. Keep it on a factual level, Pete might come back. Ruth wouldn't hint at her feelings, how the marriage worked, what she hoped for. And he was in no position to ask.

Okay, now. Tim had no alibi. He'd been home, watching TV, no one to vouch for him. Housesitting in somebody else's house, that's how he lived. Not enough money—desire?—to buy a place of his own, have to pay taxes. Too bad about no alibi. That jail record, police would be suspicious.

Willy. He chewed on his pen, looked out the window. The boy was turning another abortive somersault. Seemed gentle enough, but cross him and the temper could erupt—case of dignity, he supposed. You never knew what was inside the human. There was a case in Burlington: kid came up and stabbed a woman in the chest, she was sitting in the park, eating a sandwich. Just like that: stab. Then ran and told about it. Said she wouldn't give him a bite. That was all. Stabbed her for a hunk of peanut butter and jelly. Got off on a plea of idiocy. Justice? Jeez!

He drummed his fists on the notebook. Was he prejudiced himself? Where did it come from, this fear of strangers, somebody different from oneself? Was it archetypal? He remembered reading Jung in college. How did you unlearn it? Did you ever?

"Pre-ju-dice" he said aloud. Pre-jew-dice. Interesting when you pulled the word apart. Scary as hell. He was born after the Second World War but felt he'd lived it, the way his father talked about it. His father was one of the ones liberating the camps. They were walking corpses, he said, the Jews, the Gypsies, the homosexuals who survived. He could hardly imagine the suffering.

So where was he, this Willy? In a bar, the Alibi—there was his alibi! (Not much of a pun, that.) With his friend Joey, he said. They got silly, were thrown out. Then where? Willy couldn't remember. Home he guessed, Tim's. He could have done anything on the way. Or Joey. He'd better talk to Joey.

He guessed he'd have to hit the bars tonight, the Alibi—with Ruth, if she'd come. He stayed away from there usually, stayed away from the hard stuff too, drank mostly beer and wine now. Middle of their sophomore year at the university, when Ruth got engaged, he got drunk that night, went swimming in the lake with friends, kept on swimming, on into the mile-wide lake. But they fished him out. Jeez, would he ever forget that night? Or maybe it was worse the next day, when dawn hit. Reality: she was gone. Slam! No Ruth. He'd wanted back in that lake.

He put the Horizon into gear and reeled around out of the driveway. He'd drive past the Larocque place again. And then see Belle. He just needed to see her. Stand in the doorway and look. Did she remind him of his own mother? Dark hair his mum had, hard worker.

A red car, new Honda Civic, came swinging around the bend as he pulled out, splashing mud on his father's car.

"Mudfucker," he said.

"STOP!" Vic cried after the yellow school bus as it chugged off out of the school grounds. He and Gerry Dufours, who was faster than he, dashed after, yelling, but the driver kept on going. Vic stopped running, leaned against a tree to catch his breath. He'd stayed after school to finish a science project. He'd brought his telescope, to show Mrs. Ronsard how it worked. He thought she might show the others, he'd let them try it out if they wanted. Even Unsworth, especially Unsworth—he wanted him to see it. See what a farmer's son could do.

But there wasn't time, she said. Show her after school she said, and he did. And she seemed interested. But then she said she had to go, she had a dentist appointment. Take the telescope with him, she said, it wasn't safe in the classroom, and he did. She didn't ask him to bring it back.

But now he'd missed the bus. And so had Gerry, but for a different reason. Gerry set off an alarm clock in the middle of reading. "That was a riot," he told Gerry, "that was great. How'd you dare?"

Gerry shrugged. He wasn't even aware how great a trick it was on Ronsard. "I just did it, was all. I just set the alarm. I been late gittin' up for chores and my mother got me it."

Gerry wasn't the smartest kid Vic had ever known. It was too bad, he was another farm kid. He didn't take many baths. Or if he did, he got back in the barn afterward. Gerry got the same guff as Vic, and he smelled twice as bad. It wasn't fair. It hurt all of them. It wasn't fair.

"We got to walk," Gerry said. "Three miles. Ma'll be mad as hops. I'm suppose to clean the chicken pen."

"I'm supposed to meet a detective." Vic felt a little spring in his step as he said it. It wasn't really a detective, but his mother's old friend Mr. Hanna. But he was a detective now, his mother said, they all were, all three of them: Hanna, his mother, and him.

Gerry was impressed. "Hey, a detective?" At least he knew what that was. The Dufourses had a TV.

Vic told about the Larocques, and Gerry said he'd heard about it. "That the old guy kept his cash in his socks?" And guffawed.

"No," Vic said. He liked Lucien Larocque. The old man talked to him when they worked, showed how to do things, make a rake, for instance, even a dulcimer once, and Vic showed him his telescope. Mr. Larocque was patient when Vic got things wrong—better than his dad, who was always in a hurry for Vic to learn.

"Not in his socks," Vic said, "in his pocket."

And then was sorry he said it, he didn't know why.

"That's stupid," Gerry said. "That's dumb. My pa puts his in the bank. The Chittenden Bank, he takes it every Friday when he gets the milk money. He don't wanna get hit on the head. That Larocque, he's askin' for it my pa say."

Vic walked on ahead. He didn't want to hear what Dufours's pa had to say, he wanted to get home. It was over three miles to his house, past Dufours's turn-off, and he wanted to be there to meet Mr. Hanna. He wanted to tell the man about the money that smelled of cows. He hoped his mother hadn't already told. She had a way of taking the words out of his mouth before he could say them. He didn't always like that.

It was on the shortcut just before Gerry's turnoff that Vic heard the noise. They were walking through a section of woods that bordered the Dufours land, and the boys were quiet. It was always a spooky spot. Vic never walked through there alone; when he missed the bus, he'd take the long way around.

It was a funny noise, a kind of crackling and crunching like feet walking along in the same direction and stopping when the boys stopped. He walked faster, and Gerry said, "Hey, wait up, huh? I gotta stone in my sneaker."

So he had to wait in the middle of the spooky spot while Gerry untied his sneaker, shook out the pebble—a tiny one, hardly more than sand—put the sneaker back on, and laced it up. An hour later, it seemed, they started walking again.

It was then they came out.

There were four of them, three his size and one a big kid, probably in junior high, maybe high school. They were dressed like Indians, with bags over their heads with feathers sticking up, purple feathers like Indians probably never wore, and leather jackets, one with fringe. They had sacks on their backs, and two had boxing gloves on. "Who-woo," they moaned, dancing around the boys, holding hands. "Who-woo, we got you-hoo farmer boys."

Vic tried to break through, but they pushed him back. He heard Gerry yelling beside him, "Get away, I'll get my pa on ya!" The Indians laughed, and one of them broke the circle and opened a sack and pulled a bunch of hay out of it.

It was like his heart would leap out of his chest with the banging. Usually he could see the faces, it was Unsworth or Marsh or Southwick yelling names at him, bawling him out for missing a pop fly. Or that last time, pushing him down in the mud and filling his pockets with dung. But at least he knew who they were. His heart thumped like a dozen drums.

Now he wasn't sure. One was the size of Unsworth, but he didn't have the same sounding voice. One could be Marsh, but the bag had ripped on the back of his head, and Marsh had blond hair and this one was dark. So he didn't know. His heart beat everywhere: in his feet, his knees, elbows, throat. In a minute it would burst out of his chest, and he'd be dead.

He almost wished it, he'd be out of here, away from these torturers.

Suddenly Gerry Dufours gave a blood-curdling yell and broke through the chain of hands and started running, yelling like an Indian, and they let him go. "Next time," they shouted after him, and now there were four to one, and Vic knew he'd never get away.

He wanted to be dead, he dropped to the ground, pulled his legs up under him. But they yanked him up, ripped off his backpack. He was more angry than afraid now, he grabbed for it—it held his telescope.

The big one had it in his hand. "Yo, a farmer with a telescope," he said, and danced around, peering through it.

"You be careful of that!" Vic screamed, "you break that and I'll—"

The big one gave a high-pitched giggle. "You'll what, string bean?" Vic gave up, he didn't know what, there was no 'what.' There was a pile of hay now, at the foot of a tree, they were pushing him into it, were tying his legs, his chest, to the tree trunk. They were going to burn him alive! He resigned himself to it. He'd be dead, and no one would know who did it. Mr. Hanna and his mother would never find out.

Or would they? There was Gerry, Gerry got away. There was that hope.

"Dufours will tell on you," he screamed, and a boxing glove hit him on the nose. "He knows who you are. You better not kill me!"

It worked, they were quiet a minute. Then one of the smaller ones said, "Who's killing you? Nobody's killing you. We're just gonna tie you up in this hay, that's all. 'Cause that's where you belong, dummy. Dummy in a haystack." And they all laughed and seemed more relaxed again. Then one of them took muddy cow patties out of his sack and smeared them on Vic till he was practically covered and shoved one in his mouth till he gagged. They danced around him again, till they heard Gerry Dufours's voice, and another louder, angry one, Gerry's dad's, and they ran away, back through the woods.

Mr. Dufours untied him, cursing the whole time, and then Gerry cleaned the dung off him. Vic groped around for his telescope but couldn't find it. He couldn't see, the tears were streaming out of his eyes. He was sorry about that, but he couldn't stop, he was so pissed about his telescope. It took three years to build it, and all his allowances for the parts. He beat his fists into the tree till Gerry's pa pulled him away and said, "No good doin' that. What's gone's gone."

"Maybe you'll find it, maybe they dropped it," Gerry said, but Vic knew they didn't. They might break it, but they wouldn't drop it for him to find.

The Dufourses' house was pretty shacky inside, more so than the Larocques': beat-up lineoleum, saggy wicker chairs with blankets thrown over the backs, plastic crucifixes on the walls (Aunt Bertha would rip them down). He washed up in an iron sink full of rust. His own house, it had nice stuff in it, there were books on the shelves. He didn't see a single book here except on Gerry's back. He wanted Unsworth and the rest to see his house. They'd see he was different from Gerry, they couldn't lump him and Gerry together like this.

One of them was Unsworth after all, one of the ones with the boxing gloves, he was sure of it. Something about the voice, the laugh, the smell—that hair stuff he got from his brother (how did Emily stand it?). He smelled it when they put the dung in his mouth, didn't he? He had a good sense of smell, Vic did, they couldn't put much over on him.

No, they couldn't. They wouldn't, jeezum, it wasn't fair. He scrubbed his face and neck till they hurt. Mrs. Dufours came out with a towel. She rubbed his back, and he slumped forward and let her. She was a nice lady. She didn't smell, either.

THE GIRL WAS relaxed, Colm saw, prepping the cows—they'd have to talk while she worked. She waved to him, pulled a child's wagon to the center aisle at the north side of the barn, and wet a paper towel with something smelly—she was disinfecting the cows' teats, he supposed you had to do that. Her brother had missed the school bus. That would delay Colm, he wanted to hit the Alibi before dinner, check Willy's excuse.

She was a pretty girl, like her mother, but less intense, more fragmented somehow. Case of adolescence, he supposed, kids that age were so scattered, like kaleidoscopes: flashing green one second, red the next—you never knew where they were coming from. Of course he'd never had any of his own, what did he know?

He looked at Emily with new interest. She might have been his daughter. Weird to think about.

She was gazing up at him now, waiting for the question. He asked if she'd seen anyone around the house that night. She was out with Wilder Unsworth, Ruth had told him that. What time did they get back?

"Eleven-thirty," she said. "My curfew's eleven on school nights and I was late. We went to a movie, and then... we sat in the car a while." She threw the towel into the gutter behind the cow, then forced a stream of milk from each teat.

"You didn't see any, any activity, over at the Larocques'?"

"No, but we weren't exactly looking." She had the grace to blush, and he smiled. He remembered how it was with Ruth. A bomb could have exploded and he'd have gone on kissing her, he'd go home with a case of blue balls. His glasses slipped down his sweaty nose, and he shoved them back up. The place reeked of cowshit. He supposed you got used to it. He didn't want to look down at his shoes.

"Then Wilder returned to his car. And drove right off?"

She peered down at her fingernails, sucked in her lips. He repeated the question.

"Not exactly at once." She looked at him and then over at the window. "I saw him out my window. He was still in the car, he was watching the moon." She had a clear, high-pitched voice. Naive sounding, like Ruth.

"He didn't get out of the car, though, and you saw him drive away."

She fidgeted with a ring on her index finger. It looked expensive, more expensive than a farm girl would wear. He saw the swallow in her throat where it wouldn't go down. He leaned back on his heels, gave her time to answer. She knew the implication for her boyfriend. He wondered if she'd lie for him.

"Mother called me then, and I went out in the hall to answer. When I got back to the window he was gone. I'm sure he didn't get out. And he didn't go to Larocque's. Wilder's a good person, he wouldn't do that!"

Her face was scarlet, he had to be careful, he'd turn into the enemy. She moved on with her wagon to the next cow.

"I just needed to ask, that's all," he said. "It's possible he saw someone. Did he say anything the next day at school? About seeing anything unusual at the Larocque house?"

"No." She shut her lips tightly. She was looking paranoid now, she disinfected the cow's flank instead of the teat. A cluster fly circled her head, and she swatted at it, impatient.

"He was in school," he said and held his breath. It was just a hunch.

The eyes flew open. She was indignant. "He was sick. He was in bed. He was coming down with something the night before, he had a sore throat." She coughed, like she'd caught it. Then blushed, and he felt she was making up the sore throat. "His mother signed a note. She wouldn't sign a note if he wasn't really sick."

She squeezed a teat and the milk sprayed out, hit him in the glasses. "Sorry," she said. "Is there anything else?" There was a commotion at the other end of the barn, and he heard a female voice, a baby whimper.

He wiped his glasses, but everything was milk. He tried to keep smiling. "Not unless you remember something you want to tell us. Your mother and I want to find the assailants. It was a cruel thing to do. Belle's still in a coma."

He didn't usually play on people's emotions—he tried not to, in the mortuary—but sometimes one had to. This time it worked, tears stood out in her eyes.

He peered at her through the milky lenses. "We may have to ask Wilder a few questions. Just in case, you know. Sometimes people see things and don't realize what they've seen."

The sweat sprang out on his forehead and his glasses slipped. He could see better without them, actually. He disliked emotional encounters—maybe that was why he hadn't fought harder for Ruth. He wished it were Vic coming into the barn. But it was the older daughter, Sharon. She shouldered her way in, a pretty young woman with long reddish hair that needed trimming, a confident smile on her round dimpled face, the baby in a sack on her chest. Here, he sensed, was the boss of the family. In her own place too, he imagined, the husband away in Alaska doing something about the environment.

"I hope you told him everything," she told her sister. "No detail is unimportant. Did you tell about Wilder missing school the next day?"

"Yes I did, and none of your business, Sharon. He was sick, I said!" Emily cried, and turned to the next cow. Sibling strife. This he hadn't missed, Colm thought.

Sharon laughed. "She's so sensitive," she said of Emily. "She takes everything the wrong way. Now, what do you want to ask me?" She swung the baby off her chest and sat on a turned-over pail. When the child whimpered she opened her blouse like it was the most natural thing in the world.

And it was, perfectly natural. It was he who was outside the norm, an anomaly, could live only other people's lives, like an actor. He looked away while she nursed the child. It sounded like it was slurping peppermint tea.

There was nothing Sharon wouldn't tell him, but there was nothing she could tell. Except her opinions on the family. Her mother: a wonderful woman but overworked, paranoid since her father left, and overly protective of Vic. Sharon had told her mother over and over she should sell the farm like her father wanted. Her father: a well-meaning man but afraid of intimacy, a fish thrown up on land. "Mother never understood that."

"Your father has a sister," he said.

"Oh," Sharon waved her away. "Nobody pays any attention to her. Aunt Bertha's a freak, a fundie. Got Jesus, you know. I just laugh when she tries to convert me—so does Dad." The cluster fly landed on her arm and she knocked it to the floor, imprisoned it under a pail. Colm could hear it buzzing.

She went on. Her sister Emily: flighty, going around with blinders on, didn't help enough around the house (Sharon couldn't, after all, she had the baby). "If I so much as speak to her, she jumps on me, she's so supersensitive!"

Wilder: she didn't really know him. She didn't want to jump to conclusions. She hoped the police would question him—Colm and her mother were just people, it was laughable. Risky too, wasn't it? their getting involved in this thing? It was funny that Wilder missed school the next day, wasn't it? You never knew, that was all. Sharon read a little detective fiction. She read Jane Langton, Ann Granger, she watched *Mystery* Thursday nights. You're guilty until proved innocent.

She turned her wide green eyes on him for approval. "You have to turn over every stone. Like on a farm."

He said he and her mother intended to, and thanked her, waved to Emily, went out to his car. He realized he hadn't commented on her baby, how cute it was or whatever you were supposed to say, and then took a sharp breath. He was a man, wasn't he? Sexist thought, he admonished himself in the next breath. Maybe that was why he was in real estate. Realtors dealt with facts: basements, septic systems. They stayed away from the psychological.

Though facts lied, too. He'd think more about that tonight, at home in bed. He hoped his father wouldn't need him to lay out a corpse.

Was it his imagination, or had the world taken on the odor of feces?

He was driving out, turning onto the main road, when a battered green pickup with a shovel and broom sticking up out of the rear rattled into view. A man in overalls and red cap was driving it, a boy in the passenger seat. Colm held up two fingers in greeting. The man returned it, the boy peered out glumly, his face a pale round moon. It might be Vic—he hadn't seen the boy in a year, maybe two.

Should he turn back? He'd done enough questioning for today, hadn't he? Already he wasn't sure if this detective business was for him. He should let Sharon take over in his place.

RUTH HUMMED as she prepared to grain the cows. She hit a switch, and the feed poured down a pipe from the grain silo outside. She was using a new mix now, had everything from vitamins to sodium bicarbonate and cane molasses. She scooped the grain onto the floor ahead, to keep them from attacking the wheelbarrow with their huge pink tongues. She'd named half of them after famous females, real or fictional. Here was Florence Nightingale: Florence had her third calf three weeks ago. Here was Catherine Earnshaw, the independent. She'd been bred for the first time—what kind of mother would she make? Even now she was butting the stanchion bars with her head. And Charlotte Brontë, at the end of her fertile years, who only last week had dropped a sickly calf—maybe her last, who knew? They were all strong-minded in their own way; none of them would stand for this BST business: being pumped full of growth hormones, turned into objects that poured out the milk—up to 25 percent more, they claimed. And for what? To add to the surplus?

It was harmless, the FDA said. Sure, harmless as synthetic hormones, chemical additives, pesticides. Harmless as arsenic.

But she was getting stirred up again, just when she'd started to relax. It was worrisome enough having Vic miss the bus, Colm question her family—though she was glad to have his help in this, she was too busy to find out everything herself. And what had the police done? A dozen break-ins this past spring, and none of them solved. Not to mention the Charlebois fire. Who would have done something like that? Her neck got hot, imagining her own place on fire. It was unthinkable, that.

Three more and she was done. Emily had prepped the cows; Tim would come in to do the milking. She wasn't crazy about machine milking: she tended to overmilk, never got the thing off at the right moment. Maybe a dozen cows was enough, milk them by hand.

But there was no money in that, she had to think of money.

She glanced at her watch: 5:36. Vic should be home, even if he missed the bus. He'd call if he needed a ride. Through the stall window she saw Sharon coming toward the barn. "He was nice," Sharon said as she entered. "He was nosy. He's not bad looking. How come you didn't marry him?"

"Who's nosy now?" Ruth said. "Vic call?"

"Honestly, Mother, you've got to stop worrying about that kid. If he needed a ride he'd call."

"It's after five, he has house chores. I traded him the barn for the house because..." She paused, but it was too late.

"So he won't smell like a barn," her daughter said. "Well he lives on a farm, he's a farmer's kid. What's he supposed to smell like, yogurt and honey?"

"Okay, let's leave it. No other calls—from Marie Larocque? She promised to call if there was any change in Belle. Though she's not exactly reliable. She gets scattered."

Sharon put an arm around her mother's neck. "It's all right, Mother, it'll be all right, stop worrying." The baby whimpered on her back.

Charlotte gave a long low bellow, answered by her frail calf. Outside there was the hollow metallic sound of a truck door slamming. And then Emily's voice calling, "Mother, telephone! It's Marie. Better hurry up. She's in hysterics."

WHY DID HE turn back? Colm didn't know, but he had this feeling—he was the paranoid one now. It was Vic all right, Colm saw the boy run up to the house and then Ruth dash out of the barn in a baggy blue sweat-shirt. Sharon ran behind, baby bouncing on her back. Emily came out on the house porch, waving her arms, looking excited. The farmhouse door banged twice, the baby wailed.

He drove into the driveway—what the hell, they'd have seen him anyway. Of course he didn't want to get into a family quarrel, it could be something about Pete. He'd go in on the pretense of making a time to see Vic, for tomorrow; he'd get here early, before the boy left for school. For some reason it seemed important to talk to the boy. And Ruth couldn't do it, not with objectivity. Sharon was probably right, she over-protected the kid.

No one answered when he knocked on the back door, so he just walked in. They were all there, sitting around the kitchen table, looking up at their mother. They hardly noticed him. She was holding the phone in her hand, it was still buzzing.

"That was Marie. Belle's dead," Ruth said to the vase of grasses and pussy willow on the table. "She's gone. An hour ago. They murdered her. Whoever it was, it was murder."

FIVE

MARIE INSISTED ON laying Belle out, she wasn't to be embalmed, Belle "wouldn't like that." She didn't want Belle cremated, and she refused an autopsy. So the coroner had backed off: he'd known Belle personally, wanted Marie's vote, an election coming up. Anyway, the coroner admitted, even an autopsy couldn't prove exactly how a wound had been inflicted.

They had to have the funeral the next day, then, Colm's father said, looking doubtful, stroking back his several white hairs—"I mean, with no embalming?" and Marie agreed. Already there was that waxy look, the corneas cloudy, the body frozen, face and neck going greenish red; in thirty hours the rot would set in. Colm was relieved about the embalming, to tell the truth. He didn't think he could do that, not on Belle. Pumping in that stuff, like needling in crack or something.

Marie insisted on thick makeup: she'd do it herself to hide the bruises, though nothing could hide the distortion on Belle's forehead where the blow had landed. There were still tiny red marks—Colm couldn't think what put them there: precise as ellipsis points in a print machine or the prongs in a pitchfork, but too close together for that. His father photographed her, though; it seemed gross, but you never knew.

Marie wanted the oak coffin, the copper lining—the

most expensive at fifteen hundred dollars. When Colm suggested the pine—his dad out of the room to take a leak, he did it every hour these days—she zipped up her lips like a small purse.

"I'll pay for it out of my savings," she said, her eyebrows shoved into a V, her pointed chin risen like a martyr's. "I was saving for new carpeting. Harold knows how much I want it, but he can't find work, though he's got a lead. I won't have linoleum like Mother put up with."

"The pine lasts just as long," Colm suggested. He was getting a double message here: she wanted the best but she didn't.

The black eyes blazed at him. "The oak," she said.

"They're discounted now," he said quickly, "I'd forgotten." His father would have to accept it—jeez, he'd pay the difference himself. "You can take as long as you need to pay," he offered, and she nodded, chin up.

Neither of them, he realized after Marie had gone, her slim hips grinding inside a brown vinyl skirt, had mentioned the word murder. Pulling the lids down over the opaque eyes, he sensed something cold pass through him. It wasn't just the mortuary. It was something more. He couldn't put a finger on it.

"S'funny," his father said, coming back in the room, his pants open, he'd forgot to zip. He touched his groin: "I got some pressure down here, I don't like it. She take the oak?"

Colm nodded. "You'd better see Dr. Collier. But zip up first or he'll think you're advertising."

"Oh, shit," said his father, zipping.

WHEN SHE DIED, Ruth told Colm after the wake, she wanted to be cremated, and he said he'd been thinking the same thing. There were only the bones left, like shells picked clean on a beach. The dead could rise again, if that's what you believed, out of the ashes.

He'd give her a discount, he said, and winked. They were leaving the funeral home together. The wake was still going on, Belle in an open casket wearing makeup she'd rub off at once if she could see; Harold holding on to Marie like he couldn't stand up by himself. Lucien visibly absent—he wasn't to know yet, Marie said, in spite of Ruth's protest.

Ruth couldn't weep. Her initial shock, the sense of loss, had gone to anger. A life snuffed out over money! There was to be a funeral of course, full Mass—she'd see that Lucien got there. It would be well enough attended, like the wake. Half the people had come, most likely, out of curiosity.

"How can you live in a mortuary?" she asked Colm. "I know about your father. He looked frail tonight, though he had the old chin lift. Like a director glad his play was going well but afraid someone would blow it in the last act."

He smiled. "You've got him."

She glanced sideways at him. He was quite dressed up: gray suit, dark striped tie. He looked almost handsome: slightly beaked "black Irish" nose (the Spanish invasions, he said), the round glasses—the cerebral look. She found his thinness appealing, when once she'd been attracted to the macho-muscle type. So many of her old classmates going soft in the middle from overindulgence in one thing or another. Pete himself was heading that way. Maybe that was why he left—to be young again.

"It's not so bad," Colm said, "with the ones who die in their sleep. They're at peace by the time we get them. You fall into a kind of partnership with death. But I admit I have trouble with ones like Belle. When Dad goes, I'll sell."

"This is your first murder," she reminded him. "You're still in shock."

He didn't say anything, just lifted his chin to the night—the Irish romantic.

"So are we getting anywhere?" she asked. "Are there any real leads? Where are we going next?"

"The Alibi," he said, with a small laugh. It was a long thought from the funeral home to the local bar. The name of the place had never seemed so apt.

"To see about Willy? Check his story? Isn't that what they do in detective fiction?"

He squinted at her, like she might be teasing him (maybe she was). "I don't expect we'll find any more than what he told me, but we have to ask. And we'll want to see the bartender. See if they've passed along any barn money."

"What about the other stores in town? Out of town, Burlington. The banks. Yes?"

"The police have already done that. I dropped in this morning. But nothing yet. I hope you told Vic they appreciate his lead. They usually forget to say."

Actually she hadn't, she'd hardly seen the boy since Mr. Dufours brought him home. The call came at that exact moment about Belle. Sharon and Emily had to make supper, she could only sink in a chair and talk,

talk about Belle, ask why, why? When she finally dragged herself upstairs, Vic was in bed with the light out. This morning he'd complained of a sore throat, and though she felt he might be faking, she let him stay home.

"You're coming along," Colm said, almost shyly, pulling her out the door—he heard Bertha's voice shrilling behind them. And to her surprise, maybe because of Bertha, who'd been circling them all evening, she came.

The Alibi was crowded, though it was a weekday night. All the rednecks in town were there, it seemed: some she recognized, most she didn't; a scattering of students from the college, girls who looked under eighteen and probably were but had fake ID. She slid into a booth. She felt out of place here in her dark blue dress and blue heels (she preferred boots). She was sensitive about being out with a man, though there was no reason she shouldn't be, Pete hadn't thought twice about that, had he? It was her deceased mother-in-law's values—or should she say "prejudices"?—carried on by Pete's sister, Bertha.

Bertha had grabbed her at the wake: "I want you to stay out of this murder business," she'd said, all breathy, like she'd run a mile in her black pumps. "There's no telling what could happen." She looked up like lightning would strike any second, then she went on about Emily: Bertha saw her get off the school bus once with Wilder, at his house, no car in the driveway, she'd said, insinuating. And Vic: Vic should go to Pete—a boy needed his father in a time like this. And why was Colm Hanna hanging around

Ruth, a married woman? She didn't like "any of it," she said. The sister-in-law, warning of bad breath.

"Shut up," Ruth whispered, "shut up."

And Colm said, "What?"

"Not you," she said. "I'm talking to a ghost."

She shrank back into herself to see a familiar face: a woman who worked in the local Food Coop. And behind, at the next table, that woman who'd started the new boutique, some cute pun on *sense* and *scents*, she didn't want to remember. The town was getting too boutiquey for her taste. The gourmet restaurants popping up! The New Grub Street, Cakes and Ale: literary names, places the locals couldn't afford—only the new people, flocking into the town because it had a college, and that meant concerts, artsy affairs they could dress up for.

No one cared about the farms anymore. They were just there, pretty black and white cows to drive past on the way to the restaurants.

Colm was at the bar, ordering beers. He was leaning on his elbows, smiling, talking to the bartender, a big-bellied man with a red-veined nose—the stereotype of his profession. When the beer came she nodded at Colm and gulped it down. It had taken long enough. She felt she'd been groping about in a cave and couldn't find her way out. There was the sense of claustrophobia, of panic.

He peered into her empty glass. "I remember you used to balk at even one. You've improved."

"I don't usually. I mean, I'm not that dying of thirst. It's tonight, I guess, all that's happened."

He poured a little from his glass into hers. "Go on, you need it. Want to hear what I found out at the bar?"

"Tell me! I should have gone up with you." She felt better now, flushed, even exhilarated. These wild mood swings, was it menopause?

"Willy was here like he said, with his friend Joey and another guy from the men's group home. They horsed around some, bartender served them O'Doul's. The group-home guy came around eleven to get them, Willy went along. He might have spent the night at the home, we know he wasn't with Tim. I'll give the Counseling Service a ring tomorrow."

"Willy wasn't involved, I've told you that."

Stubbornly, he drank his beer. Of course they had to be certain. Still, she was piqued. Couldn't he see that Willy was little more than a child? How could he carry out a robbery?

She told him so. He looked at her out of those hooded Irish eyes; she remembered that stubborn streak. He didn't like to be reproved, even when he was in the wrong. It was a weakness in him. The arguments they used to have! Yet the fun of making up afterward...

She wiped her forehead with a sticky palm.

"What else?" she asked, getting businesslike. It was over, that relationship.

"The barn money. Last night, he noticed it when he was cashing up. Said he'd never smelled anything so bad, thought it came right out of the... 'cow's ass' is the way he put it. Sorry."

He was wasting his apology on a farmer's wife, she told him. "No, a farmer," she amended. She was a farmer. She propped her elbows in front of her beer. "Who was it, then?"

He sank back in his seat, pushed his glasses up on his nose. "He doesn't know, can't remember. So many smells in here, on clothing, hands. If his memory comes back, he'll call. If it happens again, he'll know—not that it's any proof."

"It was him, whoever came here to the bar. Or one of them," she said fiercely. "I know it. I feel it. If he came that soon after the, the murder, he'll come again."

"Maybe. But not if he sees us in here. Belle's friends?"

"How would he know?"

"Interrogators have a way of getting known."

"Yes. Shall we go, then?"

"Can I finish my beer? Just because you're an alkie," he poured a little more in her glass. "You can help."

She wanted to hit him, she didn't know why. But she drank the beer. What was wrong with her tonight? She watched him tip the glass to his mouth, calm as a cow chewing; any minute he'd wipe the hay off his chin. Colm Hanna!

Ha! He'd spilled beer on his shirt. He was dabbing with a paper napkin. Served him right. It felt good to laugh.

WHEN VIC WOKE the next morning the telescope was beside his pillow. He sat up and glanced about, like someone was in the room, might beat down on him. But it was only six-thirty he saw by his clock, and the house was still. Though he could smell coffee brewing down in the kitchen and knew his mother was back from the barn.

His heart jerked. Was it his mother who got the telescope? Jeezum. Had she been to see the Unsworths or Marsh's mother the way she always threatened? She was out late last night, she could have gone. He was worried now. Didn't she know she could make it worse for him? He'd decided not to tell her about the episode in the woods. He made Gerry Dufours's pa promise not to tell, and Mr. Dufours said he understood, but if it happened again he might go out with a shotgun after those snotty kids and "larn 'em a lesson." Vic didn't want that either. They'd take it out on him and Gerry afterward, wouldn't they?

The telescope was bent, he saw. The glass was broken in the butt of it. And he'd spent a month's allowance to buy the special glass. He punched his pillow. What was wrong with farmers, anyhow? His dad went to a college good as them. He'd said that once, and one of them said "Cow College," and maybe it was true. His dad studied agriculture. What was wrong with studying agriculture?

A car pulled up outside, and he squinted out his window. It was a thin man in baggy cords and dungaree jacket, that Hanna guy. His mother said he'd be around again, to talk to him. Well, he was glad. He had a theory. He had a theory that whatever happened in the woods yesterday was mixed up with what happened to the Larocques.

He didn't know just how, of course, kids that size

couldn't beat up an old man, could they? An old lady like Mrs. Larocque? But maybe enough of them could.

But how could he tell Mr. Hanna without saying what happened? The guy was too much in cahoots with his mother.

Then he remembered that Mrs. Larocque was dead. His belly ached to think of it. That was how he was able to slip past his mother without any questions. She had that phone call. He didn't like that. Jeezum. Nobody had any business beating up on an old lady.

"It's not fair," he said aloud.

"What isn't fair?" It was Emily, sticking her nose into his room, smelling of barn. He moved away, he didn't want to get the smell on him before school. "Little boy got to get up in the morning? Do chores? Sweep a floor? Poor little abused kid."

She was being sarcastic, he was annoyed. "I don't mind chores. I can work as good as you any day. And you were late yesterday, Mom was pissed. Mom—"

Then he realized he still had the telescope in his hand. He saw her looking at it.

"What happened to it, Vic?" she said quietly. She came in the room and sat on his bed, looked at the broken glass, the bent shape of it. "Somebody take it from you?"

"Who'd take it from me? I dropped it, is all. I dropped it in school and the glass broke. I can fix it. Today, after school." He slapped it down on his desk. "Get outa here now, I gotta get dressed. Tell that guy I'll be right down."

"Okay." She got up off the bed. "Make sure you go to school. Stay home, they'll think you're chicken.

Anyway, I had a little talk with Garth yesterday. At Wilder's house. I got a feeling they won't bother you today.''

"Who bothers me? Don't you talk to Garth about me. Wilder either. I don't like that! I had a cold coming on yesterday.'' He sniffed. "It's all the way on now. But I'm going to school. I always go. Now get outa here, I said.''

"I'm out,'' she said and shut the door behind. A minute later he heard the shower going. Emily didn't want the barn smell on her either.

Sisters were a pain. All these females telling him what to do, what to eat. Vic wished his dad were here. Did he think those Saturday night calls made up for his being away all these months?

"I hate you, Dad,'' he cried, "hate you. And I won't come live with you. Ever!''

He stuck his short bony legs into yesterday's underpants. His mother hadn't done a wash lately. What was going on in this world, anyway? It was all out of sync.

The door cracked open and it was Emily again, wrapped in a blue towel. "If you dropped that telescope in school, how come Garth Unsworth had it? It was in his room. Wilder found it.'' She looked fiercely at him. "Something you're not telling us? Mom won't like that.''

He kicked the door shut, hard, and she shrieked. He'd caught her bare toe.

Ha. She wasn't getting another word out of him.

COLM HANNA found a glum teenager and a sullen boy at the breakfast table. He glanced around for Ruth, he wasn't sure he could cope. As though sensing his worry she came in the room with the coffee cup that seemed an extension of her right hand. At once the atmosphere warmed. She seemed to have gotten over whatever pique she'd had with him last night.

"He was late getting his chores done," she said, excusing her offspring's attitude. "It's not you." One shoulder touched his as she leaned over to offer coffee; he felt his bones separate.

"She's right," said Emily. "It's not you, Mr. Hanna. Though I don't mind the chores. Not when I don't have a test. Today I have a test."

"What's the subject?"

"Geometry. My worst subject in the world. If I get through it I'll never look at another theorem in my life." She actually smiled, and he smiled back. She looked like her mother then, the same broad cheekbones, the wide dark eyebrows. They had a way of smiling out of one corner of the mouth like they were about to confide something to you.

He turned to Vic. "You're the scientist in the family. I understand you've made your own telescope."

It was evidently the wrong thing to say. The boy scowled. "It's nothing," he said, "just a dumb homemade telescope." He punched his sister, and she punched back, with a tight smile.

"That's not true." Ruth was standing in the doorway of the pantry, the coffeepot still in her hand. "It's a very well made telescope. It won a first prize in Field Days last summer."

Still Vic glowered, and Colm gave up on the subject. He was glad when Emily and Ruth left for the barn and he was alone with the boy. He made a few more efforts to coax a smile; that failing, said, "I want to thank you, Vic, for the lead you gave. We've already had one follow-through."

"Oh yeah?" The boy looked up, interested.

Colm told about the barn money in the Alibi. "Of course we don't know who it was, but someone's bound to show up again with it—somewhere. That was good thinking on your part."

The boy examined his cracked fingernails. "I got another idea too." He coughed, like he'd got a piece of toast stuck in his throat. He rammed a finger down after it.

Colm waited. But the boy was turning redder from whatever he'd swallowed. Colm patted him on the back. "You okay?"

Vic had hiccups, and Colm picked him up, held him high, then swung him down.

Vic was so surprised he stopped hiccuping. "Jeezum," he said. "They never stopped so fast before." He gave Colm a look of something like admiration.

"My father's remedy. Now what's your idea? Your mom and I can't find the bad guys without help from you."

"All right," Vic said finally, laying his thin arms on the table, carefully, like they were a part of his telescope. The hands at the end of the wrists were disproportionately large, like soup ladles. "I'll tell you. It's just a thought. But it might have something to do with, well, what happened to me yesterday. I mean, the same kind of bad stuff."

His eyes seemed to shrink back in his head as he told his story, like it was forcing its way out of his mouth. When he finished he made Colm promise to keep it to himself. "Not ever, ever" to mention it to his mother, and Colm promised.

Though it was true the connection was vague. What could a bunch of kids have to do with a theft of several thousand dollars and a killing? But just the same... "You can't give me the names?" Colm asked.

"Not really." The boy's voice was so hushed Colm had to lean over the table to hear him. "Just say that one of them might be called Unsworth."

Colm kept smiling. "Would any of them have worked at Larocque's after school any time? Unsworth, or any of the others? There was a high school student, Tim told me. He didn't know the name."

"Them? I guess not! Jeezum, they wouldn't be caught dead on a farm. Though Unsworth's mother has sheep. And he's stuck with them." He gave a satisfied little smile.

Then he said, "That was Gerry Dufours's big brother who worked over there at Larocque's. He's dropped out of school now, works down at that furniture factory. So does Unsworth's big brother—not Wilder, the other one."

"Thanks," Colm said, getting up to leave. He'd drop in at that factory. "I'll let you get to your chores now. You think of anything else, you get right to me or your mom, okay? I'll keep this other business, about the telescope, between you and me. Must have been a nasty business to go through."

Vic looked inward for a moment, froze. Then he

sighed heavily and took the hand offered him. He gripped it hard, the grip quite strong for a little fellow.

THE WOMAN WAS barging right into the barn where Ruth was waiting for the vet—he was half an hour late already, and she should be out mending fence. But Cleopatra had to be checked for heat, the heifers vaccinated for pinkeye—it was carried by flies, highly contagious, and Bathsheba's calf had it. But here she was, a sitting duck for salespeople, or whatever this woman was. Ruth saw a stockinged leg scrawny as a bovine's, a red polyester suit. She hated polyester. It always unraveled.

The heavily ringed hand tapped on the inside of the barn door. "I'll only take a minute," the woman shouted, as though Ruth was deaf. "I'll get right to the point. I'm Esther Dolley. I'm a broker. I specialize in farms. I called you once." She slapped a card down on the wheelbarrow where Ruth was scooping out sawdust. The fingers were thick as gloves inside the gold rings, tiny dark hairs grew on the knuckles.

"I know about your husband," the woman said. "I've had correspondence with him. He wants to sell. That's why I'm here."

Ruth looked up from her work. "You thought you'd just drop in, did you? On a farmer?"

"I thought I might find you in here." The woman's smile outshone the glare from the window, it masked her face.

Ruth said, "I've been busy. He left me with everything to do." She threw a pile of sawdust under the woman's feet. The woman gave a whooping sneeze.

"Of course," Esther Dolley said, like she was talking to a hurt child. "And he feels bad. He said so in his letter. All that next door—" she waved a polyester arm, "he's worried."

"You're wasting your time."

"I have an interested party. He's a developer. Oh, a Vermonter, yes. I have the plans here, very tasteful. Every house will be landscaped. We'll keep the vista, the mountains." She fished a map out of her briefcase, unrolled it with a flourish over the wheelbarrow of sawdust.

Ruth looked at it. Her fists pushed up inside the pockets of her jeans. "You couldn't get a hundred houses on my land. Not with trees between."

"Of course not," the woman said brightly. "This includes the folks to the west. They've already agreed. They're not making it, you know, even with both working and a hired man. They want to live a little, get out and—"

"On the north?" Ruth squinted at the map.

"On the north? Well, I haven't spoken to him yet, Lucien Larocque. It's too…" She pursed her lips delicately. "But I'm quite sure, with his wife, um, gone— an elderly man. His daughter is worried, you know, she doesn't want it. I've spoke with her husband."

"Who has nothing to do with the farm."

"Well. Well, he came in, didn't he? Yes, in my office. On her behalf. Looking for a job, actually. It was before, before the, um… His wife was worried about her mother. And now—" She gave a little sigh, the lips parted like the Red Sea. "The funeral is tomorrow?"

"Mostly family." Ruth didn't want this woman barging in in her red suit with the fancy label. It was sticking up at the back of her neck. She'd dressed in a hurry, this woman, a hurry for something. Something more than money, maybe?

The woman threw up her arms; it was all simply beyond her: death and the universe. She rolled up her map, got up, her thighs swished together in the textured stockings. The smile was replaced by sympathy. Realtors throve on divorce and death, Colm had admitted that to her, even while he kept on with it. They were like crows, she'd told Colm (and he laughed), pecking at dead things. At least undertakers disposed of them neatly, burned them.

Two barns had burned, too. She shivered.

"I can see you're disturbed by all this, and my dear, I understand. Yes, take your time, think it over and call me." She shoved a card at Ruth. It said ESTHER K. DOLLEY, BROKER. SPECIALIZING IN FARMS. PLATTSBURGH, NEW YORK.

"I just moved over," the woman explained. "I haven't got a new card yet. But I put down my phone number. There." She pointed a sharp fingernail.

Ruth followed Esther Dolley to the door. Outside Doc Greiner's white pickup was turning into the drive; she was relieved to see him. "How did my husband happen to write you?" she asked. "There are other Realtors here. Ones he knows personally."

The woman looked down at her leg—had her stocking ripped? She'd stepped in a cow pattie. Ruth smiled.

"Oh, I imagine he contacted us all," she said, pull-

ing out a cigarette. "Do you mind? I'm one of these
bad people—but I'd never smoke in your barn! Darn.
Forgot my lighter. I'll have to—" and giggling, she
galloped off, a red heifer, and squeezed herself into a
small red car.

"Most Realtors, you know," she hollered out the
window, "don't deal exclusively in farms. My daddy,
my daddy," she shouted, her voice vibrating, "he was
a farmer. My daddy, he was killed in a threshing machine. It ground him up. Like hamburg. I know farms,
all right."

She struck a large wooden match on the car door
and lit up. "I just happened to be driving by," she
yelled, the cigarette in her mouth now, "saw your barn
door open. Farmers don't have any privacy, do they?
Time for themselves? Your husband says you always
wanted to finish college. Maybe you could—"

Turning her back, Ruth went over to greet the vet.
She'd take him to the heifers and then call Colm. Pete
had contacted all the Realtors, had he? If so, Colm
would have told her. No, there was some other liaison
here.

She'd call Colm, ask him anyway. She just needed
to hear his voice. Calm her nerves.

SIX

CATAMOUNT FURNITURE was the town's third largest employer after Agway and the Branbury Cheese plant; the place was built on an acre of town land given over to "industry." The town didn't mind, just so it was out of sight. Colm smiled as he walked up to the white colonial door—he and his father could use some new furniture, replace a couple of coffins maybe.

A secretary at the general manager's office informed him that the manager was out, but if he wanted to wait, someone would talk to him. Minutes later the manager himself came in: a tanned young man with a receding hairline and a busy look on his face, he shook Colm's hand weakly, sat on the desk slightly above Colm's eye level, crossed his khaki-clad legs at the ankles, and frowned at the note Colm had extracted from Police Chief Roy Fallon.

"I read about this," he said and shrugged. What did he have to do with it?

There was something about people in a hurry that made one want to talk faster, rise to the level of their anxiety. Colm refused that. He let the man wait.

He said, "You had a furniture raffle. Someone went to the Larocques' farm, a ticket was found in Mrs. Larocque's pocket. It was dated April sixth, the afternoon of the assault. She paid a dollar for a chance to win an armchair. Can I see the person who sold her that ticket?"

The manager rocked back, folded his arms. "I'm sure we can find out for you. The raffle's still going on, I believe the cut-off date's on that ticket. A way of bringing folks into the store, you know?" He shrugged again, kicked out a foot, apologized as it hit Colm's ankle.

Colm's head ached.

The manager said, "You can't think the salesman had anything to do with a robbery?"

"A murder," corrected Colm. "Mrs. Larocque died day before yesterday." (The smile dried up on the manager's face.) "We want to follow up on everyone who went to the house, that's all. Tell your salesman not to panic. Oh, and one more thing."

"Oh?" More foot kicking.

"You have a young guy working here named Dufours. He worked off and on for the Larocques. I'd like to talk to him."

"Yeah, he works here. He'll be on lunch break in about"—he consulted a huge watch that had date, year, and probably, Colm thought, century—"Forty-five minutes?"

"I'd like to see one of them now," said Colm. "Either the raffle salesman or Dufours." He didn't think he had to explain. He hadn't read Chief Fallon's note, but it must have been a door opener. Fallon used to ask if he wanted to be a policeman one day, like his granddad. And remembering his granddad when they brought him home that day, the blood, the smell, he'd shake his head.

And here he was.

The manager looked put upon. "All right, I'll get Dufours. It'll take some to find the salesman. We had more than one selling tickets. In fact, maybe two assigned to that area?"

"I'll wait?" Colm put a question mark in his own voice and adjusted his glasses. He was used to waiting, wasn't he? He'd learned patience from the bodies brought into the mortuary. It was one of the prerequisites for undertaking.

Brian Dufours was a short-coupled young man with a pockmarked complexion and hands like hay rakes. There was something dwarflike about him, though he wasn't abnormally short. He wore gray workpants covered with thick lacquer, a mask around his neck, and the green furniture company T-shirt with a catamount on the front. Colm was reminded of the story about the stuffed catamount that snarled toward New York on the Fay Tavern in old Bennington—back in the days of the Republic of Vermont, that was. Colm always loved the idea of Vermont declaring itself a republic.

Except that Brian Dufours wasn't snarling; he was looking anxious. He stood like a child in a bearskin, wringing a red kerchief in his hands. His cheeks worked in and out, his black eyes looked startled, like he'd met up with a bear.

"I'm not a policeman, not really," Colm said, trying to put him at his ease, though Dufours was literally sinking into his seat. The manager had introduced him as "Detective Hanna," and Colm let it go—why not? He explained the situation in as easy a voice as he could. He only wanted to know the extent of Dufours's work there, who and what he'd seen. What did he know about Lucien Larocque? His habits, and Belle's?

When Dufours finally spoke, it was in a voice that might have come straight out of the spray can. "I worked, uh, weekends for a year there. Uh, last year, till I, uh, dropped out, got a job here. I been workin' here six months now. I do most of the, uh, sprayin'."

"You didn't want to work on the farm?"

"Uh-uh. No money there, old man takes 'vantage 'cause I'm his kid. Here I bring home a check each week."

"Home is..."

"I got a room. In town."

Colm questioned him about the Larocques.

"Funny old guy. Never talked much, not like my old man—orders ten to the minute. I done haying, he taught me the round bales. They got, uh, machines now, but he done 'em by hand. You tie 'em with string and then put 'em in plastic. They look like little mushrooms. Five-hundred-pound little mushrooms."

He seemed amazed at his comparison, and amused at the same time. The red kerchief was wrung into a rag.

"Five-hundred-pound little mushrooms," Dufours repeated. "Try an' lift 'at."

"He was a good boss, then," Colm said.

"Oh yeah. Bettern' pa. Pa—"

"About Larocque. Were you aware of his habits? He was frugal, they say, never spent his money."

"I don't know nothin' about that." Was there the barest color rising in his neck? "He pay me every

Sunday out of his pocket. Money stunk. Who cared? A fair wage. Miz L'rocque, she always run after me with cookies or somepin. They say she part Indian, but I don't care. Ma say she she don't mix much, don't come to Home Dem, but she always give me cookies.''

"There was no one who might have disliked her, anyone you might have seen hanging around the place? Arguing with Lucien or Belle?''

"No. No. 'Cept—''

"Uh-huh?''

"Maybe that, uh, Willy next door. He'd give an argument. Too dumb to know better. He was in my class awhile that Willy, couldn't read, do moren' write his name. He got a temper, though, when he's crossed. One time Mr. L'rocque, he say, Willy, you not diggin' that hole right. You want to get up that rock you dig around it, get a pick under it. And Willy say, I'm doin' it my way, it's only way I can, or I quit.''

"And did he quit?''

"No, but he do it his way. Mister L'rocque, he give up. Besides, that guy Tim's always there, takin' Willy's part. Spoilin' him rotten. A retard.''

Colm dug his fingernails into his palms. It was everywhere, the old pecking order. The ants hated the worms, the worms hated the birds. What could you do?

He asked a few more questions but gained no more insight.

One thing, though, Dufours was a talker. Like talking was the only way to get rid of the nerves. Dufours told about Lucien's habit of taking a beer every hour while he worked. It kept Lucien going, he said, and he "don't mind having one with him." And Belle, she let him. "My ma, she'd have a stroke, Pa's bad enough nights when he gits going. Ma keeps him off the booze daytimes. 'Nother reason I want out. I could work a place like L'rocque's, but that's only part-time."

"He may need more help when he gets out of the hospital. Without Belle."

Dufours spread his rakelike fingers. He earned more money here, he explained. Though he hated the lacquer. "Gits in my nose, mask don't keep it out. Sometimes I think, them round bales, they smell good, bettern that lacquer. But I couldn't keep my place then. I need my own place."

"Other than lacquer, it's okay here? The bosses are fair?"

"Okay. I do my work, punch in on time, and they let me alone. That it?" He glanced at the clock. He seemed nervous again, he had to get back to work. He didn't want to get in bad with his boss.

"I hear there's a raffle going on," Colm said as he rose to let Dufours go. He didn't know why the raffle was relevant, but it nagged at him. "You involved in that? They went to Larocque's, I understand, day of the assault."

"That was, uh, Smith, he's one of the salesmen. I know 'cause he ask how to get there. He's always foolin' around the rest of us guys, only salesman who does. Fat guy. Makin' jokes and all. Rest of 'em think they're somethin'. College guys. They don't ask me to do stuff like raffles. I just spray."

"So you talk to Smith. Might have told him about working there, at Larocque's?"

"I might. He likes a laugh. He thought that beer every hour pretty funny."

"He's here today? Smith?"

"Oh no, he quit. Quit couple days ago. He don't like being bossed around, he said. Wants to be his own man."

"I see. Thanks then, Brian. Thanks for your help."

Colm's hand was still sticky with lacquer when Brian withdrew his. He rubbed it on his pants, but the stuff wouldn't come off. Voices sounded in the hall, and Brian looked panicked, almost ripped his kerchief in two.

"Oh, one more thing," Colm said, and Brian wheeled about, a bicycle in a grease spill. "Did you see much of the daughter, Marie, when you were working there? Marie and her husband, Harold?"

Brian thought a minute. "Know Harold from, uh, fire department. But never met her. Not once. You can ask Smith, though. He's a cousin or somepin', I dunno."

"Cousin to who, Marie or Harold?"

But Brian was gone.

"It was Jules Smith," the manager said.

Colm said, "But he quit, Brian told me. He worked alone, then?"

"Naw, there would've been somebody else with him, but we don't know who. Nobody claims the privilege, right?"

"Then where can I find this Smith?" asked Colm.

"He left no address, okay? He was a good salesman

though, smooth. But nobody knew much about him. He came from somewhere across the lake. Drove a red Alfa Romeo. Spent a lot of time with the spray crew. He told jokes and they laughed. Comical guy. We wrote him out a good reference, okay?"

RUTH STOOD on the doorstep a long minute before she knocked. She hated herself for being in awe like this, it was against her principles, all money was tainted in her scheme of things. But the big white house, the well-kept lawn, the bronze sculpture in the front garden—a peregrine falcon it looked like, grasping a sparrow. If she had to wait another minute she might pass out.

And then the door opened. A woman stood there, in jeans like herself, a blue striped sweatshirt, Reeboks on her small feet. Her blonde hair looked freshly set, there was something frail about her, determined.

"Ruth Willmarth. Victor's mother. Is this a bad time? You said one-thirty was okay. I had errands this way. I brought you this."

She held out a pint of syrup. A peace offering. They'd discuss this amicably: no tears, no anger. One reasonable mother to another.

"Come in." Mrs. Unsworth's fingers trembled as she took the syrup. She looked fit for little more than sitting behind a porcelain tea set.

The living room was filled with teak furniture. It looked uncomfortable, all angles and peaks and pastels. Not like a room for three active boys, except for the TV that squatted in the middle like a giant snap turtle. Ruth lowered herself into a lemon upholstered chair. The hostess offered coffee.

"Let me help," Ruth said, not used to being waited on, but the woman was already gone, her footsteps went click-clack on the hardwood floor.

Her hand shook slightly as she offered the coffee, a plate of cookies. "They're store-bought," she apologized. "I thought, when we got up here, I'd have time for baking. At home there was all the volunteering. Junior League, the hospital."

Ruth imagined the charity scene: heads freshly coiffed, the chatter about clubs and children and recipes—she'd take Home Dem over that. Of course, they were doing a service, they were good women. But you couldn't help thinking of them driving away in their expensive cars.

"It's my sheep," Mrs. Unsworth explained. "I thought I wanted to raise sheep. And I love it, I do. I didn't know it was so time-consuming, that's all. The boys complain they don't have any clean laundry. George complains—he's my husband. He's with IBM, if he survives the cuts."

"Do you have help? I wasn't brought up on a farm either. I learned. And now…" Ruth hesitated. She didn't know how much to say about her own life. Though this woman seemed unassuming, holding her cup in two hands like it might fly away.

"Emily told me," Mrs. Unsworth said. "About your husband. I'm sorry."

Ruth was piqued. Emily. Her daughter's name coming out like that, in one familiar breath. How much had Emily told? She felt the red creeping up, tingling her ears.

"I came, Mrs. Unsworth, about my son. And yours. They're in the fifth grade together. There's been... some trouble."

"Carol," the woman said. "My son is named Garth."

That made it more difficult. The first names personalized things. Ruth steeled herself, rushed on, a caught fly, she'd blundered right in. "Your son, and some of the others, are victimizing my son. They call him names, do things."

Mrs. Unsworth—Carol—sat mute as a sheep while Ruth talked. She drew her fingers through her thin curled hair. "I know about the telescope," she said. "Wilder told me. I didn't like it."

Ruth said, "The telescope?"

Outside in the street an ambulance rushed past, its siren quickened her breath. She imagined Colm riding in it, his glasses jumping on his nose.

"Well, Garth had it. They took it from your son. Or your son dropped it. I don't know exactly how it happened. But Garth is sorry. I scolded him. I didn't tell his father because, well, he gets carried away. He worries about his older son, Kurt."

Her laugh was as thin as a spoon dropped in a saucer. She'd said "his" son. This was a second marriage, then?

"I'm sure things will be better," Carol went on. "I told Garth he's a farmer's son too. He laughs, of course. I have to prove he is! It's not easy being a woman with four men, one of them—well. You have a daughter, you're lucky.''

"Two. And a grandson."

"Oh." Carol Unsworth couldn't imagine such luck.

They went out afterward to see the sheep. There were twenty of them, new fencing, a red painted barn, everything neat as a doll's house. Carol picked up one of the lambs, she'd had four freshen in March. A look of wonder came over her face as she talked about it, like she'd witnessed a miracle.

"How nice," Ruth said of the fencing, the barn, the lambs.

The other woman smiled her china smile and offered a trembly handshake. "I don't know many women in town. Will you come again?"

"Sure," Ruth said, though she doubted she would.

They walked out together to Ruth's pickup. "Just what I need!" Carol exclaimed. "To carry the sheep in. To the vet's, you know."

"Vets will come to you if you need them." Ruth smiled. "It's twelve years old," she said about the pickup. "It's rusted out already, our harsh winters, salt on the roads."

"But the size, the make. It's a Ford?"

"You could probably get a new one at the Ford place in town. They make them in six colors." She smiled at her irony. When she went to leave it took two slams to shut the bent door (Pete skidding into a tree, in his cups). Her breathing came easier as she drove out to the road and finally into the dirt road that led to her farm.

She thought she'd never smelled anything so sweet

as the new grass, pushing up beside the porch steps. Already a pair of orange crocuses poked through the unmowed grass (when would she have time to mow?). She stood there, breathing it all in.

And what had she accomplished anyway, from that visit? She went to the phone to try Colm. Where had he been all day? She found a message on the answering machine. But not from Colm.

It was Bertha. "Get Vic to his father at once," the voice demanded, sounding raspy, tinny. "I had a vision. A terrible one. He's in terrible danger here." And the machine clicked off.

"That woman," Ruth said aloud, "belongs in a nuthouse." She dialed Colm.

WILLY'S SEEN the fellow before, here at the Alibi, but there wasn't no talk between them. For one thing, the fellow always joking around, slapping people on the back, and Willy don't like that. He don't like to be touched like that. His first foster father joke around, and then come the beatings. It was the way the drink work inside him. First the jokes and then the beatings. The next seventeen was better, but not a whole lot. The last didn't laugh at all, man nor woman, just work all the time. They kept calling up Tim to take him away, and Tim did. And Willy liked that. He even kept his rabbit in Tim's apartment. Now when Willy has his fits Tim don't mind. Willy likes being with Tim more than anything.

But this guy tonight, he start slapping Willy on the back. Start asking him questions, big red face lit like a sign. ''Where you from, boy? You know how to read, boy? Hold your liquor can you, boy?''

And orders Willy another beer. And not O'Doul's either, though the bartender knows.

''I only drink two,'' Willy says. ''That all I can have.''

''Big strapping boy like you? Come on.'' The man's face beams into his like a headlight.

''Two beers. And I had 'em. O'Doul's.''

''This strapping boy's drinking O'Doul's,'' the man tells the woman on the other side of him. ''Imagine that. O'Doul's. Might as well be milk. And him all of—how old you, boy? Twenty-two? Twenty-three?''

''Twenty-one,'' says Willy proudly. ''February twelfth. Tim say me and Abe-ham Lincoln.''

The man thinks that's just too too funny. He laughs and laughs, his fat sides pulsing. ''Four score and twenny years ago,'' he says, and gasps with laughter. ''Finish it, kid.''

Willy doesn't know what four score is, but he knows what twenty-one is. He's twenty-one years old. That means he's a man, Tim says, and this guy better not make fun.

''I couldn't help I was born,'' he says. ''My mother born me and then she die. And my father he go away. And then I got my first home. It not my fault.'' He feels a burning in his chest.

''Simmer down, kid, I didn't say it was. Here, I'll buy you a Pepsi.'' And the man pulls out a wad of bills. ''You want to make some money? You want to make all this money in one short time?'' He flaps the wad at him.

Willy can use the extra money. He has a rabbit now, he needs paint for the rabbit's box, and food. It's a beautiful rabbit. Beautiful. All pure white. And pink eyes. Pink eyes!

The man pulls out a package. "Take this down to the bakery, down by the creek. You'll see a blue pickup there, it's got a big dent in the passenger door. Put the package on the seat, that's all you gotta do. For this."

It's old smelly money, the bills wrinkled up like they'd sat in somebody's pocket for years and years. Willy don't know if he wants that old money. He drinks his Pepsi, his hands clamped around the glass. The bartender is moving closer, and the man slides the money back in his pocket.

"Yes or no?" the fat man says. "Take it or leave it."

"Two fifty," says the bartender, leaning over the counter, looking into the man's face.

The man slides his tongue around his lips. He reaches into an inside pocket, takes out two fifty. The bartender sniffs it, and then takes it to the register. "I gotta go," the man says. "You want this money, you follow me out," and he gets off the stool. The stool keeps rotating after he's up.

"Say, what's your name?" the bartender calls after the man. "I've seen you in here before."

"Jasper," the man calls back. "Jasper Magillicuddy."

Willy knows he's lying, nobody named that. He's not going to follow the man out. "He want me to take some package,'' he tells the bartender. ''I don' like his money, all smelly.''

''Like a barn?'' the bartender says, sounding very interested. When Willy looks at him he says, ''Go out and get his license number, okay? For another Pepsi? Copy it down. The way you see it.''

''I don't want another Pepsi,'' says Willy. ''Tim say two beers and one Pepsi enough.''

''For this,'' says the bartender, and holds up a crisp new dollar bill.

When Willy gets out there he can't see the man. But in the far end of the parking lot the rear lights of a car shine like cat's eyes. He goes down to look at the license plate. He can't write but he remembers how things look—that's one of his special talents, Tim says, he remembers how things look. Willy's proud of that. Four numbers on the license plate and only two different letters: HAHA. Looks funny, but that's what it is. The car is bright red. Willy plans to paint his rabbit hutch red. The dollar will pay for the paint. He thinks how his white rabbit will look in that red box.

''You're here, are you?'' says the man, coming out of the trees, zipping up his trousers. ''About time. Now take this envelope where I told you. Can you remember? Down to the creek there. Put it in the blue pickup. It's the only blue one with a dent in the right-hand door.''

He holds out two crumpled bills. Even from here Willy can smell them. Something about the way the man stares at him, like looking right through him into the building behind, not seeing Willy at all, that brings up a stone in Willy's stomach. The stone says no. Don't take the envelope. Don't take the money.

Willy says, "You take it."

The man says, "I got new shoes on, it's muddy down there by the water. Now I'm offering you money. Make it three fifty."

Willy turns back toward the bar. His fingers feel the new dollar bill in his pocket. "I gotta better one," he tells the man over his shoulder. "I gotta bran' new one, don't smell."

The man's hand comes down on his shoulder like a clamp, like that foster father's fingernails in the flesh. "Why'd you come out here then?" the man demands. "Who sent you, you fucking retard? Was it that bartender?"

"He give me this," Willy says. "I'm telling."

He's not going to be afraid, not going to be bullied. The foster father said not to tell, not to tell what he was doing to Willy. Now Willy would. He'd tell. He's with Tim now. Tim won't let anybody hurt him. Tim—

"Tim say don't do that!" he cries as the hand slams down on his head. "Tim say—" as the boot kicks up at his belly.

The pain is a bullet in his groin, shoving him down, his arms shoot out like pieces of metal, released by a spring, but meet nothing, like he's fighting air.

The man lets him go then, Willy staggers down behind the bar, down the embankment, he needs air, he needs to breathe in the fresh creek air. He runs hard, like he can outrun the pain that's knotting him into a ball. The ball kicks, drags, rolls him over and over, down and down the bank.

And there they are, the others. He holds up an arm, his teeth clatter like breaking dishes, "Don' wanno fight, don'—" He hears the voices now, voices in his head like when it comes on, the fit. He tries to speak, but only squeals come out, like his rabbit when it hit its head once.

"Hey, dummy, get up and fight." The voices crackle like lightning, seize his bowels till he can't control himself, he'll let go and they'll see... Then the water, cooling at first, then hot and he gasping, sinking.

Tim-mm, he cries inside his head, Tim-mm-mm, and the word soaks into the creek.

LUCIEN TESTED his ankles out the side of the bed. They quivered like pudding at first but then held up, and he was standing, holding on to the iron bar of the hospital bed. For that's where he was: in a hospital. He had it all straight now. It was the middle of the night, there was a knock, and then the two masked figures. The struggle, and then Belle, lying on the floor, blood running down her eye, her unraveled braid.

How long had he been here? A day, two days, three? More? He had to find Belle, she had to be here.

He flipped aside the curtain, but the lax face of an old man lay nose up in the bed. He remembered about this place: they kept the men from the women, husband from wife. They didn't care. Mother of God, they didn't care.

He lurched to the metal closet and groped for his coat. It was there, thank God. He jammed his hand into the pocket, felt for the ripped lining, reached deep down.

Where was his money? Jesus-Mary, where was his money? His six—no, seven thousand dollars! More maybe, not always time to count.

They took it, that's why they broke in like that! Beat him up then took his money. His money he made with his own sweat. Those bastards, they got no damn right! The money he and Belle worked their guts out for. The money in the barn, the rafter hole—was it still there? He had to get out of here, go look... Belle.

Where was Belle?!

He limped out into the hall. It was morning, must be. Light coming through a far window. He hurt like hell, his bones felt banged in, his head a zoo. He had to find her.

"Just a minute here, sir."

He pushed past the restraining hand, down to the nurses' station. He was here when Marie was born, then that hernia, a quick in and out, Belle had her hysterectomy. They were always tearing you apart, patching you back together. Charging you plenty. Fleecing you. The health insurance a racket, bleeding you dry. Hell, he has no insurance now, only that Medicare—not worth a damn.

He has to get out of here!

"Here, you, Mr. Larocque. Get back in bed. You're not ready to come out." She was a big one, hands like shovels, pushing him back down the corridor. Treating him like a child. When he was a man, a man!

"I want Belle," he shouted. "Where's she?" And then all the whispering, like the creek swelling up late April, behind his farm. And calling Dr. Somebody, and then they were on him, shoving him into a wheelchair, jamming in needles, clucking and clicking till the noise got farther and farther away and his head was heavy as a full pail of milk; and far down the corridor like it was coming out of a loudspeaker that wasn't working right someone said, "Belle's gone, Lucien, Belle's dead."

And his head swelled up again like a drum that beat and beat and beat, like a whole goddamn army, a whole parade drumming through his head, thundering: Belle's dead, she's dead, she's dead dead dead. Sweet Mary Mother of God, Belle's dead!

THE HEAVENS could be falling in and the animals had to be grained. Thank God she had this routine to hold on to. Regular as the sun: five-thirty in the morning, five-thirty at night. One of them bawling now, a big protest, next down the line: Bathsheba, who refused to wait. She had a half grown calf now—would it change her? The pinkeye, at least, hadn't spread to the others.

Charlotte was next, getting old, not giving so much milk anymore, even to her new calf, but still ornery. The old girl butted her head softly into Ruth's shoulder.

"That's it," Ruth said. The feed dropped into the manger. "That's all you get. You just think you want more. Typical woman, not wanting to compromise. But that's it, you old independent. Till tomorrow."

She patted the cow's rump, closed the bars on her

and the thin calf. It was still too frail to go in a heifer pen. The cow was impatient, she stomped, blew bubbles on her breath, lashed her tail. She wanted to be outdoors.

"Spring's coming," Ruth told her, looking at the mud on her boots. "Just like clockwork. The grass, I can smell it already. Next week maybe, you'll be free."

Charlotte went on butting and snorting. She wanted action, not words. Some days Ruth wanted to hug her. Some days she did.

Outside the barn the sun was melting over the mountains, spreading a pinky-orange glow, like cheese. A transparent moon was creeping through a curd of clouds. Ruth let it fill her, calm her. The natural world was in order at least. If she waited, so might her life be. Murderers would be caught, victimizers brought to justice. Wouldn't they?

But Belle was dead.

And what now? Colm Hanna's Horizon was steaming into the driveway. "Colm!" She ran toward him. "Where have you been? I've been trying all day—"

Colm looked grim, the sun glared red in his face. He climbed out and squinted at the sunset like it was trying to fool him somehow, like he was suspicious of it. He spied her and tried to smile. He acted as impatient as Charlotte, as unsettled, grouchy. When she went to him, wanting him in a good mood, he grabbed her arm. It pinched.

"Better come in," he said. "I have news you won't like. Is Tim around?"

"He left early. He's looking for Willy. He didn't

come home last night. He's usually at the group home, but not last night. I hope nothing—'' She examined his face.

He put a hand on her arm to guide her inside. "Is it something about Willy?" she said, putting out a hand to ward off bad news.

He took the hand, squeezed softly, sat her down on a kitchen chair though she didn't want to sit. She wanted to take bad news standing up. She was in bed when Pete defected. Afterward she'd felt sat on, squashed.

He sat beside her, still holding her hand. "Willy was found an hour ago," he said. "By a canoeist, in the creek, half a mile below the Alibi."

She didn't understand. Found? She felt guilty that she was half relieved. That it wasn't Emily, who was out with Wilder. Or Vic. Or Sharon and the baby. Oh, God...

And then that swimming sensation in her head. Willy? "What was he doing in the creek? He can't swim. Tim never could teach him to swim. He knows enough to stay away from there. Unless he had something besides O'Doul's. That bartender knows better! Willy always obeys. He won't go near the creek unless—"

"He wasn't trying to swim, Ruth," Colm said, his voice gritty as dust. "He was dropped in there. He could have had a seizure before—or after, I don't know. He was epileptic, right? He'd gone after a number on a license plate, the bartender said. Why send him when the boy couldn't read? But we don't have the license plate."

The end of the story staggered past her ear. Something about a license plate, a strange man, Willy drowning. She stared into Colm's eyes. They were bright with sun.

He was still talking. He was still gripping her hand.

SEVEN

THEY BURIED BELLE in the small Revolutionary cemetery behind the farm. Lucien gave the plot to the town when he bought the place, but he still maintained it in his unorthodox way. "There are only two French names in there," Ruth told Colm, "but he puts flowers on the graves every July fourteenth—Bastille Day, you know. One of the families is still around, but they let Lucien do it."

They were standing by the new-dug grave: Lucien, Marie in black pants and brown suede jacket, her shy gaunt husband Harold, and little Michelle, who was diving after grasshoppers. Even now the husband was running after the girl, it gave him something to do, she supposed; he seemed ill at ease with this funeral, with Ruth and Colm, with Pete's sister, who as Ruth feared, was full of comments.

"These Catholic funerals," Bertha said, hitching up her panty hose. And then, trying to shield Vic again, her vision: "It's no place for a child. If Pete were here—"

"But he's not," Ruth said, and heard a sound like a hiss, in return. Was literal religion the snake in the garden? Maybe so. The way some saw life, anyway.

"You'll be sorry," Bertha warned. "I had a telegram from Pete. The Lord—" But when Colm moved closer to Ruth, Bertha quieted. Her cheeks turned apple pink.

Conscious that her elbows were touching Colm's sleeve, Ruth moved a step back toward Bertha, eyed a contingent from the Home Dem that Belle had avoided. They stood there in drab dark dresses, eyes cast down on the budding crabgrass like they'd put down their own roots. They were carrying out their duty, the folded hands said; patience stuck out in the knucklebones.

It was a warm April day, the cedar tree that shaded one corner of the burial ground bore fresh willowy sprouts; an early robin was digging in last year's crushed leaves. The world: in bloom at the graveside. And Lucien, left behind, leaning forward as the coffin was lowered. He looked dazed, like a small boy in school for the first time, awkward in a blue suit that had shrunk in the legs. They'd let him out of the hospital only this morning, he was to report back tonight—though Lucien said no: Belle was home now, he'd stay till they put him under, too.

His lips moved with Father Benoit's prayer. When the priest was done Marie handed her father a flower to drop on the coffin. He stood there, staring at it, till she tapped him on the arm, and he took a tottering step and tossed the flower on the casket. Michelle picked up the flower her mother had thrown and held it up triumphantly. Marie nudged Harold, but his flower missed the casket, and Marie scooped it up, with a frown. A pair of female cousins looked on shyly, in sturdy shoes and dark rayon dresses. The Home Dem straightened their shoulders to a woman.

Bertha had an enigmatic smile on her lips, like she knew where Belle was heading, and it wasn't heaven, not for Indians. Ruth's heel caught in a hole as she shifted position; Colm steadied her elbow.

Colm's eyes were shifting—looking for something? Relatives, friends? No one was sacrosanct. She'd drowned in his questions.

Drowned—there was that, too. With Belle's burial she'd almost forgot poor Willy. Tim was too distraught to come, he was collecting Willy's things, making burial plans. There was no money for that, it would come out of Tim's pocket. She'd help; she could sell one of the calves.

At last it was over, Marie and Harold supporting Lucien back over the uneven grass, Father Benoit stooping down to the granddaughter, hoisting her onto his shoulders. He seemed a jolly sort: short, pugnosed, a smile bubbling on the lips. Pete's sister would disapprove of the smile. But Bertha was talking with the women, one of them likely in her church: animated now, hands describing something—her vision, maybe?

Belle had never said, but Ruth knew: Belle wanted freedom of thought, choice above all else, in her life. Choice! What was life without it?

Now Ruth and Colm were the only ones left at graveside. Ruth stepped forward, she had her own prayer. "Go with the spirits," she told Belle, the Indian words rising out of something she'd read about the Crees. The Crees thought one was descended from the trees, returned to the trees, to the earth, to nature. Ruth liked that.

"Go with nature," she said and, kneeling down,

laid a switch of cedar on the coffin top. Colm didn't try to break her silence, just put a hand on her elbow. They walked back together across the pasture that was planted with winter wheat, past the gray weathered barn, the unpainted silo. Past the rusted machinery that Lucien would make run until, like himself, it wore out and was dragged off.

They moved in silence up to the back porch of the house where the blood stains hadn't wholly washed away from Lucien's crawl to the road; into the kitchen where the women were unpacking plates of cookies and small sandwiches and a jug of lemonade onto the white metal table. They were good women. Even Bertha meant well, didn't she? She'd had her disappointments in life—Colm, for one. She was offering him lemonade, practically dancing on his toes, her cheeks pink balloons. Colm flashed a distress signal, and Ruth swallowed a smile.

If Pete were here he'd insist on beer. Well, he might have come up from New York, he didn't live on the moon! But he wasn't here, and it was a relief, really. His weekly call to the kids was due tonight. She might have to talk to him herself, about that broker, for one thing. About Bertha's visions. They were getting on her nerves.

Why was it she resented, more than ever, speaking to him?

TIM WAS HOLDING up a shirt of Willy's. He was giving the clothes to the group home, he told Colm. Tears crowded the crevices of his craggy face, dampened his beard. "Jesus," he kept saying, "Jesus. What in hell's goin' on here, Hanna?"

It was the fourth time he'd said that, it was nothing Colm could answer. "We don't know why," Colm said, "but we think we know who. It has to be the fat man in the bar, the one who handed over the smelly money. But no one can identify him, or the car. Only Willy knew that."

And died for it, he thought.

"He was smart," Tim said. "Smarter than people realized, see? It takes time, that's all, to get rid of the bad stuff inside. He had more smarts than anyone knew."

"I know."

What else could one say? It was a lousy business, this. Colm wanted to punch out the wall! But it was Tim's wall, and covered with posters: views of the Grand Canyon, the Taj Mahal, David Bowie in concert. Colm had some old 45s at home of Bowie.

"We'll find this guy," Colm said, feeling the hornet in his chest. "Somehow. We got his description from the bartender. We'll get the guy." Or guys—he had to be connected with someone else, didn't he? There were two men that night?

"It won't bring Willy back."

"No. Or Belle."

The murders had to be connected, he felt sure of that. Willy had found out something the murderer wanted to hide. Or murderers. Yes, he had to keep thinking, double.

"Look, if you hear anything, anything that can help us. Maybe talk to the bartender yourself. He might

remember something more. Sometimes people do."
He handed Tim his business card.

Tim stuck it in a pants pocket. "Willy can't swim,"
he said, like Willy were still alive. "I never could
teach him to swim. He's afraid of water. He
wouldn't've gone in it himself."

Even if he could swim, Colm thought, he wouldn't
have had a chance. He must have been half unconscious before he was thrown—or pushed in, maybe.
The embankment behind the Alibi was steep. A snow-
ball would roll on into the creek. And there were the
seizures. The police were calling it accidental for want
of evidence. It was impossible to determine the exact
manner of death from drowning, he knew that from
his father. Epileptic seizure or not, the drowning victim had to breathe, take in more and more water until
respiration stopped.

Drowning was a slow, agonizing death—he didn't
tell Tim that. The water was cold, Willy's body already in advanced rigor mortis when they found it
floating, full of gas. The question remained: Was
Willy dead before he hit the water? There were abra-
sions on the head, odd red marks on the abdomen. But
some might have come from sand and weeds. A
drowned body was usually facedown, the face and
limbs dragging on the bottom.

The police had found only a child's boxing glove
on the waterfront, a couple of Pepsi bottles—wet,
nothing they could get fingerprints from.

"You might like to keep this," said Colm, picking
up a snapshot of Willy and his rabbit from the floor.

Tim took it and turned his face away.

"WILDER GETS HOME around three-thirty," Carol Unsworth said when Colm asked for the boy. Her voice was stiff, her lips set in a thin lavender line. "I don't let him take the car to school. He goes on the school bus like the rest."

The implication was that he wasn't like the rest but that she wanted him to be. Colm sat down in the only hardback chair he could find. He'd wanted Ruth with him, but she'd already been here, she said—enough. Besides, it was a delicate matter, speaking to Emily's boyfriend. It took an objective listener. The woman served tea, then sat opposite in a yellow chair. The whole room was yellow, it was like sitting in the middle of a squeezed lemon. She perched on the edge, like she was ready to spring. What had her son to do with a murder?

"He's a good boy," she said. "We've had trouble with the older one, I suppose you know that. I told Ruth Willmarth. He got in with the wrong crowd. His father and I tried, but what can you do? It's like the sixties: don't trust anyone over thirty. I was never a part of that. Do you have children, Mr. Hanna?"

"Colm," he said, "my name is Colm. No, I'm not married." He left it at that. There was always that twinge of guilt when women asked. Like he'd somehow shirked responsibility or was to be pitied. He straightened his glasses, his shoulders. His father complained of his posture.

But he wasn't here for small talk. There'd been two murders. Wilder had left the Willmarths' the night of the first. Colm wanted to speak to him—alone. He made that clear.

The door opened and Wilder came in, a green book sack on his back. He was a tall, good-looking boy, the kind you'd place above suspicion because he looked like the all-American kid, down to his green and white Proctor Academy Soccer T-shirt. He narrowed his eyes at Colm. Then, as they were introduced, the look changed to a forced smile.

Carol Unsworth was politic, she retired to the kitchen. Still, the boy seemed nervous, kept glancing in that direction. Colm suggested a walk.

"A walk?" The boy frowned.

"Out back maybe. I see you have sheep."

"They're mother's." The tone was deprecatory.

"My mother kept sheep too. It was a long time ago."

The boy nodded, he didn't look very interested. But he got up and went to the back door. The mother was peering into a cupboard. From the rigid way she stood, Colm knew she was aware of them. The boy never glanced at her, led Colm out back to the sheep pen. A dozen sheep were lolling about: they turned in unison to stare at Colm. He felt, well, sheepish.

The boy was waiting.

Colm got to the point. "You were with Emily Willmarth that night. I thought you might have seen something."

The boy shrugged, spread his hands. Stared ahead, slightly beyond the sheep, like he'd pretend they weren't there.

"Emily said you didn't leave at once, that you sat in the car. There was a full moon."

This time he'd connected. Wilder turned his head:

a blaze of eyes. A little miffed maybe that Emily had told his secrets.

"Maybe I did," he said. "Maybe I looked at the moon."

"Sure. Any guy would—with or without his girl."

Wilder's cheeks pinkened. Maybe he didn't like a middle-aged man, a bachelor, "understanding" him. But he said nothing.

"This would have been just before midnight. That you got to the car, I mean. When did you leave?"

The cheeks deepened to red. "I don't know. I didn't look at my watch. Maybe ten minutes later. Fifteen. Twenty. I don't know. I was thinking, that's all."

Colm was careful. He didn't ask what the boy was thinking about. He could imagine that. He remembered how it was with Ruth. He was more interested in what the boy had seen.

"What was I supposed to see?"

"A car? Two men? Anything different from the norm. It wasn't the first time you'd taken Emily home, was it?"

"No."

"Well then?"

The knuckles were white where the boy was gripping the fence. There was the same rigidity of spine he'd seen in the mother.

"Nothing," Wilder said. "Nothing different." He turned to Colm. "Emily would have seen something if there'd been anything. She was looking out the window. What did she tell you?"

"She only looked for a few minutes. Then her mother came in the room."

"Oh. Well. I told you, there was nothing. I looked at the goddamn moon and then I left. Okay?"

The boy was irritated, he looked like he might cry. Colm was sure he'd seen something. Something or someone. Someone he didn't want to tell on.

Unless—he hadn't left that night, not for a long time anyway, till he'd accomplished what he came to do. Hadn't his father cut off his allowance? Emily had told Ruth that. He might not have meant to hurt anyone. But if Lucien fought back, the blood would go to his head.

The chin was quivering slightly, the hands still gripping the fence, small for a boy's hands. No, it was hard to imagine Wilder Unsworth beating on an old man and woman. Unless he was the one who stood by. Let the other do the work.

Whoever the other was. The one who'd killed Belle, and maybe poor Willy Beeman.

"I left my cap in your living room," Colm said. "If you don't mind I'll go back in with you."

"Sure." Wilder's hands were red and serrated where they'd held onto the fence.

"My mother's sheep were Scottish Blackface. Black noses and feet, real shaggy. I have a sweater made of the wool. Warmest one I own. Full of holes though now."

"Mom's knitting one for Christmas. If she can stand to cut off the wool."

"Fleece."

"Huh?"

"Fleece is what they call the wool. They shear it

each spring. It's a time-consuming process. I helped as a kid.''

The boy looked at him with some interest. The eyes were intelligent, the mouth was mobile, sensitive. There was the flicker of a smile. Then the mouth went dead again.

"We call it Mother's folly," he said, and led the way to the back door.

Carol Unsworth was at the window, examining a tiny break in the pane. She'd have stood there, watching the interrogation. She'd have seen how nervous her son was.

"Garth threw a softball," she said. "I have to get a new pane of glass.''

"I hate to think how many windows I broke as a kid," Colm said.

She smiled back, she seemed grateful. "It went all right?" She was looking at Wilder.

"What'd I have to tell him?" said Wilder, and strode through to the front of the house.

A second later he was back. "This your cap?" he said. He turned it over in his hands.

Colm had two dozen of them, all bought in Ireland. Different blends of tweed. Not to mention derbys, baseball caps, a green Rogers Rangers hat, though he felt foolish wearing it.

"You want it?" he said. "Hats are taking up my whole closet. My father complains.''

Wilder examined the cap. It was handmade tweed, autumn colors, brown and gold with a reddish cast.

"You'd give it away?" He looked suspicious.

"Honest." Colm threw up his hands. "It's not my favorite. I just grabbed one on my way out."

Wilder hesitated, then stuck out his hand. "All right." And clapping it on his head, he ran outdoors and disappeared into the garage.

"I can't pay you?" said Carol Unsworth, looking embarrassed, and Colm said, "It was my gift." Then, "I have to be going. Appointment with the police chief."

She looked upset when he said that.

She showed him out the front, through the pastel living room, past the porcelain and fine bone china. It wasn't until he was out on the front porch, by the stone sculpture of the falcon, that he realized what he'd seen.

Three books of raffle tickets from Catamount Furniture on the hall table. Who but a mother would indulge her son, buy up the tickets the kid hadn't been able to sell?

THE GUYS HAD already begun the recess soccer when Vic went out. He'd been kept after by old Ronsard again, he wasn't doing the arithmetic right. He hated arithmetic. He might even hate Mrs. Ronsard. She was so sweet—sweet as sour cream. Joe Piezzo was running after the ball, two other guys bumping into him, one of them Garth Unsworth. He kicked the ball away from Joe, it bounced out of bounds and hit Vic in the head. Everybody laughed. The girls laughed on the sidelines. One of them, Sue Ellen Brewer, grabbed the ball and ran with it and the guys tackled her, knocking her down. Her shirt hiked up out of her pants and they guffawed.

Vic was mad then. The guys never let any of the girls into the soccer game, though Sue Ellen was a faster runner than any of them. He went to help her up, though she was practically twice his size, and when she was standing again, the tears flying out of her eyes, her chin bleeding, the jeers began.

"Manure loves Sewer," they chanted, "Vicky Manure loves Slimy Sewer." The gibes swelled the schoolyard. Vic felt the shadows fall over him. A finger poked his arm, a foot stung the tender crease of his knee. He hit back at it.

"Shut up!" he screamed. "Shut up, you bastards." He got coughing, his nose filled up. He couldn't breathe, it was the asthma.

"Victor Willmarth, repeat that word and you'll march straight up to the principal." Mrs. Ronsard was mad, so mad her two chins were waggling. Vic saw the kids were glad, too, glad he was getting it from Ronsard.

"They knocked Sue Ellen down," he told her, gasping out the words. "It was Unsworth and that gang. They're after her and they're after me. You never see that. You think they're just perfect. You think everybody's just perfect! Well, they're liars. They steal. They stole my telescope."

"Liar. Dirty little pigfucker. Dumb farmer boy. Cheap—"

"That's enough!" Mrs. Ronsard screeched. "Get back inside, every one of you. You'll stay after school, the whole class. We'll have this out once and for all. No one talks like that in this schoolyard."

"I can't stay," Vic said, getting his breath back. "I have to get back."

"Don't you backtalk me," she yelled, she'd lost it now. "I'm your teacher. If I say stay, you stay."

The kids poured back in the school. Sue Ellen walked close behind him. He could hear her raspy breathing in the back of his neck. She blew her nose practically in his ear, she had a cold.

"You wait," a voice crooned. It was Marsh. "You'll get it for that." He knocked Vic in the elbow and walked on.

Sue Ellen caught up with him. As they entered the classroom her body squeezed against his and he pushed her back.

"Your father works in a sewer," he said softly, and saw her give him a swift hurt look.

AT NINE THAT evening the phone rang: Pete was right on time. If he made the weekly call he was fulfilling his fatherly duties. "Emily?" she hollered. "It's your father."

Vic appeared at the head of the stairs. "She's in the bathroom. Emily? It's Dad. Hurry up! I need to get in there."

The phone went on ringing. A little breathless, belly aching—she was about to get her period—Ruth picked it up.

"Oh, hi." Pete's voice sounded small, properly subdued.

There was a silence. Then, "How are you? How's the farm going?" Voice getting stronger. "I was going to write, ask about the trees, suggest Tim make some kind of irrigation system. You can lose the whole thousand in a drought."

"It rained last night," she said.

"Oh. Good."

Another silence. Where was Emily, for God's sake!

"So how is everybody up there? The kids? Tim and Willy?"

Of course he didn't know about Willy. "Willy's dead. He drowned in the creek. Tim is distraught. We all are. We think it might be connected with—the other. We don't know."

She heard the long slow whistle of breath. Pete had been fond of Willy, he'd tease him, he was good with him. Pete was a natural with children—other people's children. 'Careful now,' he'd say, 'do it this way, that's it, good, man.' And Willy was literally puffed up, pleased with himself. Pete knew how to make people feel good about themselves. Other people, not his wife.

"Better keep the doors locked at night," he said. She could picture him, furrowed brow, stiff upper lip: don't let the emotion show. "Until it blows over. Bertha tells me... "

"It won't blow over." He could annoy her so with a word. "Deaths don't 'blow over.' They leave a hole that can't be filled." What was it about death that brought on the clichés?

His sigh made a hollow sound in the receiver. She knew he was annoyed, too. She was being prudish, precise again, like her mother; he used to say that in the early days of marriage. "Just like your mother," he'd say, "down, woman." A fist squeezed her bones, bore into her flesh with five fingers. He could say what he wanted, she couldn't.

Then relented. At least he was thinking of the family, suggesting they lock the doors. He never used to believe in locked doors. Vermonters don't lock their doors, he'd tell people from out of state. "Do you lock your door down there in New York?" she asked, trying to sound light. It was hard to talk to Pete without the tears pushing through.

He gave a half laugh. "Yeah, we do." She noted the 'we.'

Emily was coming downstairs with Vic. "You talk first," she told the boy. "I need a soda."

"Here's Vic," Ruth said, and added, in rapid succession: "We had the funeral this morning, Belle's funeral. It was hard for everyone. Vic is still having trouble in school. I hope you're having a good time in New York."

It was cruel, the juxtaposition, she couldn't help it. She went to the refrigerator and got out a beer. She heard Vic say, "Hello, Dad," and then stand there, the phone held away from his ear. She could hear Pete from here, something about a movie he'd rented; he wanted Vic there to watch it with him. The boy's thin, angular face was expressionless, feet splayed apart in the ripped sneakers he insisted on wearing, though he had a brand new pair in his closet.

Emily reappeared with a can of Pepsi, stood behind Vic, erect, her young face smooth, impassive, not looking at her mother. "I can't come to New York, Dad, I just can't," Vic said into the receiver; and then "Here's Emily," and he ran upstairs.

Ruth took her beer into the living room and sank into the old maroon sofa. There would be no money now for a new slipcover. The room looked so ugly with its ancient wingback chairs, her mother's narrow black rocker, the scratched bookcase, the blue carpet, worn to the nub in places. She put her head back and let the beer ease her belly. Emily could say the final good-bye. Emily was closer to Pete than Vic, Ruth didn't want to hear the conversation. Sometimes Emily looked at Ruth as if it were Ruth that had made him go away—and maybe it was. She finished the beer in one long guzzle. And felt her stomach turn over.

Pete couldn't take Vic away from her! He couldn't—could he?

POLICE CHIEF Roy Fallon seemed amused that Colm was involving himself in this "investigation." "Maybe you'd consider coming on the force," he said. "We might have an opening. One of our detectives, Wisnowski, thinking about retirement—after he solves this one, that is. Of course you'd need some, um..."

Colm, who'd lately been thinking of that very thing, was turned off by the offer. For one thing, he'd just seen Mert Downes walk past. He remembered Ruth's distaste for the man, his officiousness. The way he'd lift one arrogant eyebrow when you said something, like it was all wrong. The way he wore his hair, combed over from the back to hide the bald spot. It seemed a metaphor for his whole self.

"Possibly," he said. "Though I'll need your official stamp again, in this, um, investigation."

"And how did it go, then, at Catamount? Place has been around a long time. Employs a lot of people. They wouldn't like it if—I mean, a raffle ticket. Well, we'll fingerprint. You think?"

Roy Fallon had a way of not finishing sentences that left one's head in a cloud. But Colm didn't mind, really. The man was solid at bottom. For one thing, he'd admired Colm's grandfather.

Colm told him about the fat man. "Fat Man, I call him for lack of a better name. You realize we have two murders now."

"Well, the second is questionable," said Fallon, lighting a cigar. "Do you mind? My father lived to be ninety. I don't see why I should..." He looked apologetic.

"It's on your conscience," Colm said. "My grandfather died at fifty. Of course he was helped along."

"I'm aware." Fallon nodded at the portrait over his head. Colm's grandfather looked like he wanted to be someplace other than on the wall: in the street, or the saloon. He looked the quintessential Irishman: hat shoved back on the head, the sly grin. Maybe Colm resented that, the stereotype of the Irish drinker. At least the Hannas had been able to hold it, he prided himself on that. Three good drinks and still sober as an owl.

There was little progress to report on the detective sergeant's work. Visitations to the local businesses— no one reporting an exchange of barn money. Interviews with Marie and Harold (Colm made a mental note to see them), with Tim and the Dufourses' son who'd worked for Lucien. No real leads, though Tim wasn't "out from under" yet, according to Fallon. No alibi there, for one thing. Some "iffy" stuff back in the sixties.

"I guess you made the most of it?" Fallon said. "At the Alibi?" He winked at the wall.

"What would be helpful," Colm said, "is a check on the fat man, Smith. Is that his real name? Who he really is, was, where he comes from—anything you can find on him. Where he is now, of course."

Fallon stuck a finger in his ear, ran it around, examined it. "We're trying. Nothing yet. We've no proof of anything there, but you know, we'll... We're not used to murders around here. Domestic squabbles, rape or two at the college, petty thefts, you know. But murder? In Branbury, Vermont?"

Though he looked quite pleased. He was to appear on WCAX-TV tonight, he told Colm. Even now he was going home to shave. "Town's back on the map," he said, and Colm assumed by "back" he meant the Ferraro boy's drug case, the famous son set up by a local detective. Fallon grinned, spread his hands, like it was a holdup.

On the way out Colm ran into Mert Downes. The man was a puffed up martinet, a primitive, something out of Aesop's fables, the frog that blew himself up. Now he was bouncing up to Colm, confiding in him, the chief had bawled him out. Nothing was happening and it was three days already. The townspeople were nervous, there were fifty calls a day: women locking themselves in, walking their kids to school.

There were sightings on the red sports car, of course, Mert said, in his too-loud voice, at the rate of four a day, and the chief wasn't doing a "goddamn thing 'cept running off to TV shows." Mert looked disgusted. He'd apply for detective when Wisnowski left—the guy was too old for this, he said. Did the chief want his murderer to get to China? Mert grinned at his joke. That would take care of him all right. The Commies would chop him up for Sunday dinner. They'd make chopsticks out of him. Hee-hee.

Colm squeezed past the man, smelled something as he went. Had the man let out wind?

They had to find that guy, Smith, solve this thing. Had to! He couldn't name all the reasons.

WHEN HE LEFT the station, Colm went back to Catamount to see Kurt Unsworth. The boy (or man—already the hair was thinning, the forehead lined—cocaine, whatever else, though Kurt was just nineteen) appeared in the door, a forced smile on his face, the lips set like they'd let no negative come across the tongue.

"You know why I'm here," Colm said. He held out a letter Fallon had given him.

Unsworth didn't bother to look at it. He just stood there, tall and lean as a birch tree. Hands in his back pockets, lips pressing together till they turned porcelain. When Colm posed the question, about the fat man and the red car, the lips quivered, like they'd try to come unglued but couldn't. Good-looking fellow in a dead way, the face around the lips was marble.

There was still no answer, and Colm repeated the question. "You delivered brochures together, didn't you? For the raffle?" He didn't want Unsworth to

GET FREE BOOKS AND A WONDERFUL FREE GIFT!

TRY YOUR LUCK AT OUR CASINO, WHERE ALL THE GAMES ARE ON THE HOUSE!

PLAY **Roulette!**

PLAY **TWENTY-ONE**

Turn the page and deal yourself in!

Welcome to the casino!
Try your luck at the roulette wheel ...
Play a hand of Twenty-One!

HOW TO PLAY:

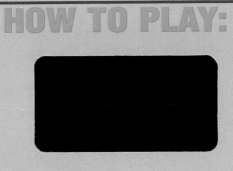

1. Play the Roulette and Twenty-One scratch-off games, as instructed on the opposite page, to see if you are eligible for FREE BOOKS and a FREE GIFT!

2. Send back the card and you'll receive brand-new, first-time-in-paperback Mystery Library novels. These books have a cover price of $4.99 each, but they are yours to keep absolutely free.

3. There's no catch. You're under no obligation to buy anything. We charge nothing—ZERO—for your first shipment. And you don't have to make any minimum number of purchases—not even one!

4. The fact is, thousands of readers enjoy receiving books by mail from the Mystery Library Reader Service™ before they're available in stores. They like the convenience of home delivery, and they love our discount prices!

5. We hope that after receiving your free books you'll want to remain a subscriber. But the choice is yours—to continue or cancel, any time at all! So why not take us up on our invitation, with no risk of any kind. You'll be glad you did!

PLAY TWENTY-ONE FOR THIS EXQUISITE FREE GIFT!

THIS SURPRISE MYSTERY GIFT COULD BE YOURS FREE WHEN YOU PLAY
TWENTY-ONE!

It's fun, and we're giving away FREE GIFTS to all players!

PLAY Roulette!

Scratch the silver to see where the ball has landed—7 RED or 11 BLACK makes you eligible for TWO FREE novels!

PLAY TWENTY-ONE!

Scratch the silver to reveal a winning hand! Congratulations, you have Twenty-One. Return this card promptly and you'll receive a fabulous free mystery gift, along with your free books!

YES!

Please send me all the free books and the gift for which I qualify! I understand that I am under no obligation to purchase any books, as explained on the back of this card.

Name (please print clearly)

Address _____ Apt.#

City _____ State _____ Zip

Offer limited to one per household and not valid to current subscribers.
All orders subject to approval.

PRINTED IN U.S.A.

(U-M-L-03/98)

415 WDL CF4N

The Mystery Library Reader Service™: Here's how it works:

If offer card is missing, write to: Mystery Library Reader Service, 3010 Walden Ave., P.O. Box 1867, Buffalo NY 14240-1867

BUSINESS REPLY MAIL
FIRST-CLASS MAIL   PERMIT NO. 717   BUFFALO, NY

POSTAGE WILL BE PAID BY ADDRESSEE

MYSTERY LIBRARY READER SERVICE
3010 WALDEN AVE
PO BOX 1867
BUFFALO NY 14240-9952

NO POSTAGE
NECESSARY
IF MAILED
IN THE
UNITED STATES

think he was coming after him—just the other guy. He wasn't prepared for the response.

"I was always alone with the raffle tickets, man, when I took 'em—but not that often." His mother, he said, was a "sucker" for "that kind of thing." Kurt had a thick voice, like he'd been drinking gravy.

Yes, another man, Jules Smith, had worked here, Kurt said. Yes, he left. No, he had no idea where. "We hardly spoke, I mean everybody tells jokes, man, it's how we get through a coffee break."

Anyway, Kurt Unsworth didn't care much for jokes.

As for the Larocque house: no, he hadn't been there with tickets. If any were found it would have been that other one, Smith—"serious guy actually," he said with the barest lisp to his gravy voice, "a loner, overweight, yeah, some."

But not Kurt Unsworth. "I've never been in the place," he said and turned up his nose like he could smell it now, in this small white office. The lips relaxed, he seemed to feel he'd exonerated himself, he turned to go.

"We have the tickets," Colm said. "They're down at the station. We'd like to have you stop for fingerprints."

This time he scored. Unsworth wheeled about in the doorway. His voice came out cracked but angry. "Anyone's fingerprints could be on those tickets. We all handled them for chrissake. It was my job to divide them up for the guys to distribute. I'm not going to any fuckin' police to be fingerprinted!"

Colm breathed in the way he'd taught himself to do in real estate. One had to deal with all kinds. Time wasters, young couples who "might." "We'll see," he said and nodded pleasantly, though his Irish was up inside.

He didn't have the temperament for this job, to tell the truth. There was that sudden anger up and he was off. It almost killed him once, up in Montreal, that anger, when he'd got out of his car to respond to a driver's finger, and the driver pulled a knife. It was maybe that anger that brought on his granddad's death.

Well, he should never have mentioned the fingerprinting. Of course he couldn't make this boy-man be fingerprinted. He had no evidence. He wasn't even a policeman. Besides, there'd be any number of fingerprints on the tickets: probably Belle's would cover the rest, and Unsworth knew it. He was smart. Though Colm was certain he now saw fear in the eyes. The eyes looked, well, haunted. He'd seen eyes like that on the dead, on the suicides. His father got a suicide once, twice a year.

Unsworth took a step toward him. "If you must know," he said, "it was my brother Wilder. He was the one sold those tickets. I was, well, under the weather. Wilder took them over to Larocque's for me." He headed for the door again.

Then said over his shoulder, "He's my half brother. He's straight. You understand?"

EIGHT

WHEN COLM FOUND Ruth in the heifer pen, flying at
the end of a rope, he wondered if he'd stumbled into
a rodeo. Seconds later she had it around the neck of
one beast while two others charged about the pen.

"Go, girl," he shouted as she slid through the mud,
or worse.

"Don't just stand there," she yelled back, and he
took a deep breath and plunged in, helped her drag
the roped heifer to a corner post. When the animal
was secured she took a metal ear tag out of her jeans:
"Now get a headlock on this girl."

He said, "What?" and she said, "Hold her tight
while I get this tag on, or it'll rip her ear."

"Darling," he said, and grabbed the heifer. He
hoped Ruth had good aim, he didn't need a yellow tag
in his ear.

The heifer leaped: stood on two front legs, embrac-
ing Colm; then, as the tag sprang shut, sank down on
all fours, staggering Colm back against the edge of the
pen.

"Is that all?" he gasped, "I came to tell you something, not—"

"One more and we're done," she said. "Hang on
now." She roped the neck of a large heifer with a
mean-looking black patch over one eye. When Colm
tried to get the beast in a headlock, she lunged at the

rear of the pen. Colm lost his footing on the shit-slippery floor and skidded six feet on his knees.

The laughter behind him might have come out of a canned game show.

Tim said, "Nice choreography." He pulled Colm upright and brushed him off. Easy as swatting a fly, he grabbed the reluctant heifer and Ruth jammed in the ear tag.

"Where were you when we needed you?" Colm said.

Tim grinned. "Fixing fence. I told you to wait for me, Ruth."

Ruth said, "Oh, but I had Colm."

Colm smiled feebly and stumbled out of the pen. Maybe he knew now why Pete had quit the farm.

It took a full five minutes to get back his breath, never mind his dignity. He couldn't think why he'd come at all. He was wet and miserable, it had snowed two inches the night before—almost mid-April, jeez. One thing he did know: he had to get his boots resoled if he was to keep on seeing Ruth; the wet manure had soaked up into his socks.

"Any news?" she said. Now she was bent over a cow, feeding it something from her hand. He had to admit, she had a fine rump—should he make comparisons?

"I was thinking how good you look. Like that." Then kicked himself for saying it. They weren't students anymore.

She dove back into the cow to hide the flush that was spreading over her face. "Just tell me the news. No backhanded compliments."

There was the red car, that's why he'd come. "The call came an hour ago. They found it in a used-car lot in Plattsburgh. Jules Smith—I doubt Smith is the real name, how obvious can you get?—Traded it in for a tan Honda Civic. Generic looking car, every other car on the highway is gray or tan, a Honda. Of course he doesn't know we're looking for him, but he'd suspect. He knows the bartender would talk. Temporary plates—he'll trade them in. He could be in Kansas by now. Or return here. We only know the trade-in was two days ago."

He'd said it all in one breath. He smiled to meet her smile, patted the cow's rump. "This is Jane," she said. "Jane Eyre, my yearling. Expecting soon, you might gather."

Artificially inseminated, he assumed. There wasn't a bull on the place that he'd seen. Pete came to mind, and he stuck his tongue in his cheek.

He said, "Pleased to meet you, Jane. But I don't want to dance."

The cow turned a wary eye on him, flicked her tail. A fluff of hay flew in his face and he coughed.

"Allergic?"

He moved back a step in case Jane decided to re-lieve herself.

She laughed out loud. The laugh lit up her face, took off years. Though the lines were there, even in the dim-lit barn: the past week had hurt. He was glad he'd come, she needed the support. Her kids had their own lives, they wouldn't help that much, except to keep her busy, worried, frustrated.

He told her about his meeting with Carol Unsworth.

"What did you think of her?" she asked. They were leaning against Jane's stall, like it was a natural place for friends to meet (he'd started to think lovers and slapped his hip).

"Nice lady," he said. "I think 'lady' is the word. The sheep look well cared for. Tell me about your visit."

"Oh, we had coffee and cookies. I was angry when I went there, to talk about school. Her son was one of the ringleaders."

"You mentioned that."

"I was mad, but I calmed down. She made me. She was nervous too. She seem nervous with you?"

"Yeah, I was going to say that. She kept fluttering her eyelashes."

She didn't smile. "Why did you go, really? Because of Wilder's connection to Emily?"

"Basically, yes. I was there to see Wilder, but he didn't have much to say. But I found something interesting."

This time Jane Eyre lifted her tail, and Ruth said, "Oh," and they moved away from the stanchion. Outside the barn, standing in two inches of muddy snow, he told her about the raffle tickets. "A pile of them, mama bought what son couldn't sell."

"Wilder?"

He thought of the liaison with Emily. Besides, Kurt might have been lying. "The older one. Works at Catamount Furniture."

"Oh. I know about him. The druggie. Emily told me. One of the reasons the family came to Vermont. You think he's connected?"

He said, "We have to look at everyone, Ruth. Kurt says Wilder sold the tickets to the Larocques. We have to look into that."

"Ask him. Sounds innocent enough."

"I hope so." He saw her lips press together. "I thought you could ask him."

"Maybe. It's delicate. Or get Emily to."

She came back to the fact of the traded car, the only tangible in hand. "That's good news, anyway. It means the man was guilty, trading in cars like that. Though he must have known he'd be checked on, as you say. I suppose he'll keep trading?"

"Possible. Latest car is six years older. He may just abandon it, buy another. So we're checking everything. Police, FBI. They're alerted across the country, Canadian border."

There was a silence. He saw how attractive she was, even in her muddy shirt. Her neck was palest pale. Celtic skin, he'd read, was especially vulnerable to sun—to feeling, too, maybe. The blood was reddening her nose, or maybe it was the damp air. Anyway, he had to smile. In a minute he'd be ear to ear. He coughed again.

"Got any coffee in that kitchen of yours?" he asked. "I mean, I'll make it if you don't."

She looked confused and said, "Oh, sure, I should have offered. Popovers, too. That is, maybe. Vic's home."

"I'll take my chances." He followed her up to the house, stamping the manure off his feet into the snow. He guessed he needed a shower more than a popover.

She turned by the porch. "Plattsburgh?" she said.

"A used-car lot in Plattsburgh? That's where that broker comes from. I have her card. Plattsburgh, it said."

He tripped on the porch step, thinking about that.

TIM ASKED, "Anything else you want done?" and Lucien shook his head.

Cows milked, barn swept, nothing for it but to face another night. He might have said to the fellow, "Toddy? Come in then," but his tongue wouldn't wrap around the words. Lucien wanted company and he didn't. What he really wanted was up there on the hill. Willmarth's hired man was hardly Belle. Mother of God, hardly!

The beagle Marie got him nipped at his heels, and he pushed it away with a foot. He told Marie he didn't want no other dog after Raoul, but she went and got it anyway. He refused to give it a name, just called it Dog.

But then when Tim was gone, his squarish back moving across the field toward Willmarth's, he wanted to call him back. Maybe he would like company.

"Tim?" Heard his voice, croaking like an old frog.

But too late. Tim kept going. He allowed the dog to come in the house with him anyway. He locked himself in every night now since Belle's death. It was getting familiar, pushing the bolt. He'd filed off the rust, it worked all right. He yanked the shades—Belle'd put them up, he laughed when she did it: "Don't want heifers seeing you in your nightgown, woman?" But he was glad of them. Never thought he would be, but he was. He went to the Kelvinator for ice, tray was all crusty, poured himself a drink. It was Marie's husband brought him the rum. Just handed it to him in a bag, wouldn't look him in the eye. Drank, Harold, but held it, up to a point. Heard him sound off once or twice, mostly about farms. They smelled bad, he said. Well, that was all right, each to his own. No, himself he never drank much. Just a beer off and on.

But there was something in it, he saw why they did it. After the first jolt, the lip pucker, went down smooth, better than any hot plaster on the chest.

He sat down opposite Belle's chair and then pulled himself up again, turned his rocker around to face the shaded window. God, he had to get used to this "alone" thing. Dog wasn't gonna help, he saw that, just sitting there by an empty dish. There was a French-speaking station out of Montreal and he got up to turn on the radio. But it was all talk and he switched it off. Ear didn't pick up French the way it used to, as a boy.

Anyways, with the radio going he couldn't hear. He needed to hear. Loose branch rapping the window, more like a trap sound, trap, trap trap, he'd cut it down tomorrow. If someone came he wanted quiet, wanted warning. He went over to the corner, got his stick. It didn't help much that night, but then the other got to it first. When he had his stick he felt okay. It wasn't gonna happen again. No one gonna get him off guard, by Jesus, get him again, his money. Christ, how he slaved for that money!

He sank back in the chair, red braided mat Belle made, and sipped his rum. If he fell asleep it was all right, he was ready for them. He took a long swallow, it trickled down to his toes—not quite, he had cold feet, poor circulation, Belle used to rub them, they'd never warm up for all the rum.

After a while he got so he didn't start every time the tree branch trapped on the window.

Just every other time.

RUTH DIDN'T walk him to the door afterward, she realized that after the Horizon started up in the driveway. It seemed a long time before he actually pulled out, like he was sitting there, contemplating the stars, up over the silos. Something like a small rain showered through her and she crossed her arms hard across her chest. It was ridiculous, she was acting like a schoolgirl, she should stick to realities.

"Out," she said to the thought, "out." He was only doing his self-appointed work, thought she might remember something, give them another clue, that was why he came. Good Lord! There were two murders in her life, a defected husband, a troubled child upstairs. How much could a woman take?

"Vic?" she called at the foot of the stairs, "Vic?"

There was no answer. She climbed the steps and found him in his room, bent over his homework. He didn't look up when she went in, she saw he was drawing a map. "Of what?" she asked, "where?" Her voice came out loud, bright, she made an effort to be cheerful, make out that life was normal, in spite of two murders. Of course Vic knew it was a charade.

"Australia," he said and bore down with a yellow pencil.

Australia, she thought, Australia, where nothing really new had happened—had it?—since the landing of the convicts in the eighteenth century? Eastern Europe had exploded out of the Communist yoke, the old Yugoslavia was cannibalizing itself, China was still groaning under the old guard, Africa dying of AIDS, South America in the yoke of drug kings. And her son was drawing a map of Australia.

It was wonderful, somehow. Pick a peaceful country, pretend. Pretend, while you're young.

"I've always wanted to go there," she said, "see those furry koalas. You had a koala when you were little, you remember that? I think it was Mimi gave it to you. She went there, you know, when granddaddy was alive."

"It wasn't Mimi," he said, speaking of his mother's aunt. "It was Aunt Bertha. Daddy told her to give it to me."

"Oh." Bertha always did Pete's Christmas shopping for him and attributed it to "Daddy." She wondered if Bertha was buying Pete's gifts for the new woman this year. Did she have a name, this new woman? Oh, yes, one of those popular names, Dawn or Dewdrop or something. Ruth didn't care to remember.

"Tell me about Australia," she said to Vic, and he recited what he'd learned in school. About the climate: desert in the western half, wet jungle in the north; population: 19,508,186 (excluding aboriginals); chief animals: the kangeroo and platypus.

"Any cows?"

"Mostly sheep," he reported. "They got 'em in the outback. I might go there one day and help shear. They live like cowboys. I saw that movie."

She'd forgot the name, something about a crocodile.

They'd seen it together on a rare Saturday night out, she and Pete and Vic. Laughed all the way through. They'd had fun together now and then, the three of them.

"Maybe we should have sheep here," she said.

His face was long and pointed in the lamplight, the chin looked shadowy, like she could see through to the beard that would soon emerge, too soon. She put a hand on the shoulder and thought it trembled. He didn't respond about the sheep.

"Maybe we could, in a small way," she said again. "You could have your own lambs, would you like that?"

"My own?"

"If you take care of them. Just two. Boy and girl?" she suggested slyly, and heard his soft giggle.

She lifted her hand from his shoulder, saw him shiver slightly. Moved across the room to inspect the bed: plaid comforter up over the crumpled sheets, pillow case dragging on the floor. Motherly things were called for in times like these. They were mother and son. There was that fierce animal love.

"Why not sheep?" she shot back over her shoulder. When she turned back he'd finished the map, was shoving it into an orange folder. "Guess I'll go to bed now," he said without expression, and she knew she was dismissed.

She didn't shut the door all the way, it cracked open again, needed fixing like more things in the house than she could count. She'd let the house go to concentrate on the farm. But Vic didn't say anything, he'd left it open every night since Willy's death, and she understood.

"Holler when you're ready for bed," she said, and he said, "Okay," and she went down the scuffed steps, hand balanced on the wall. Pete never got around to installing a railing.

The telephone was ringing. She was glad of that, it was a connection with the world. Vic was safe in his room, Emily with Wilder (safe? Colm had her worried now), Sharon home with her baby—what was there to worry about?

Still, her fingers trembled to pick up the receiver.

The voice was high and sweet, like a little girl's: "Carol Unsworth, Ruth. I know it's late, but I wanted to catch you before morning. I want to have a few kids over after school tomorrow. I thought maybe Vic would come. I'd pick them up myself. Getting to know each other on a one-to-one might help..."

The voice drifted off, low, apologetic for having called so late.

"Oh. Thanks. Well, I'd have to ask Vic. He's in bed now." She felt annoyed, for some reason. Though it was nice of Carol, thoughtful, of course.

"You can let me know before school's over. Actually, I have to go out your way tomorrow. I could stop by. I mean, I'd like to see your setup. I was thinking, I saw a small farm for sale, couple of miles down your road. Maybe I could interest George."

Voice trailing off again, knowing she'd never interest him, Ruth thought. She knew the farm Carol was talking about, either selling or turning into development. She'd wanted it sold as a farm herself, didn't want a bunch of condos rising up there, cars rushing down her road, city people.

But now she was sounding prejudiced. There were fine, sensitive people, too, wanting, needing out of the city. She had to remember that. It could have been her, moving up here, following some kind of gleam.

She heard herself inviting Carol to stop by—what else could she do? "Not before nine," she warned.

But Carol had her sheep, anyway. "Could you get away to look at this farm with me? It's all a pipe dream, I guess, and here we've just bought this place."

Finally, she hung up.

"Vic?" Ruth called, climbing the stairs again, feeling her legs lighter this time, "that was Mrs. Unsworth on the phone, she wants you to come after school for a get-together with her son—Garth? You don't have to, of course," she added when there was no answer (water was running in the bathroom). "Vic? Did you hear me?"

She stood outside till the water stopped running.

At last he said, "I heard you."

THE WOMAN entered Poore's Country Properties where Colm shared an office with two others, and asked for Colm. He'd called her, Esther Dolley said, loud, confident: she was busy, but she happened to be coming this way, took a chance.

She could open a can, he thought, with those fingernails. They were false, he supposed, stuck on. Was that an indication of personality? "I'm looking for an office," she said, her voice at odds with the nails. "Rents are high here."

"Maybe." He felt small enthusiasm for this woman, wouldn't intercede with Helen Poore for a new associate. Unless he decided to get out himself, of course. He looked at her with new interest. He'd called her, yes.

"Meanwhile I'm operating out of my house. I bought a place on Seymour Street. It's next to that group home." She raised an eyebrow. "But it will do for now." She handed him her card. "Nothing going on in Plattsburgh," she said by way of explanation. "That side of the lake, depressed, you know."

"Not much going on here," he said, concentrating on the name Plattsburgh. "Why did you decide on Branbury?"

"Well," she said, like he ought to know. "Well. The farms of course. That's my specialty, you know, farms."

"There are farms all over Vermont. Were," he corrected himself.

"A college town. Things going on. People needing homes, professors, you know."

"You said farms, not homes."

"That's just it. This is the future. We have to face it. The small farms are going, the Midwest will feed us now. The farmers here realize that, they're wanting out. I happen to have a client ... I thought you knew that. I left a message two weeks ago. I thought that's why you called. You might have listings."

"I might."

She looked annoyed at the brevity of his response, then smiled again, recrossed her legs. She was wearing pink stockings with little black cows on them. She was in the game, all right.

"I'll get right down to it," she said. "The Larocque farm, the Willmarths'. Too small individually, you know. But together?" She whacked the palm of one hand. "I might already have Willmarth's. I saw her, she might do it. Husband's gone, too much for a woman. And the Larocques," she looked sorrowful. "Poor man. Alone like that. He'd be better off—"

Colm interrupted before she could say where. "I know him. I'll speak to him." He didn't know why he'd said that, he just wanted to buy time. "Plattsburgh. You don't happen to know a man named Smith, Jules Smith, in Plattsburgh?"

He thought he saw her start. The fingernails fidgeted with the clasp of her alligator pocketbook. Then she said, "Wasn't that the name of the Mormon? I saw the monument somewhere. Smith? There must be a hundred Smiths in Plattsburgh."

"That was Joseph. He led a troop out to Salt Lake City. He was born here."

"Anyway." She pursed her lips, got up to go. She was suddenly looking busy.

When he checked his desk afterward he saw she'd left a second card. Was she forgetful, or just nervous when he mentioned Jules Smith?

But the phone was ringing again. "Hanna?" he said, abstracted.

"Colm?" The voice was familiar. His heart sank. "It's Bertha, Colm. I'm calling because—"

There was an audible intake of breath, like she was suffering a heart attack. He waited. He wouldn't give her any encouragement. He never had really, he didn't know why she persisted. He'd thought it was over, actually, this crush. In high school she was young, naive, maybe he was flattered, he'd felt sorry for her. The fact that she was Pete's sister, and Pete his rival—all those things. But later, on weekends when he was home from university, she'd begun the phone calls. Harassing him. He finally had to be rude. It was after that, he guessed, she got religion. One obsession to the next?

"Colm. I was wondering. If you could come for dinner. I, I need to talk to you. It's important, Colm. Oh, horribly!"

She sounded distressed. "About what, Bertha?" he said, heard his voice gruff. "Can we do it by phone? It's all that's been going on. I'm in a rat race, you know." His glasses were slipping down his nose and he shoved them up. Outside it was snowing again, fat lazy flakes on top of the mud.

He was full of clichés today. His own obsessions.

"If it's Ruth," she said coolly, even cruelly, "Pete's coming back. Oh, he is. He'll see the light. He wants the children, he wants Vic—he's worried to death about Vic."

Then why isn't he here in Branbury? Colm thought. "Is this what you wanted to tell me, Bertha? I've a client outside."

There was a silence. Then, "Never mind," she said, still cool. "I thought you'd be interested. I thought you'd be able to help. I see you're too busy." And the receiver clicked off.

When he called Ruth afterward, needing advice about Bertha, she laughed. "It's probably another of her visions."

"What visions?"

"Oh, she never says. Just hints at these sinister revelations. They used to be purely religious. Now they have something to do with the murders, with the children. She wants me to send Vic down to Pete.''

"That wouldn't be a bad idea, under the circumstances?''

"Oh, my God!'' she shouted. "You too? You think he'd be better off in the city, with that woman?''

He'd put his foot in that one. "No, no, of course not. Just don't let her get you down.''

"Oh, I try to ignore her, she's a little wacko. She just wants to get you in bed, that's all.''

"That's being wacko?'' he said, and waited for the response.

But after a quick laugh, she changed the subject.

VIC WANTED to go straight home, but before he knew it he was in the back of the Unsworths' station wagon, driven off like one of the woman's sheep. Garth sat on the far edge of the seat, staring out the window like Vic wasn't there at all. It wasn't Garth's idea to have him come, he figured it was cooked up by the mothers. He suddenly missed his father, this was something his father would never do. His father never interfered. There'd been times when Vic didn't like that, but now he thought it the right way.

But he'd have to get through an afternoon alone. When they arrived, Garth jumped out of the car without a word.

"Garth,'' his mother called, "remember your guest,'' but Garth was already in the house. Vic was told it was a party but it turned out to be only Garth and the mother. He didn't even see Wilder. There were thumps, and loud rock music somewhere upstairs, it could be the older one—Emily said he'd lost his job, he came in stoned or something. He didn't want to run into that one.

They spooned up ice cream and there were chocolate chip cookies; he ate three and felt sick to his stomach. When he asked for the bathroom, Garth pointed to a door that turned out to be a pantry and then laughed, he thought it funny.

"Piss in the pantry," Garth said, "and mother will be fu-ri-ous." So Vic held it, which made him feel sicker. When the mother tried to give him more ice cream he wanted to throw up in the bowl.

"Garth," she hissed, "be nice to your guest, we talked about this." She thought she was speaking softly, but Vic could hear every word. "Now take Vic up to your room and play."

Garth scowled, but he said, "Come on," and what could Vic do but go? It was only four o'clock by the kitchen clock, another whole hour before his mother would come get him and he didn't know how he'd last that long—either from having to go to the bathroom or from plain misery.

Garth's room was twice the size of Vic's, and every inch was covered with posters of baseball figures. There were yellow curtains with dancing green bears on the windows. Garth saw Vic looking and ripped them down.

"Mother put 'em up," he said and threw them out in the hall. Then he raced around the room tearing up paper and pulling off spreads and throwing books on the floor. "Down, down," he hollered while Vic looked on, his hands behind his back, his mouth slightly open. He squeezed his knees together, the swelling in his bladder worse.

When Garth had made a shambles of his own room he moved to Wilder's. It was a different sort of room, there was no mother's touch here, just paneled walls and blinds instead of curtains, and plain wood floor and books covering one wall and sports equipment in a corner.

"Catch," Garth said, and hurled a softball at Vic. Vic caught it against his belly, it almost released the flood in his bladder. He couldn't throw it back.

Garth was amused. "Toilet's across the hall. You want to go? Don't be bashful," he said, like he was all concerned, and Vic said, "No thanks." Afterward he wanted to take the words back, but he couldn't. Somehow he'd manage to wait another twenty minutes and then go, at least he knew where it was.

"Want to do a puzzle?" Garth asked, sounding more pleasant now, and dragged a box out from under Wilder's bed.

He dropped on the floor with it and grabbing out some of the pieces, pushed it over in Vic's direction. The box smelled musty, like it'd been under the bed for a long time. Vic liked puzzles, it was neat to find the right piece, see it fit into another, watch the picture grow. This one seemed to be a moonscape or something, Vic liked that. It was like looking through his telescope.

He almost forgot his bladder, working on it. Garth liked doing it too, once he added a piece to the part Vic was doing. It made Vic feel good, maybe they could be friends after all.

"That's good," he said, pointing to Garth's half of the puzzle, "that's a good job," and Garth grunted.

What was missing now was the sky, the hardest part because it was all pale lavender-blue, you had to keep trying this piece and that one. There was an envelope under the puzzle, there were probably more pieces inside and he opened it.

And sneezed. He was glad the sneeze was out because Garth looked away and covered his mouth. It gave Vic a chance to close the envelope, stick it back under the puzzle bits. And when he stuck it back he saw something else that had nothing to do with any puzzle either. He couldn't think though, why it looked familiar. He was all flustered then, said he'd use the bathroom now, he didn't care. He needed to be alone.

He saw his face in the bathroom mirror, pale and bluish like the sky he'd been putting together, his eyes were dark holes. He couldn't believe what he'd seen in that envelope. And that other thing. In Wilder's room, under Wilder's bed. He remembered how late Emily came in that night of the murder, how she said Wilder waited outside in his car, she was all thrilled with that, that he didn't want to leave her.

But there was another reason, he bet.

He took his piss, he'd almost forgot why he came in! It went on and on, he felt he was in a dream, or a trance. When it finally stopped he zipped up and washed his hands and looked in the mirror again.

You have to see Mr. Hanna, he told himself, not Mother, she'll get upset. You have to see Mr. Hanna straight off.

And then felt a sharp stab in his left temple. Wilder was Emily's boyfriend, they were all lovey-dovey. But

he had to do what he had to do. He'd make Mr. Hanna
promise not to tell who told. Hanna seemed a determined kind of guy, maybe even more than his mother.
He'd find the murderer, even if it was his own father.
You had to be that kind. You had to be tough. He
balled his fists.

He was itching to go now, he didn't want to be in
this house anymore. What if Wilder came home and
discovered they were doing the puzzle?

"I don't want to do this anymore," he said to Garth,
standing in the doorway of Wilder's room. It was a
quarter to five anyway, his mother would be here,
she'd be prompt, she had the cows. He might even
help her, after he called Mr. Hanna.

"I'm sick of it anyway," Garth said and took his
foot and jumbled up the puzzle.

"Aren't you going to put it back in the box? Won't
Wilder be mad?"

"Nah, he lets me," but Garth put it back in the box
and left the box on the floor.

Vic didn't help, he didn't want to see that envelope
again, smell it. He started downstairs, he felt better
there, he'd be ready the second his mother came. As
he went down the hall, a door opened and rock music
shrieked out. It was the older brother, he figured, but
thinner, taller than Wilder, tall like a flagpole. The
brother brushed past Vic like he didn't exist, peered
into Wilder's room and bellowed.

"Get the shit out of here," he screamed, "you hear
me, stay in your own goddamn room. What you doing
in Wilder's room anyhow?"

And there was a scuffle and a lot of whining and

then a shriek from Garth. Vic felt almost sorry for Garth. He stood on one foot at the top of the stairs.

"I hate you, hate you, Kurt. You leave me alone, you hear? Wilder lets me play in here, he lets me play with his puzzle, he's not like you, he's a real brother. You're not, you're just a half brother. A half—"

Vic flattened himself against the railing as Mrs. Unsworth dashed upstairs. She screeched at the top of her lungs and then things went quiet. Garth thumped into the bathroom. Mrs. Unsworth looked at Vic, her eyes were bright. "I'm sorry, I wanted this to be nice for you. I promised your mother. I want you and Garth to be friends."

"It's okay," he said.

It wasn't Garth's fault, Garth didn't know about the envelope or he wouldn't have opened the puzzle box. It wasn't Garth's fault. He had a sudden rush of warmth for Garth.

Then he heard a car door shut and the front doorbell ring and Mrs. Unsworth smeared her eyes with her sleeve and said, "Heavens, time flies. It's your mom," and ran down the steps.

When his mother appeared in the doorway Vic was composed. He'd come to another decision: he'd tell Emily first, yes, Emily had to know, it might save her from—from what he couldn't say, really. From something dark in his mind, was all.

He greeted his mother, he was glad to see her. When she nodded, he turned back.

"Thank you very much, Mrs. Unsworth," he said, "for a nice afternoon."

BUT EMILY didn't get home till after Vic's bedtime that night and though he tried to stay awake he couldn't. He woke up with his mother's shaking him for chores. Then he couldn't get Emily alone except for a few minutes at the breakfast table and he decided it wasn't a good time to tell her, just before school when she was cramming for some quiz. So he left a note that he wanted to talk to her. She'd find it after school. In the meantime, he'd call Mr. Hanna, "cover all bases" like he'd heard his father say. But when he went up to his mother's bedroom to call the number, a gravelly voice said Mr. Hanna wasn't in, and Vic didn't want to leave such an important message with somebody else. It was even more important than he'd thought at first—that other thing, all dusty and beat up he found under the bed by the envelope.

He remembered now, where he'd seen it before. And he shuddered.

So he decided he'd call from school. There was a pay phone there, he jingled the change in his pocket, he had a quarter and two dimes. He'd phone during recess, old Ronsard would have to let him, that's all. If she gave him a hard time he'd say it was information for the police, none of her business.

He went to say good-bye to his mother, but she was on the phone. He waved at her and walked out to the school bus stop. He was a few minutes early but that was all right, he had lots to think about. Besides, his map of Australia was due today, he held it against his chest in its stiff folder. He was the only kid on this part of the road for the elementary, they had to make a special stop. The woman bus driver was usually in a bad mood in spring because the road was unpaved on this stretch, and the bus had to lurch in and out of the muddy ruts the state truck couldn't seem to straighten out.

But real spring was coming, he could smell May in the air—something about the grass. It was good to smell it, and he jumped up, twisted his body about, kicked his heels together. He'd seen a character do that on TV. He did it twice more and giggled. When he landed the third time, a tan car was coming up slowly; looked like two people in it, maybe looking for the Manleys' farm that was being sold—by that developer, his mom said.

Yeah, he could smell spring, and he didn't even mind going to school. He looked forward to it, actually, looked forward to seeing Garth Unsworth. He'd walk up to him and say, "That puzzle was a tough one, I have a couple hard ones at my house. Maybe we can work them together some time." And Garth would say, "Why not? Maybe Sunday?"

He picked up a handful of pebbles and tossed them into the road. The car was stopped now, a man got out, he walked into the field—to take a leak probably. Vic smiled, he looked the other way, where the bus was coming from. He thought he saw it, a fat yellow blob, like a duck, waddling down the muddy road, stopping far up, maybe half a mile for Mike Gold. He squinted, cupped his hands over his eyes. He was in no hurry—or was he? Well, he'd be there soon enough, recess'd come, and he'd call. Would Mr. Hanna pick him up? Yep, that would be best, he didn't want to risk the information over the phone. Anyone could listen in. They'd go down to the station together, he'd face Wilder across the desk, fold his hands on his knees, and then...

"Hey, young fellow, know anything about that farm? Hear it's for sale. How about that one up there? Dairy?" It was a deep voice, though the man was only medium height.

"Not that one," Vic said, "that's my place. That's where I live. Other one up the road past Larocques', that's Manleys'." He pointed. "My mother wants it farmed, not developed. You a farmer?"

The man laughed. He didn't look like a farmer. He didn't look like a tourist either. He looked kind of flaky. Except for the eyes, tiny bits of glassy light inside the puffy lids. And Vic didn't care for the way he squinted, like he'd peer into Vic's bones. He wished the bus would hurry up. It was getting bigger now, not a duck anymore, but a goose, a fat yellow goose. He took a step toward it.

And was pulled back. The hand crushed over his mouth: "Easy, boy." He heard a woman's voice calling out, muffled, like she had a scarf over her mouth. The car zoomed up beside them, the rear door opened, he was shoved in the back, the man beside him.

"Go," the man said, and the woman driver skidded about, roared back down the road. Couldn't see where the car turned, the cloth over Vic's face, he fought for breath, pounded his fists in flesh; then was stuck, held down by the man. "Easy, boy," the man kept growling. "Easy. Easy."

Vic thought he'd drown, this minute, in his fear.

NINE

WHEN THE TELEPHONE call came that afternoon, the one about Vic, after they all realized that he never got to school, was nowhere, Ruth went into shock, she could hardly breathe. "Say that again," she shouted, "repeat that, please!" and Chief Fallon went into his refrain: "Nothing for certain. Seen getting into a tan car—bus driver never thought to mention until—well, that's all we know. Want you to stay by the phone, in case. Call if you hear anything. Sorry, that's all we can tell you for now."

And at nine that night, when Ruth was slumped over the kitchen table by the coffee pot, by the phone, her daughters hovering about, telling her to go to bed when she couldn't, she couldn't! a second call from the chief. "Our fat man, Smith—well, uh, if he is our man—just spotted in a convenience store, outside Detroit, could of traded in that Honda, you know. And trade again. But, well, we'll contact all the used-car lots we can locate in, uh, Michigan. Though there's always the private, uh, what, ma'am? Oh, well, Detroit storekeeper read our advisory. Kidnapper—if he was, uh, paid barn money for gas and cigarettes. That's what's suspicious here. You can thank your son, uh, Vic, for telling us about the barn, you know."

Vic's name triggered the panic again, the giddiness, the sickness in the belly, like overwhelming PMS, though menstruating was never so bad, was it? She might die, the feeling was there, and her Vic in limbo. But she had to keep on till they found him.

She sensed he knew more—nothing conclusive maybe, just some bit of information. She pressed him. "He's all right? They've been feeding him? They haven't hurt him?"

But he couldn't tell her that, and she knew it. He couldn't even say it was that man—Smith, she remembered now, Smith, who had Vic. The "jobs," as Fallon called them, could be unrelated, and if so, she'd be the first to know, a ransom call—she knew about ransom calls only from the movies and TV. The chief sounded pleased with the word: "Ransom call," he repeated it. Kidnappings didn't happen very often in Vermont, almost never, he said, like that fact made it easier to bear, put it in the realm of make-believe, denial. She'd wake up tomorrow and Vic would be home, patching up his telescope, complaining about barn chores.

What the other information was, she didn't know, but it didn't pertain directly to Vic, was probably conjecture. Policemen were like doctors, they wouldn't say their hunches, in case they were proved wrong, she supposed.

She was exhausted now, could hardly hold the receiver up to her ear, her body was separate from her mind, but she clung to it like it would bring Vic back to her. "When you know more," she said, "I'll be here, I'll have a phone put in the barn."

"I'll call you," he said. "Wait, here's Colm, just walked in my door. Wants a word—"

And then Colm's voice, far away, like a shell held up to the ear. "Hang on," he said. "Are the girls there? Are you okay?"

She murmured yes, though she wasn't, she wasn't okay at all.

"I'm going to Michigan," he said, "Detroit. I want to be on hand when we connect with that guy." Under his own jurisdiction, he added, Fallon wouldn't authorize the trip.

"That's dangerous!" she cried, "on your own?" But then, hardly hearing her voice, "Thank you." Then, "I want to come!"

"You've got to stay home," he said. "It's your job now, you know that. We don't know this guy has Vic. It could be somebody else, anybody. You have to stay by the phone, Ruth. The police will have a man nearby."

He was right, of course. She had to stay by the phone. She held her hand down on the receiver for a long moment after they hung up. To keep Vic's name on her lips, her baby, Vic...

Why? she said aloud, though the phone was dead, why would they take Vic? Who? She gave a shout. She was alone now in the kitchen, the girls upstairs, she'd lied to Colm. The word echoed. Vic...

It could be anyone, yes, she thought. Even Pete. Pete?

She dialed at once, too hysterical to be nervous. "Pete," she shrieked when the woman answered down in New York, "I want Pete!"

When the woman said he wasn't there, he was off at a four-day sales conference, could she take a message, Ruth couldn't think what to say, she just hung up.

Already they were banging on the door—at this hour of the night!—a pair of reporters from the *Free Press*. "Leave us alone!" she cried. "You'll know when we know."

And then screamed to call them back, to give them Vic's picture. She fished one out of a drawer. It was a bit out of focus, why hadn't she taken more pictures of the children? What kind of mother was she?

She had to be rational about this. Someone might have seen. She might have to go on TV herself, to plead—whatever one did. Was there no end to all this?

For the next day and a half there was no news. There was only the media, the police with questions, a man from the FBI with the compassion of a fish. Neighbors, townspeople, bearing casseroles, desserts, people she hardly knew. They meant well, but they kept her from chores: farm life went on, like breathing and peeing. The cows had to be grained and milked, meals prepared—for Tim and for Joey, who'd taken Willy's place, for Emily, for the grandson, because Sharon had moved in now, taken over the house. "Stop worrying, Mom," Sharon would say. "It'll be all right, just do your barn work, I'll get the meals."

Sharon was wonderful, a comfort, a rock. But Ruth wanted to do the meals, she had to keep working, working! It was her only sanity.

Colm called from Michigan, almost stopped her breath, but had nothing to report. Pete was still out of town, she had Emily try to get him, talk to the new woman. Nothing to report. The fat man seemed to have vanished again.

On the afternoon of the third day of Vic's disappearance, the phone rang and she felt the shock waves in her spine; she and Emily ran for it together. She practically ran Emily down.

"All right! Who would call me up anyway?" Emily yelled and slumped back in her chair.

There'd been some quarrel with Wilder, Ruth thought. And she was glad, she was suspicious of all the Unsworths now. Did Kurt have something to do with the kidnapping? Was his mother shielding him? She couldn't trust anyone, Colm had taught her that.

She kept coming back to Pete—wanting the boy down there, lonely for the children, hadn't Bertha tried to tell her that? Didn't it happen all the time, this custody battle? She warned Chief Fallon. She even hoped it was Pete, didn't she? It meant Vic was safe?

It's Pete, Pete has him, she told herself.

But here was Carol Unsworth on the line. There was no time for small talk, though she'd have to thank her for the turkey sent over when the news broke on TV. She'd stuck it in the freezer with the other stuff they didn't have time (or desire) to eat. It was hard to be pleasant under the circumstances. And Carol Unsworth with those three sons. Bad seeds?

But a mother loved a son on death row, defended him, covered up for him. She'd read about that.

Carol was calling about the Dolley woman. "She's been everywhere, the smallest pretense of a farm. Aggressive! Wanting to incorporate. She said she'd seen you, that your answer was indecisive, but she thought maybe. I hope you won't sell." She took an audible breath. "That's why I called."

That got Ruth's back up. Why shouldn't she sell if she wanted to? It was her own damn business. Did someone take Vic to try and make her sell? There was a new angle. Oh, she'd sell then, she'd sell everything, to get Vic back.

"When this is over, when you have Vic—I know you will," Carol said, her voice sounding small, apologetic, "I mean, I'm praying every minute, Garth too, he's upset, he's so sorry"—Ruth stiffened—"I want to talk to you. I'm thinking, well, things aren't working out here... Oh, I can't talk about it over the phone. I thought, see, I'd like to talk to you about maybe renting a couple acres of your farm. I figure you could use the money. I mean, forgive me, I know you're hard-pressed, I could help you keep the farm."

She kept on, she was a bee thrashing in the inner ear. Though Ruth got the part about renting; for a minute her heart quickened, like when Colm had called: "I have some news," he'd prefaced the call, and her heart somersaulted in her chest, beat against the bones. And it turned out the news was no news, really. Almost three days Vic had been gone, and no word, nothing. Only the small verification at the start: the sharp eyes of Nedda Bump, the woman bus driver. Nedda had seen a boy Vic's size pulled into a tan car as she rounded the bend, her lights already flashing red. "First I thought, well, a neighbor couple," she said. "Then later I got to thinking. The boy looked upset, real upset."

At last there was silence and Ruth said, "I have to

hang up, Carol. I have to keep the line open. They'll want money maybe, if they have Vic. Why else would they take him?"

And then she stopped talking, she didn't know why. In case no one ought to know, in case the phone was tapped, someone listening on another line in the Unsworth house. Didn't Vic say the oldest one had his own phone?

How paranoid could she get?

But with reason, right? The oldest boy sold raffle tickets for that furniture company, she knew about that. Wilder sold some, too, anything suspicious about that? Belle bought them when Lucien was in the barn, Lucien didn't know who'd sold them to her. He was in full denial, he didn't want to think about anything to do with Belle's murder, it was over and done. It was bad, she'd told him, to let it gnaw away inside. She knew what it was to have things eating inside. Lucien could be the next victim: his father had died in his fifties of a heart attack, Lucien had told her that.

Was there no end to the victims? Where was she, anyway? Her mind was a labyrinth. Yes, the broker.

"I told that woman I won't give an answer till I get Vic back," Ruth said. "She knows that."

She felt suddenly faint. Was the fat man connected with this woman? What was the name? Esther, yes, Esther with the scarlet fingernails. Something about Plattsburgh...

Crime turned everyone into a victim! Her temples were on fire, sweat smoking out of her pores. She saw that Emily had a fire in the woodstove, the flames appeared to be licking the walls. There was the illusion that the house was burning. And all those barn fires this spring.

"Turn that stove down!" she hollered at Emily.

"We'll talk another time," Carol Unsworth murmured. "But call if I can help. I don't know much, but I'm a good learner. I love animals. I'm a country girl at heart I guess. I'm sorry to go on like this when your mind is—I won't keep you."

And mercifully, the conversation was over. Ruth sank into a chair, felt nothing. Emily was moving the food around on her plate, she wasn't eating.

"How does that help?" Ruth snapped. "If you don't eat? I can't have you sick. Now eat, damn it!"

"Listen to Mother," said Sharon, back in the room, sticking a spoonful of squash into the baby's mouth.

Emily ate grimly, her eyes on the forkfuls of beans and rice she bore to her mouth, distastefully, like she was sipping worms. Then dropped her fork with a clang on the plate, and Ruth jumped. "I can't eat another mouthful, I won't," Emily said. "I have a test tomorrow."

"You always have a test," said Sharon.

Emily said, "Yes, I do. I always have a test," and stomped up to her room.

Ruth yelled, "When I need you, you desert me!"

And took ten breaths to calm herself.

A moment later she heard a noise, like an explosion of wind through a pane. Warned, she ran upstairs. Emily was on the bedroom floor, sobbing into the braided rug, her body bunched like a snail on the hard pile. When Ruth stooped to put her arms around her, the girl didn't move.

"Tell me, talk to me," Ruth said. "Come on, baby. We can't fight among ourselves. We have to be a team."

She helped Emily to the bed, sat there with her, her arm holding up the girl like a rag doll.

It was Wilder, Emily spoke between gasps of breath. "I wouldn't speak to him, and now he won't speak to me. He walks right past me, in the corridor, like I'm invisible."

It was that phone call to Colm Hanna, Ruth thought, she'd known when she made it. She'd betrayed Emily: telling about the car the night of the murder, about Wilder with time enough to... she couldn't finish the thought. The father gave a pittance of allowance, Emily said, and she'd told Colm. Wasn't that a motive? And then Colm confronted the boy with the suspicion.

But it was important that Wilder tell what he knew! It was Vic's life at stake now, no lovers' rift could count. Emily must see that. They had to find the killers, the kidnappers.

"I'm sorry," she said. "I'm sorry, Em. But if Wilder knew anything about that night, saw anything he's keeping back, it has to be out. It's too late for the dead, but for Vic—"

"How did you know?" Emily said.

"What?"

"About Wilder. How did you know it was because I accused him of holding back? Of lying? Isn't that an awful thing to say to anybody? Not just anybody— someone you love! Mom, I love Wilder! And I told him he was a liar."

Ruth's heart was a propeller inside her chest. Any minute she'd take off. And dive-bomb.

"At first I said nothing, just ignored him. Then one day he caught me by my locker, made me tell. I was relieved, I know he didn't drive away when he said he did. Then I saw another car come up, slow—I didn't tell you that—and then I pulled the shade. I didn't think anything of that other car, I didn't actually see it stop. I guess I thought it was Marie or somebody. I never thought it might have been—might have—"

She was sobbing again, and Ruth tightened her hold. "It's all right, all right, darling." Feeling guilty, though, that Emily didn't suspect her mother's interference: "You had to say it, you were brave. If Wilder's hiding something he'll have to tell. And maybe he isn't. Maybe he was just sitting there."

"Looking at the moon, thinking of me. That's what he said. That's what I was doing, too. I didn't want to think about someone else spoiling our moon together. Maybe that's why I pulled the shade."

"Em, what did he say when you told him what you saw?"

They had to quit being emotional about this, there was Vic. The boy would be suffering, alone, this minute, while she and Emily were together, touching, mother and child. She shoved her knuckles against her eyes.

"Nothing. He didn't say anything. He just looked all pale and unhappy, and that was the last we spoke. He's avoided me ever since. He thinks I've broken our trust. Trust is important to Wilder, Mom. I've written him notes, asked him to meet me. We'll talk it out, I told him. I said I loved him no matter what he'd done. Because I do! He didn't hurt that old couple, I know that. If he's shielding somebody, maybe, maybe—"

She paused, drew a gasping breath.

"Do you think it's that older brother?" Ruth heard her voice coming from a far corner of the room.

"I don't know, I just don't. Wilder won't say anything. It could be a friend he's—oh, I don't know."

Ruth wiped the girl's cheek with her sleeve. She hadn't realized how thin Emily was, like the bones weren't strong enough to support her head the way it flopped down on her chest. She drew the girl closer. They'd always found it hard to touch, she and Emily. But she'd make amends, she would! Just get this horror over with, she begged, and things will be different.

She was filled with new resolve. She'd call Colm tonight, he'd left a number. Find out what he'd said to Wilder, what the boy's response was. Then decide how to tell Emily. Because she had to tell, nothing could come between them: there had to be trust between mother and daughter, too. There'd been little enough with Pete, though some of that was her fault. If they'd communicated more, if she'd told Pete her concerns, made him listen, got it out whether he wanted to hear it or not, maybe...

Oh, she couldn't believe Pete had Vic, without telling her.

But she'd never thought he'd leave, either, not altogether like that. No, nothing was impossible.

But it couldn't happen with her daughter, this break, her flesh and blood. Emily was all she had at home now with Vic gone. Sharon had her own life, her child, she'd escaped somehow, she had some inner strength. But Emily...

"It will all work out," she murmured, rocking the girl, "it will all work out." Emily was rocking with her now, the two of them rocking to the easy words. And Emily sighing in reply, like any second her heart would break.

Downstairs the phone was ringing again, it was a siren in the inner ear. When she got there Sharon already had it, was holding it up. "That woman again, very excited," she said.

"Wilder," shrieked Carol Unsworth. "They came for him. They're holding him down there."

Ruth, dumbly, said, "Who? Where?"

"The police," Carol screamed. "I need your help. Tell them he had nothing to do with that, that—He's a good boy. He's my son!"

"I'll talk to them," Ruth said, her head reeling. And after she hung up, realized she didn't know why Wilder had been arrested. They couldn't prove he was involved, could they? Was there new evidence? The nausea was starting, down in her toes, making its way up to her throat. What would she say to Emily?

She ran for the bathroom.

COLM DISEMBARKED in Ann Arbor with a dozen university students: young men with backpacks and baseball caps on backward; women with skintight pants and colored combs in their long frizzy hair. He'd sat next to a stunning black girl who refused to talk to him, held her chin high, her hair in a hundred tiny snakes. He wondered how often she had time to do it—once a month? But she wasn't telling, just swept up her canvas sack of books and moved swiftly down the aisle. He wanted to yell after her that he was black Irish, that his great-grandfather came over on a coffin ship, boxed for a living, till he got knocked out once too often.

He imagined the girl's look after he told her. "Talk to me about coffin ships, white man!"

There had been a dozen sightings phoned into the Branbury police station. It seemed Vic was everywhere: in a Vermont shopping mall, a New York subway, an Ohio post office. A kidnapped child rang an alarm in the minds of the compassionate. But a more recent sighting, not a sighting exactly but a phone call from a used-car dealer in Ann Arbor, Michigan, who happened to be a radio buff, sounded the most authentic. And so he was here. He was a private detective, Colm told the Ann Arbor police lieutenant, and flushed when he saw the man's lip curl: he couldn't produce a business card. But when he flashed a copy of the photo he'd conned for Fallon from Catamount Furniture—thirty employees, with Smith grinning beside Kurt Unsworth in the back row—the officer grudgingly gave out a little information: a fat man trading in an '86 Dodge Colt. This time the fat man, if it was Smith, had made a mistake: the contact rapped all over the world, picked up the latest police reports, sent for copies of their "Wanted" photos. Now he was hooking into the World Wide Web. How unlucky could a criminal get?

The fat man had answered an ad for a Honda Ac-

cord that the dealer, whose name was Petronelli, was
selling; had been to the place once, where Petronelli
had recognized him, and contacted the local police.
Smith would return that evening to trade in the Civic.
All they had to do, the lieutenant said, was surround
the place. For that the Ann Arbor force was prepared.

"I've an even better photo than the one Fallon sent
you," Colm said, pulling it out of his wallet. "A
close-up. One of the fellow workers took it, farmer's
son. Caught him with his eyes wide open." Colm
wanted in with this lieutenant, he wanted to go along
on the hunt.

The lieutenant barely glanced at it. He knew he had
the right man, "no mistake." Colm had to hope. There
was no invitation for him to come along. But no turn-
down, either. He'd have to follow in his rented car.
The police were on their way now to "case" it, form
a plan.

The dealer lived in town, practically on top of the
university: he operated out of his house. Ten or fifteen
used cars in the yard. The house was down the street
from a white pillared building, archaeology department or something. Colm was impressed with the university: it was the kind of place he'd always wanted
to be part of, but there was never money. It looked
like the pictures he'd seen of Athens, one Parthenon
after the other: library, art gallery, Eisenhower ar-
chives—Eisenhower, a military man, in this lane of
temples. He smiled at the irony. But wasn't the play-
wright Sophocles a general, too? He'd read that somewhere. Jeez, he was jumping to conclusions again.

He shivered, he was nervous, he couldn't help it.

He'd never done anything like this before. He'd make a lousy policeman. It was a bleak day, winter's last blow in mid-April, even the mud had frozen. Ann Arbor seemed a city of wind. He wouldn't be surprised to see snow. His shoulders hunched against the possibility.

The dealer identified Fallon's photo of the fat man, and the lieutenant looked smug, Colm was a fly on his shoulder. He might yield to praise, but Colm wasn't ready to give it. He was worried about the plan. Four police stationed around the house, one inside. What if Fat Man had a gun? He probably did. And the boy in the car? But Vic wouldn't be in the car, would he? to be transferred? Wherever he was, Vic would have to be gotten out safely.

Nothing must happen to Vic—if Vic was alive. Christ, there was that, too. There was always the abductor—for sex, he hadn't mentioned that to Ruth, he couldn't, though of course it was in the back of her mind. Her face had been sick with worry, the ripe body bent forward. She'd wanted to come, it took all his bullshit to keep her in Vermont. A sensible mother, but emotional, a parent (that waste in his own life).

If the boy was dead, how could he face her? It was easier to telephone, not have to deal with her one on one. Her eyes, blurring to sea; the breath, caught in the teeth. It had to turn out all right, that was all. He bit hard into his lower lip. And tasted blood.

The fat man was due at six thirty. Of course he'd wait until dusk, want to make his getaway in the dark. There was most of the day to plan. They stayed long enough at the dealer's only to make a map of the house.

"We'll meet here half-past five," the lieutenant told the others. "Leave the cars in that parking lot over there." The way he said it meant, Just the four of us. We don't need a fifth.

So Colm went back to his motel and downed a Manhattan, he needed it. He'd be at the dealer's by five, just in case. It was going to be rough, he didn't have a gun, couldn't defend himself. What was he doing here, anyway? What if someone was killed? All the dead men he knew were brought to the funeral home by relatives. It was going to be rough, yes. Interesting word, *rough*. Sounded like ruff: elitist dress, obscuring the ears maybe, suggesting doublespeak, hypocrisy.

What good were words without a gun? No one was going to give a pseudodetective a gun. He couldn't shoot one anyway, could he? He hated guns. Jeez, a detective without a gun!

BRANBURY WAS a small town, the few criminals were housed in the old red brick courthouse—mostly break-ins, now and then a drug bust. Wilder would be out on bail already, Ruth bet; Carol's new green pickup was pulling out as she arrived. The husband was with her, they walked apart like each was teetering on a separate tightrope. The husband looked mad enough to kill, another reason Ruth wanted to be here alone, to see what she could find out.

Wilder had been picked up on a drug charge, she discovered, not the assault at all, though there was some question about the other, the officer looked meaningfully at her. Still she was shocked: a drug charge. And Emily? Was Emily into drugs? The thought panicked her, she needed to sit down. She barely made the contact room; found Wilder half crouched on a wooden bench, his head in his hands like a melon he could hardly heft.

"Why am I here?" He answered her unspoken question. "Not the cocaine. I made a delivery for my brother, that's all. Kurt was... indisposed. But promised he'd try to quit. I think he means it this time. Does that involve me? I think I was set up, they've been watching us, like we're some—"

He made a noise in his throat. She waited. "But the other—don't think— Look, Ms. Willmarth, I sold them a raffle ticket. Yeah, sure I did, she gave me a dollar. I don't recall it smelled. I did it for Kurt." He cleared his throat. "He's my brother. But sometimes—"

"Sometimes?"

"Sometimes I can't find him at all. He doesn't know I'm in the room with him, he's that far gone. I sense he wouldn't even know how to be the old Kurt, who the old Kurt was. He says he wants to change. But I don't know if he can."

"Even if it means you take the blame for something he did," Ruth said. And waited.

But the boy turned his face away.

"The fact is you lied to the police." Ruth was calmer now. She believed him about the drugs, she had to. "You told them you'd never been there, you went back on your story. You were there that night."

"With Emily! In the car." His hazel eyes pleaded with her.

She had to think tough. "After you dropped off Emily, too. Your car was still there. Another car stopped. Emily saw. I saw."

Now she was lying. She hadn't really seen, but she'd felt, she'd felt something out there. That moon, she could never sleep on a full moon night. She'd gone to the window in the bathroom; she'd seen something in the road, hadn't she? A car, or merely shadows—who knew? Or was it because Emily had seen a second car?

Was it a lie if it brought out the truth?

He dropped his head back in his hands. "Emily told you," he said, like he'd been betrayed so often he hardly cared anymore. "Sure, I was there. Dreaming, sure. Can a kid dream?"

"And saw nothing else?" Her voice was softer now. She'd dreamed her way through high school herself, those two years of college. It was marriage, money worries that killed the dream.

The flush crept up his neck, his chin, spread over his cheeks. He looked like he had something to tell her, wanted to tell. She waited.

But the color cooled, the lines went stubborn in the face, like he'd been caged all year, was damned if he'd give in now.

"Nothing. Nothing but the moon. Oh, another car going past, slow, you know the road, nothing more."

She got up to go, then turned back, he was still slumped on the bench. "Your mother's worried sick about you, Wilder. It's hard, having a son—" She stopped, something was filling her throat.

"I know. I know about Vic." He appeared to be shrinking into his shoes. If she didn't leave she might run over and embrace him, cry on his bony shoulder. He was just a boy.

She left.

Out in the parking lot she stopped short, her heel caught in a crack of the pavement. What a softie she was. Wilder was hiding something, someone, she knew it, knew it!

She yanked her foot out of the crack and felt something rip. The rubber heel had torn off and now she'd have to stop at the shoe repair shop. There wasn't time, she had to get back to the cows, her best milker down with ketosis, it was putting her off her feed, she'd have to call the vet.

"Shit," she said, "Shit. Shit shit shit."

And felt better when she'd said it.

COLM HAD TO admit he was nervous, waiting. Jeez, what an amateur he was. The lieutenant looked at him like he was a girl. "Better stay back then," he said, a concession to speak to the interloper. "We'll do the hard stuff. You identify the boy—if Smith brings him."

He wished now he had a gun. But it was too late. A Colt was coming up the drive. He flattened himself against the wall. The dealer, Petronelli, was nervous, too, he was sweating waterfalls. He might give the whole thing away, they might lose everything. Was anyone else in the car? Was it Vic? It was a police-

man's job to get Vic out—if he was there—while Fat
Man was inside the house. But what if there was an
accomplice, someone else in the car? Had they thought
of that?

Colm could barely see, it was stuffy in here, he
could hardly breathe. The plan was for Petronelli to
meet the fat man at the door, invite him in. Then the
police would close in from outside. If the dealer didn't
give them away. Colm heard the bottle clink down on
the table, the guy was fortifying himself.

The door banged. It sounded like an explosion. His
head was coming apart. He heard Petronelli yell,
"Come in," he wasn't going to the door, he was too
nervous. He'd give it away for certain.

The door opened. The voice was jovial. "I'm in,"
the man said. And Petronelli called from the next
room, on cue: "Minute. I got Cairo on the air, gotta
sign off. Car's around back. Beside the green Chevy.
Keys inside, you can—"

"I'll get it then," said the voice. And the door
slammed.

This wasn't in the plan, to let him leave. The dealer
had done them in, the idiot! Colm was sweating, his
face was a steam bath. He heard the lieutenant swear.
He heard a shout, a lot of shouts. He ran to the back
door.

And there was the fat man, running toward the new
car. Colm plunged out after him, it was like diving
over a cliff. And then crashed. There was a flash of
pain, and the air turned blue and then green. And then
black.

When he opened his eyes, sat up, sank down again

from the pain, they had the guy. There were three men on him: the lieutenant was screaming, they'd almost lost him. Smith had whirled away, he was agile for his size, fired a second wild shot and got the lieutenant in the elbow. The lieutenant was screaming with outrage. He'd aimed his pistol and Fat Man stumbled, fell against the fender of the green Chevy. Beside Colm. Colm stared into the small blue eyes. He couldn't get up himself, something had struck his ankle. They were a pair.

Colm said, "Where's Vic? Where's Vic, you bastard?"

"Who's Vic?" growled the fat man, and squealed as he was yanked up and onto his feet, his wrists clapped with handcuffs.

Colm got up on one knee, he had to see for himself. The lieutenant was yelling at him, yelling how stupid he was, running out at the man that way, unarmed. He said it served him right if he was shot.

And the world went blank again. The world had landed, solidly, on Colm's left foot.

TEN

RUTH WENT TO the Unsworths' "on business," she told Sharon, sitting her down by the phone. She wanted to meet Kurt for herself, see what he knew about Vic, watch him with Wilder, who was out on bail—all that Unsworth money! But "watched like some criminal," his mother had despaired over the phone. And Ruth wanted to see Garth, though how could a fifth grader arrange a kidnapping? No, it was too sophisticated for that.

Besides, she had to get out of the house, she was stir-crazy. Do something, anything, that might remotely lead to Vic.

But how awful to suspect the children of a woman she liked, even admired. Admired, yes, the word surprised her: a woman up from the city, raising sheep, though she hardly knew the first how-to. You had to give her credit.

She was greeted warmly at the door, though she couldn't return it. She wasn't ready to be friends, not yet. They came from different planets, didn't they? The living room was empty of boys, but she heard noise upstairs. It was a Saturday, Kurt was still laid off work. But he was at work the day Vic was taken, Carol had made that clear, he had the alibi. She squeezed her eyes tight, it was hard to think of Vic without her heart flopping over, her stomach throwing up in her throat.

When Carol offered a tour of the house before "tea," Ruth said yes at once. She didn't want to go, didn't want to see the boys, yet she had to. But then there were rooms they couldn't enter, it was like Bluebeard's castle. Locked rooms—were there bodies inside? Rooms with noises behind the shut doors: scraping, buzzing noises—what were they? Garth's room was open, though, he was making a model of something, not looking up when they entered, used to his mother's tours maybe. His nose an inch from the glue he was squeezing between delicate wings. She tried to imagine him with Vic, working on the telescope.

"Garth," Carol said, "this is Vic's mother."

The boy glanced up, did he flush? Looked like he might speak, or protest. And then with a frown he swooped low to his project again, stuck the glue in the wrong place.

"Fuck!"

Here was a new Carol. A swift step and the boy was yanked up to face her, eyes stunned, mouth open to a missing tooth.

"Don't you say that word again!"

And he was back on the floor, facedown in the furry rug, crying. Ruth wanted to be away, far away. The boy sat up: "See what you did?" He held up two frail pieces of the airplane.

Carol said, breathless, "See why I keep sheep?" Then taking Ruth's shoulders, pushed her back toward the stairs.

"Same reason I keep cows," said Ruth, trying to appease, though it wasn't because of her children, who weren't like this: stubborn maybe, disobedient sometimes, but never vindictive. This child wasn't sorry at all, he was spoiled rotten; he needed discipline, probably had little. No wonder Carol preferred sheep. Sheep obeyed without backtalk.

Then on the stairs, one she hadn't seen before. Looking nothing like Wilder: different coloring, larger features. He nodded, wordlessly, and when Carol introduced them, her voice small like she was afraid of this one:

"Hello," he mumbled, but didn't look at her, only stared past her, into the distance. Afterward Ruth remembered the lips, white as parsnips, the stare of the blue, blue eyes. There was something missing here, because of the drugs she supposed. Carol didn't detain him, she was used to it probably, had long ago given up.

And then Garth's voice, "Hey! Kurt! Come up here, I need help with my model. I'm outa the right glue. Kurt!"

And Kurt moving slowly up the stairs, hangdog, his back humped like he bore a weight he couldn't lift; no good-bye, no "nice to have met you," just a slow, labored exit. Would he help Garth with the model?

When they sat down again in the kitchen, Carol made a valiant effort to entertain: tea, homemade biscuits this time. "I add bits of dried pineapple, you see, Wilder loves them, he's my bake boy. Has he used your stove, too?"

Ruth spread her hands. She couldn't remember things these days, not even what Sharon had made for supper the night before.

"He wants to see Emily, I know that. Probably he's, well, afraid. Do you think that's it?"

The woman was ingenuous, Ruth thought, the

wrong woman for these three sons. Too bad one couldn't match parents to sons, after they'd grown up a little.

Ruth said, "There was some rift, even before the police got to him." She didn't want to get into it, didn't want to betray Emily again. "I don't know, except that Emily's unhappy."

That much she could say for Emily's sake, knowing it would get back to Wilder; he should know he'd made Emily unhappy. Though it might be best if they stopped seeing each other, wouldn't it? But she couldn't say that to Carol, could she?

Ruth wondered about the husband she'd seen only that one time by the courthouse: gray-brown hair going bald, inaccessible, made Emily "uncomfortable," she said. Emily, the romantic, maintained he was something of an autocrat. She didn't think the parents got along.

"Kurt was George's son, by his first marriage. Wilder and Garth are mine." Carol looked like she wanted to say more but didn't know if she should. Ruth waited.

And here was Wilder, coming in the back door, flushing to see Ruth; her throat tightened. But when his mother scolded him for the mud he'd brought in, he carefully removed his shoes. He was carrying a bag of groceries, as though, like Kurt's shoulders, it weighed a thousand pounds.

"I hope you got something for yourself," Carol said, and he said, "Yup," and they both smiled a little.

Was this young man a killer? It didn't seem so, yet he'd lied. Ruth had to remember that.

The boy dropped the bag on the counter, began unloading potatoes, mayonnaise, bread. He held up a half gallon of Ben and Jerry's. "Heath bar crunch. I need to indulge myself. Want some?"

Carol shook her head. "Watching my diet. Ruth?"

"No, thanks, I make my own. Plain old vanilla."

"I've sampled it," Wilder said. "With maple syrup, not bad." He started out of the room, turned back.

"Ms. Willmarth? Is there any news about Vic? I wish I could help."

Carol went to Wilder, hugged him. Was this planned? Had she told Wilder to say that?

Was Wilder laughing or crying? Ruth squeezed her tea bag, set it beside the cup. It was time to go, leave mother and son, their arms around each other now, though Wilder was already breaking away. It hurt to see them, made her think of Vic. And what had she accomplished? What had she learned?

Nothing, she answered herself. She was nowhere. She'd been thrown in quicksand, was sinking down, and down. She thought of Willy drowning in the creek. For the first time she knew his panic.

COLM WAS BACK home in the local hospital. He was a bird with a busted wing, his leg was trussed to the knee like a hockey stick. He'd asked his father to call Ruth, he wanted to tell her himself, before the police got to her, to say it wasn't the fat man who had Vic. It wasn't fair to keep her hopes up. They'd grilled the fellow in Ann Arbor, could prove only an illegal weapon, they were sending him back to Vermont. There was no Vic.

Then who, she'd want to know, who did have him? And he'd have to shake his head like a kid in school who couldn't answer the question, who didn't even know what the question was.

His mind kept coming back to Pete, but he couldn't push that, she'd think he had an ulterior motive (did he?). There'd been no ransom call; Pete was still a possibility. The police hadn't ruled him out.

"A visitor," the nurse said. "Are you up for it?"

He didn't feel ready, but it might be Ruth. His heart was doing screwy things in his chest, it wanted to get out. One more day here and he was leaving. There were things to do, like seeing the man Smith for himself, he had his own questions to ask. He had crutches, he could get around. The Detroit surgeon had done a decent job on him. He didn't want to think of the cost: he had no health insurance—one more thing out of whack in this country. What could even a president do? Congress? All those interest groups. Lousy politics!

He hiked himself up on the side of the bed, he wasn't going to see her on his rear end like this, a man back from a failed mission, the abductor still loose, the boy in limbo.

The ankle hurt like hell, the bullet had split bone, he was taped up like a Christmas package ready for the mail.

And knocked flat by the perfume.

"I heard from your father," she said in her high sweet voice. "We were supposed to meet for that supper, remember? I didn't know you'd gone away. He said you were hurt, I was worried. I baked you some cookies, gingerbread."

He felt trapped in her scent, like she'd sprayed

something lethal into his neck. "Leave the door open," he said. "They don't like it closed."

But Bertha was already on him, door shut, thrusting out a package wrapped in foil.

He didn't need cookies, he needed a drink. "Got any Guckenheimer?" he asked, but she just tittered.

"Your leg, Colm, what happened? What were you doing that you got shot? Shot!" She zeroed in on the bandaged leg like it was the feast of Christ, a holy communion between herself and God. Her permed orangy-red hair (did he remember it that color?) wriggled out of its careful confines.

"I was in Ann Arbor, looking for Vic. You know about Vic."

She was quiet a minute. "Ann Arbor? What would Vic be doing in Ann Arbor?"

"Nothing. He wasn't," he said, pulling himself up from the bed. He had to get to the chair, he had a helpless feeling, like this woman was about to bake him into a cookie. He didn't want to go into it. It was none of Bertha's business.

Halfway to the chair he stumbled, he didn't have his crutch. She grabbed him like a hot pan, hustled him into a chair.

"Poor kid, you need someone to help. How you going to get to your appointments? I'm not doing anything now, 'cept church work, you know, I have time. Too much." She gave a nervous laugh.

"I'm fine," he said firmly. "I don't need help. Look, Bertha, I've got someone coming. I can't talk anymore right now. Maybe later."

And cursed himself for giving her even that opening.

"All right," she said. "I just happened to be going this way. I'll keep in touch. You may need a willing hand. Jesus—"

"Keep Jesus out of this, Bertha, please? Jesus wasn't around when Vic was kidnapped."

"How do you know he was kidnapped? How do you know he didn't go on his own, wasn't scared to death, poor child, with what's going on around here—he just left, wanting peace?"

"Bertha, I need to close my eyes a minute. I'm worn out from the trip over to this chair." He closed his eyes, he was spinning through a revolving door...

When he opened them again, Bertha was gone; in her place, Ruth, a rainbow after an acid rain.

"I ran into Bertha in the hall," she said. "She looked daggers through me when I came in here, said you were resting, you needed your sleep, you'd been looking for Vic. She said to tell you to stop looking, God's watching over him. If I could only think so. Good Lord."

"Lord?" he said, holding out his arms. "Yes, I'm here."

And when she grimaced: "At least break out her cookies," he said. "I got Jell-O for lunch. I hate Jell-O."

"No, thanks, I'd choke on them."

Ruth. She was Florence Nightingale in a green beret. She pulled it off and her hair went wild underneath, uncombed, like she had other concerns these days. He wanted to drink her in.

She was quiet for a time. Then, "You didn't find Vic. That man didn't have him."

And he nodded, hearing the break in her voice,

reached out for her. She dropped heavily to her knees, by his chair.

Here was a woman who cried out through her silence.

LUCIEN LIVED one day at a time now. Today it was Marie come to visit, just when he wanted to get the chores done, relax after milking, lock up for the night. She had Harold with her, he didn't need that, Harold'd complain about that Joey. Joey here with Tim, bringing in the cows: Joey or Willy? He wasn't sure which now, something missing up on top, anyway.

"Dad, we was driving out this way, Harold's got a job offer, that new firm—whatsa name, Harold?" And before Harold could open his mouth, "We'll be in the money now. I won't say 'bout time, but. Oh, well. Look!"

She whirled about, landed with one leg stuck forward like a mannequin. He couldn't see what it was— new dress? Harold touched the pink stuff, like he'd wove it himself. What was that fairy tale, Rumple-something? Belle used to read it to Marie. Rumple stole some baby, it ended bad.

"Little Michelle, too. Show grandpop, doll. Harold bought it. He likes to see us look nice, he got taste, Harold."

Lucien squinted. The girl was in something blue, it had lace. He held out his arms. She shied away.

"All right then," he said, hurt. He knew he smelled of barn. If they'd said they was coming. But no, they just arrive, like he's nothing to do but sit and yak.

"Leaving you a ham, Dad. Harold cooked it, didn't you, Harold?"

Harold nodded, took a step backward. Harold wasn't a talker. He didn't like to come here, Lucien knew it. Harold knew he knew it. Harold was, what was the word? Fastidious. Fastidious. Marie taught Lucien that word. Fastidious. Humph. Lucien and Belle was fastidious they'd've gone under the first day of farming! Now the grandgirl was catching it. It made Lucien angry. He lunged after the child, grabbed her, he wouldn't be rejected. Held her, squirming, against his stained overalls. "Grandpop's a baby."

It was too much for Harold, he rushed in, yanked the child away. "She don't like that." He held her to him like a bag of gold. "We gotta get going," he told Marie. "I can't keep her waiting."

Lucien turned his back.

"Dad, you gotta understand. They bring kids up different these days. You don't force 'em to do things like you did me."

That did it. He confronted her. "What'd I ever force you to do? You was the little princess! Go ask your mother."

"Dad, Mother is—" She sighed. "Okay, Dad. Okay. I was. Now sit down, Dad, we wanna talk a minute." She turned to Harold. "Hold your horses, Harold, it's important."

Lucien was suspicious. "I got help in the barn. I gotta supervise. They don't know the way I do. We'll talk some other time."

"It's always 'some other time,' Dad. Five minutes. Sit down five minutes. Put that ham in the fridge, Harold. Dad, when you gonna get a new fridge? Mom wanted a new one. You could've afforded it. All that money they took—how much?"

He shook his head. He didn't know how much. He only knew there was always some to pay the vet, the plumber, machine repairs. Most things he did himself. He burned his own trash, buried on his own land. Why'd she want to know how much money?

"The broker was here, right? Esther Dolley?"

He tried to get up out of his chair. She put a hand on his shoulder.

"Well, she was, she told us. She's a smart lady, Dad, right, Harold? Harold knows. She got big clients. One especially. He's land hungry. Got all he wants now 'cept this farm and Willmarth's. Esther thinks Ruth'll sell, being Pete's gone and that boy, you know—God, that gives me the willies! So that leaves you."

He managed to get up now, all the way. He'd forgot about the feed, the blend of it. Willy wouldn't know, Tim would give too much. Ruth spoiled her cows, gave 'em names. Lucien didn't hold with that, he didn't give names. He knew 'em by their looks, their quirks. They were all Bossy. *Vaches.*

"Dad, they're saying milk's bad for you now, it's on the TV. Bunch of doctors speaking up. Already people drinking skim, soon it'll be powdered milk, you watch, or none. Even babies, Dad. Mother's milk and then—"

"Pepsi Cola," Michelle said, and giggled. She was sitting on her father's lap, Harold holding on to her like she'd get contaminated if she moved. His chin down in her hair.

"Pepsi Cola, sure, you silly." Marie diddled the girl's chin. "Anyway, you're alone now, Dad. You're seventy-one, or is it two? You can't do like you used to. And without Mom..."

"I gotta go," Lucien said. He'd feed 'em too much, that Tim. He couldn't afford the waste. He got up to go.

"Dad, it's for your own good. We care about you, Daddy."

He swiveled about in the doorway. "You care, then leave me be," he said. And plunged out.

When the siren sounded, the fire trucks rushing up his road, past his farm, past Willmarth's, he just held his ears. Noise pollution.

COLM WAS ALONE with the fat man, in the Branbury police station. He'd had to get Chief Fallon to allow the interview. They'd charged Smith with an unlicensed gun, that was all they could do. Fallon looked sorrowful, like Eeyore with his tail cut off. In the motel room where Jules Smith had checked out, there was no sign of a boy, the room clerk saw nothing amiss; the man had entertained them, told jokes in the lobby, had a leisurely breakfast in the coffee shop, checked out at noon. He'd paid cash, and no, it didn't smell.

"You were alone," Colm said, and Smith nodded, there was no joking now, he was pissed, his cheeks wobbled, the bulgy blue eyes waxy, indignant. He'd done nothing—just trying to buy a car and suddenly all these men and guns. He was going to report it to...

"The police?" Colm said.

The man saw the joke, for a second he smiled. He drummed his plump fingers on the chair arm. His hair lay in gray threads along the pink skull, the face was the color of ketchup. He'd go fast when he went: overweight, the blood pushing at the thin skin. You could see the veins jumping, he was that nervous. It gave Colm heart.

"There was a murder," Colm said, "two murders. You were seen before the second one, the boy, Willy. He went after you, the bartender saw that. He was found in Otter Creek."

He tried to keep calm. He gripped his fingers to keep them from shaking.

"Sure, I was there," the man said coolly. "But I didn't off any retarded kid."

"Did I say he was mentally retarded?"

"Well he was! Ask anybody, ask the bartender. I was gonna pay him for a favor, but he refused. And I left. I didn't do no killing."

Colm fought to keep his temper. The man was lying. "The Larocques. Night of April sixth. Around midnight. An old man and woman—farmers, defenseless. You had nothing to do with that?"

The sweat squeezed out of the man's face. His cheeks shook as he spoke. "What would I want with farmers?"

"This," Colm said, fishing in his pocket, unfolding a wad of money. "You gave this to a used-car dealer in Plattsburgh. This to the bartender at the Alibi. Smell it."

He held it up to Smith's nose. The man jerked his head back.

"Smells like money," he said. "Old money. So? Maybe I got it as change. How can I remember?"

Colm had to admit the smell had faded, but holding it close, there was the barn. No question. He could hear the mooing.

"Lot of barn money around," said Smith. "I was born on a farm myself. I seen other farmers at the Alibi, their money smells. I play cards, I win sometimes, you know."

"Most farmers don't carry eight, ten thousand dollars in their pockets. You paid barn money for that Colt. It smells like a herd of Holstein." He held out the money and the man turned his head.

"You can't prove nothing," he maintained. He crossed his legs, the feet seemed crushed into the heavy boots, the legs swollen above the black boot tops; the silver points that decorated the boot right to the toe glittered in the slant of window light. The man looked calmer now. The red was fading in his cheeks.

"We'll see," Colm said. "Meantime, I understand, you're to stay around town."

"I'm a salesman," the man said, getting up. He rolled on his feet, it was an effort. "I got appointments all over."

"They'll have to wait."

There was something about the boots, the thistle-shaped filigree on the sides. Somewhere, Colm thought, after the man had left the room, he'd seen those silver thistles.

Chief Fallon was on the phone when Colm hobbled in on his cane. Fallon had the phone in his hand, his face was red with frustration: his beeper was malfunctioning, it sat on his shoulder like a dead beetle. "We're working on, uh," he said into the receiver, "uh, look, Miz Asher, we don't know who set your— if it was set, I mean we're tryin', I know, I know, what you lost."

"Barn fires," he said when he hung up finally, his

own face on fire, "three of them now. One over to Asher's—gol, we haven't a clue. Know anything about electronics?" He tapped the dead beeper. Colm shook his head.

"We checked Plattsburgh," Fallon went on. "Jules Smith is an, uh—real name's Kosciusko, Jules Kosciusko. Worked as a salesman for some furniture company. Let go and came to Branbury, worked for, uh, you know. Left suddenly, three days after the Larocque uh—"

"That broker," Colm said. The woman's card flashed into his mind's eye. "Esther K. Dolley. Find out what the K stands for, would you? Granny's second sight," he said when Fallon looked at him blankly. "And by the way," he said as he hobbled out—the ankle was like pulling along a tree stump, he had to get home, take a shot of Guckenheimer— "Smith, I mean Kosciusko, killed Belle. I think I can give you proof."

"Yeah? And I'll give you a job," Fallon said. "If you'll learn how to shoot a gun. That Ann Arbor officer, uh, he said—"

"Oh, hell," said Colm.

RUTH HEARD the phone ring: she couldn't answer, Sharon was screaming, there was something wrong. Her heart leaped in her knees, the knees gave way. Was it the baby? Was it Vic? She raced out on the porch.

Flames were licking at the north side of the barn, it looked like the milk room. There was only a swinging door between it and the heifers. They were bellowing, the mothers bawling from their stalls. "Call Tim," she screamed back. "Call the fire department. Emily! You hear me? Ohmigod! Get out here. Get out!"

Sharon had the barn door wide, she was flinging open the stanchions, the cows were alarmed, smelling smoke, they were charging into one another. There was no time to think how, why. The flames were in the milk room: "Get the calves out first!" she screamed.

Here was Emily now, and Wilder—where had he come from? The four of them shooing the rearing heifers. They stampeded out, panicked by the rising smoke, the shrieks of their fellows. The newest, still with her mother—Charlotte! In the back of the barn.

"Mother, we'll get them, stay here. Don't you go."

"It's Charlotte, her calf. They're still inside!"

"Too late, Mother."

"I have to. It's Charlotte!"

"No, Mother, no."

They wouldn't keep her back, damn it. She broke through, raced to the rear of the barn while they shrieked at her heels. The smoke was a gritty tent, smothering her nose, her eyes, she could only grope, low, for the bars. Charlotte was squealing, a high-pitched noise she'd never heard before, it was like a warren full of rabbits. Her calf could be on fire—what would they do? Her fingers failed her, her brain was sucked into a vacuum. The bellowing, the shouts, farther away now. She felt herself stumbling, flailed her arms, pitched forward...

When she came to she was flat on her back, on the grass, the air filled with running men and sirens. "Charlotte," she gasped, and Emily shook her head. "Wilder got the calf. That was all we could do. Charlotte was like frozen, in shock. She was a dead weight, Mom. It was too late. Go in the house.''

Behind them the flashing figures, a cascade of water, voices shouting: she saw Tim, with Joey. And Bertha—what was Bertha doing here?

"Get away!'' She waved her hands, but the woman just stared, her eyes lit up like small grass fires.

Emily cried, "Wilder. Over here. Wilder!''

Charlotte's sickly calf was crying for its mother, licking at Ruth's legs. "Get her in the pasture,'' Ruth shouted, up now on her knees. "Never mind the mud. Give her to Bathsheba.''

But no one was there to hear.

She'd go herself, set the calf by Bathsheba, if she'd take, if the old girl would let her. The barn was out of her control. Was it gone? Her barn gone?

Something was ringing. Her ears? The phone? If it was she had to answer it. But her legs wouldn't take her there.

ELEVEN

KURT UNSWORTH was already in custody when Colm arrived with Kosciusko. Faced with the photographs of Belle's face, the marks that matched the boots, the fat man had burst into a waterfall of sweat, and named Kurt. It had been crazy getting here, Colm pulled aside twice for fire engines, the chief would be in a fury. Fallon was on the phone again: the farmers were hysterical, demanding police protection, a fourth barn today. He waved Colm into the meeting room, his neck pocked with hives. Kosciusko was already there. He had the boots on, the boots with the shiny thistles.

When they brought in Kurt the boy gave a shout and raced over to the fat man, an officer had to grab him. Kurt seemed grounded, sober, they'd had him six hours: no time to shoot up, pop a pill. Colm couldn't imagine it, that dependence on a drug, like being anchored to a slippery rock in Dead Creek.

The creek made him think of Willy, his drowned bones. The boots had struck Willy, too-his stomach, though the marks weren't so clear.

"Get him out of here," he ordered, and they jerked the fat man to his swollen feet. "Take those boots off him," Colm said. "They're evidence."

"He named you," Colm said to Kurt. "I see you know that." He nodded at the sergeant to turn on the tape recorder.

Kurt was quiet now, slumped into a chair. The words coughed out of him.

Kurt and Smith were doing drugs during lunch hour at Catamount; Kurt asked the latter for a loan, Smith said he could use some cash himself, and Kurt told about Lucien Larocque.

"But he already knew, he already knew about Larocque," Kurt said. "He just decided to use me."

He squinted at the ceiling, like he couldn't think for a minute who Lucien Larocque was, the name had just slipped out.

"How did you know about the barn money?"

"Barn money. Oh, yeah, from Dufours. He'd worked there once. Happened to mention it, we thought it was funny. He said everybody knew. The wife paid for groceries out of barn money."

"Smith—his real name is Kosciusko—said he'd never been to Larocque's, had nothing to do with barn money."

Kurt laughed. The laugh came up slow and hollow out of his caved in belly. It looked like he drank his meals. "Sure," he said, more animated now, like his memory was jumping back at him, knocking him out. "He had nothing to do with it. Oh, wow—it was his idea, man! We smoked together once, he had the stuff. But it was running out, he said. He knew about Larocque's, like I said from Dufours—anyway, it was common knowledge, man, the cash never hit the bank. Christ, I never thought he'd do what he did. I just wanted the drugs. I was just the driver. I never went in."

He was lying, Colm thought. Lucien had seen two men.

Kurt dropped his head in his hands, he looked like a runner dropping out of a race, like an old man, the hair was thinning on the back of his head. Cocaine, who knew what else?

The sirens screamed through the open window, pierced Colm's temples. "You went because you needed drug money. Okay. Wilder saw you, didn't he, after he dropped off Emily Willmarth? He saw you and tried to stop you. Or didn't try—"

"I told him to leave. I said if he didn't I'd tell something else he got involved in. Never mind, something to do with Dad. He left. I'd've killed him if he didn't. I mean, at first I worried, I couldn't think what he was doing there, I thought maybe Smith had got to him, too." He jerked his thumb at the door where the fat man had disappeared.

"But he wouldn't, Wilder just wouldn't. It was me. But I never touched that woman, I swear! I was the driver, I was only getting drug money out of it, damn little. I hid it in Wilder's room, Dad's always searching mine. I didn't think Smith would hurt them. He seemed, well, the kidding sort. You know, funny. I knew where he hung his coats, I told Smith. Wilder'd told me, he sold the raffle tickets, I got it out of him. That's why he waited that night, suspicious."

Colm glanced over at the tape recorder, he didn't trust machines. No talent for them. But it was grinding away, and a good thing. His head was spinning too fast to record all this.

"If he hit her, the Larocque woman," Kurt went

on, "I didn't see it. I guess he must've. But I didn't see it. I kept the car running after they went in, and, I don't know, ten, twenty minutes, they came back. Smith said everything was okay, he got the coat money, some in a drawer, some in the barn. I didn't want any then, I could smell it. It smelled like shit. I wanted out of there."

Colm said, "Kosciusko kicked her. With those Medusa boots of his. It eventually killed her, there was an aneurism. My father took a picture. You can see the marks on Belle's face."

Kurt dropped his face in his hands, his shoulders heaved like he'd throw up. He'd said all he could for now.

Colm needed to get out of here himself, he buzzed for the officer. He needed to see Ruth, it was important. Something was beating in his left temple. His ankle hurt, bad. Did he imagine it, or was his vision blurred? Was he having a stroke?

When the policeman came back for Kurt, Colm caught the echo: "they," the boy had said, "they." There was a third person involved? He grabbed Kurt's sleeve. "Who was it? Who was that other person who went in?"

Kurt lifted his head like it was holding up the whole universe. "I don't know, I never saw his face. There was a moon, but I was stoned, I had to psych myself up, you know. He must have come on foot, met the car. Then he put on the stocking."

"You know more," Colm said, still gripping the arm. He needed to keep his balance, for one thing.

"I don't! Well, I mean, Smith, um, Kosciusko, mentioned some guy, someone who knew Larocque, needed the bucks. Though he said the guy didn't deserve a share, he was a jerk. He was, too, the guy was blubbering like a baby, wanting his split right off, wanting out of the scene. We dropped him off at an intersection. He ran down the road like he'd been goosed. You better find out who.''

Afterward, Colm couldn't remember exactly what Kurt had said. Someone else involved? A third person?

Was it Wilder after all? Kurt would lie through his teeth for his brother, anyone could see that.

WHEN THE SMOKE cleared, the mud settled, it wasn't as bad as she'd thought—the barn at least. The fire was concentrated in the milk room, they got it before it caught the entire barn. But the heifer pen was destroyed, the whole north end, smoke and water damage everywhere. It would take hours, dollars and dollars, to build it back up. She didn't know how much insurance there was, Pete took care of that, she'd have to dig through a file.

And they'd lost Charlotte. She groaned at the irony: Jane escaped the fire in Charlotte Brontë's novel, it was the madwoman who set it—what was her name? That movie on video Emily had wanted her to see, Wide Something Sea, she couldn't think now. Her mind was a sieve, her brain burned out.

Why was she thinking of a book, with a quarter of her barn in ashes, her son gone—more important than any barn. She sank down on the porch steps.

And now what? She squinted at a commotion over by the barn. It was—who? Her sister-in-law? Yes, running at the smoking barn in her black pumps, Sharon dashing after, trying to pull her back.

Bertha—that was the madwoman's name, it came to her in a rush. Whoa, she thought, it was so apt. She ran at Bertha, shouted at Sharon: "Go back to the baby, I'll take care of this."

She grabbed the woman by the neck. Bertha clawed at her hands, she was trying to get to the ashy barn: "God told me," she bawled, "in a dream."

"Told you what?" Ruth shouted. "To burn my barn? Is that what he told you?"

Bertha was there before the fire, Ruth remembered now: "for a visit, for tea," she'd said in her sugary voice, dressed up like she was going to a rendezvous with some lover. After six months she was back on the nicotine. Sharon asked her to smoke outside because of the baby and she'd said, "Oh, of course, dear," and left.

Left where? The house, yes. For the barn?

"Too late, sister-in-law. Did you leave your purse in there when you set it? You'll have to get a new lipstick. Is this how you get your kicks? Your kinky sex? Setting fires? Watching people's lives burn away? How many have you set? Huh?"

She yanked the woman, still muttering about a dream, back to the house, surprised at her own strength, Sharon yelling, "Mother, are you out of your mind? Let Aunt Bertha go." Wrestled her up the porch steps, into the kitchen; Bertha sinking down, a doll in polyester with a charred hole in the back of her lilac pants. She rubbed at it, wailed.

"It got you, did it? In the rear end? Well, you're

lucky. Another Bertha I know went up in the flames. Here." Ruth threw a hunk of butter at the woman. "Heap it on. Like you heaped on that kerosene or whatever you used. Where'd you get it, anyway? In your church? Is that what you used on that family of Italians you tried to run off your street? Colm's a Catholic, you must know that. Huh?"

Bertha sat up, the skin tight over the thin bones of her face. "It was God's fireworks. I told you, Ruth, I had a dream. Pete wants you to sell, you wouldn't. So God set that fire." Her finger waggled at Ruth, accusing.

"You did it for Pete?" Ruth sat down, incredulous.

Here was something out of *Mad* comics; she took a long breath. No, it couldn't be Pete, it wasn't like him, he wouldn't order his own barn burned, would he? But Bertha's confused mind...

She stood over her sister-in-law's chair, shook the sagging shoulders. "Did Pete tell you to? Did he? Tell the truth!"

Anything could happen now, anything was possible. It was mud season. No, blood season, Colm's pun. No-mad season! The world had gone stark raving mad.

Bertha wept. Remorseful? Or just self-centered. Ruth yanked her up out of the chair, held her, a Raggedy Ann, in her two hands: hands that milked cows, gave feed, picked stone; she was proud of all she'd done since Pete left, she felt seven feet tall.

"He wanted to sell, he did! But the barn? No. It was God's fire. The burning bush!" She was almost triumphant. Ruth could hear Gabriel's horn blast. Or was it a fire engine, rumbling out of the drive? She let the woman go.

"It was God," Bertha warbled again and threw back her orangy head. Her lipstick had leaked into her chin, it was a little red sea.

WHEN COLM GOT to Ruth's, his father driving, his father who never went over forty, the north end of the barn was a pile of steaming embers. He'd found out only as he left the station, he was in shock. A town truck was wheeling about in the driveway, there was nothing left but smoke and grit. And mud. A sea of mud where trucks, hoses, men, ladders, had dragged through. Ruth and Emily were at the barn door looking in, their arms limp at their sides. Tim was looking out: it seemed a film in slow motion. Emily's arms were around her mother's shoulders.

He got out of the car and stumbled over to her. His father shouted, "Watch out, Colm, it's not gonna heal, you running on that leg."

There was a free shoulder left, he encircled it. "I didn't know," he said, "I heard the sirens, I was at the station. I didn't know it was your barn. Oh, jeez, I would've—"

Ruth looked at him like she'd just gotten up from a long sleep. "Vic," she said, "was there any news of Vic?"

"It wasn't Kurt. Or Fat Man. It wasn't related to anyone we know about, the kidnapping."

And then he had both shoulders, was turning her slowly in his arms like a drugged child. Until she broke away.

"Hey!"

"Hey," he shouted again, and rushed at the house. He hobbled after. His father was yelling from the car, and he waved him off. He wanted her to know about Kurt anyway, what he'd done; about the fat man, about the assault, the murder, the third person involved. He wanted her to know it wasn't a wild-goose chase he'd been on while her barn was burning.

"Ruth, wait!" He wanted her to know he'd help, build back the barn. He could use a hammer, he'd helped his father build a garage once. And groaned, thinking how it blew down in the next big wind.

She halted in the kitchen door, then glanced about wildly, like the kitchen had disappeared, gone up in flames with the barn. Like there was nothing in the world left.

"Ruthie," he said, using her old pet name. "What is it, Ruthie? What are you looking for?"

"Her," said Ruth. And when he said, "Who?" she said, "The kidnapper."

And then she grabbed his arm and said, "I left her in here and she's gone. We've got to go after her. If she hasn't run off somewhere, we'll maybe—"

"Find who, Ruthie? Who?"

But she couldn't get the name out, she was dragging him over to her pickup, telling a reporter to "bug off," shrieking orders at Emily and Tim about milking; shouting at Sharon to get supper, to stay by the phone. They shouted back, but she didn't say where she was going.

"She?" Colm puzzled. Marie? That broker? They

were all the shes he could seem to think of. His mind was a maze.

"Go home, Dad," he yelled at his father. "I'll get back on my own." And his father threw up his hands. At least corpses were quiet, they didn't run off on wild-goose chases.

When Ruth calmed down a bit, when she said, "To Bertha's," Colm stared at her. She was leaning into the wheel of the old pickup, her mouth was set like a windup alarm. Bertha? What did Bertha have to do with anything? Bertha was the last one he wanted to see.

"Bertha, jeez," he said. "Do we have to?"

"Madwoman," Ruth hissed, and Colm agreed with that at least; limped up the steps at 9 All Saints Lane with his cane, thinking he was involved with two madwomen.

Then here was Bertha, at the door, in a prim gray skirt, purple sweater, like she'd come from a tea party. The scent was thick as insect repellent. You could smell the smoke—or had they brought it with them? It clung inside his nostrils.

"Kidnapper," Ruth said, and shoved Bertha back in the house.

"Wait a minute here," Colm said, but Ruth ignored him.

"It was God," Bertha said, the words spitting out like she was choking on a hunk of meat. The mouth split into two pink lines. The gray skirt hiked up, sank into a plum velvet chair. The house was as pristine as its owner: the ruffly curtains, the matching doilies on the chair arms, the flowered carpet, everything in

Good Housekeeping order, even the lipsticked cigarette butts, laid in rows in the ashtrays.

Except Bertha: she was fighting off Ruth. Her
sweater was popping its buttons. Ruth had one in her
hand, flung it on the floor. "Where is he? Where's
Vic? Is he in this house? Vic!" she screamed, her neck
flung back like a crane's.

Bertha looked stunned, like someone had thrown a
rock at her head. Colm wasn't sure of his role, if he
should intervene. Bears killed for their cubs, he
wouldn't put it past human mothers. But thought he'd
wait and see. Under different circumstances, he might
enjoy this.

Ruth was shaking the purple shoulders while Bertha
held herself stiff. "Where did you take him, Bertha?
Was this God's idea too? Like burning my barn? It
wasn't Pete. It was you, you, Bertha. Leave God out
of this, dammit. One more word about God and I'll
strangle you!"

Bertha could be a third casualty, Colm thought. He
tugged on Ruth's shoulders, was sorry when she
swung back and elbowed him. He had to fight for his
breath.

Bertha was talking, she was appealing to Colm:
"Get her off me! Off, Ruth! Get off!"

Ruth had Bertha over the chair back, she was yelling, "The truth, dammit. I want the truth!"

And Bertha: "I'm trying—to—say it."

"She's trying to say it," Colm told Ruth.

"To Pete's," Bertha choked out. "I took him to
Pete's. You wouldn't do it," she accused. She pointed
a ragged fingernail at Ruth's nose.

Ruth relaxed her grip. Her nose was bleeding. She knelt on the chair edge, her knees against Bertha's chest, amazed.

Bertha yelled, "You kept him here, he could've been killed. It was child abuse. I told Pete. He agreed. He—"

"He didn't tell you to kidnap him!" Ruth leaped back out of the chair, dug her feet into the flowered carpet like she'd root there. Bertha shrank, a pink pincushion, into the plum chair.

"It was your idea, right?" And when Bertha said, "God—"

"God didn't kidnap my son, you did. You, Bertha!"

Bertha held up a purple arm. "I took him, yes. I got a man in my church to help. It wasn't kidnapping. You don't *kidnap* your own kin. He's my nephew, we're close, Vic and me. He's like my own. I had a vision, I tried to tell you that. He needs a father. He needs Pete. Pete was away, we had to wait three days."

Ruth uprooted, flew to the phone. Dialed. Bertha jumped up behind her. "Go ahead, call," she squealed, digging her fingers into her hair—Colm was reminded of a squashed orange. "You'll see I'm telling the truth. Talk to him. Vic hasn't called you, right? He's glad to be with his father! Glad!"

Ruth wheeled about, head down, like she'd charge. Colm was a broken stick between a pair of she-wolves. "Keep dialing," he told Ruth. What was he hoping to hear? That Pete helped plan the kidnapping? He wanted to inculpate Pete, did he? Win Ruth, like a prize pig at Field Days?

But the boy was the thing. He wanted Vic back. But

why didn't the boy call if he was with his father? He'd know his mother's worry, it didn't make sense. It could be another of Bertha's visions, hallucinations. "Ruth," he said, trying to offer reason.

Ruth's eyes were granite. It was a woman on the other end, he could hear the voice, saccharine, like something out of the thirties films. Ruth said nothing for a minute, just listened. It seemed like the room had no air. And then she hung up.

They all waited, even Bertha was waiting.

"It was that woman," Ruth said, her face pale as milk. "Pete's woman. Pete is out looking for Vic—he ran off early this morning. Pete was away at some conference, the police located him, he came back last night. He wasn't even there, Bertha, when you dropped off Vic, Bertha, you bitch! The woman said she tried to call us, it was during the fire. Why didn't she keep trying! But Vic's gone now, trying to come home, I know it. Through that jungle! Pete will call me, she said, he didn't want to worry me. Worry me. Worry me!"

She rushed at the door again. "I have to get to my phone. Vic will call now, he'll find a way. That woman had him locked in a room till Pete came back. The lies you told her about me, Bertha, you godly woman, you bitch!

"And don't you dare leave this house!" she shouted back at Bertha. "We'll figure out what to do with you. Kidnapping. Setting fire to barns. You can't plead insanity on this one. Or religion, either."

Bertha looked paralyzed, like she'd heard the words

kidnapping and *fire* for the first time. Her eyes were squashed grapes.

"On second thought," Ruth yelled, swiveling about at the door, Colm behind her, his ankle a burning bush, "you should."

"You're lost," Bertha wailed out the door. "You too, Colm. You can be saved—it's not too late. I can save you, Colm. Colm, come back, I can save—"

"That woman set the fire?" The reporter was out on the sidewalk, she'd followed them here, was holding up a notebook.

Ruth waved her off, ran for the pickup.

"Possibly," Colm called back. He believed in freedom of the press. "We'll need proof."

"I didn't burn your barn," Bertha screamed out the door. "I didn't burn any one of them. Don't you accuse me of that! It was God told me to take Vic. You'll pay for this, Colm Hanna, you'll burn in hell!"

The reporter's camera flashed, twice.

He already was, he thought, in hell: the ankle shooting pains up and down his body. Ruth screeched off in the pickup before he could slam the door. "Jesus Mary and Joe," he shouted, "you're trying to put me back in the hospital."

"We have to find Vic," she said, "he's trying to come home, I know it, he's running away from Pete. We have to tell the police."

She took the corner of All Saints Lane on two muddy wheels, while Colm hid his face in his hands.

VIC CLIMBED in the rear compartment of the old green Ford, stretched out his small body, and drew his father's coat up to his chin. It was headed north, this car, he didn't know how far, he'd watched them go into Kentucky Fried Chicken, two young men in jeans and dirty T-shirts. He wanted to go in, too, he was hungry, he hadn't thought of taking any food—just left, while the woman was on the toilet. Got a bus to 125th Street with his only dollar, the dollar he took to school that day for his chocolate milk and cookies. They left the car unlocked, and he got in.

When they came back, the two of them were laughing. "You did good, man, nice trick," one of them said, heaving a bag in the back, licking a strawberry cone. Vic's heart flipped up in his teeth. In a minute they'd look, they'd see him. He didn't want them to see him. He didn't know what they'd do, he'd been warned about these things. He didn't know how far they were going. They had to be students, though, didn't they? There were books in the back of the car: a sticker on the rear window said Marist College, Poughkeepsie, N.Y. He didn't know about Marist College, but Poughkeepsie was north. If he got to Poughkeepsie he'd find another car, a car with a Vermont license plate. Someone in Poughkeepsie, New York, would be headed to Vermont. Someone had to be. He'd get there, he'd get home.

The car screeched off, the radio blared. "Sto-len car," the boys sang, "ridin' in a sto-len car..."

Vic was suddenly so hot, so closed in, he couldn't breathe. Any minute, he thought, he could die. They'd find his body in the rear compartment of a stolen car. "Kidnapped boy dead of suffocation," he saw the headlines in the Branbury *Independent*.

His aunt would be sorry then. Aunt Bertha: he balled his fists to think of her. Closed up all those nights with Aunt Bertha and that kooky man, while they sang hymns and read aloud from the Bible. And talked about how he'd been saved. Saved!

And then that woman at his father's place. Locking him in a bedroom that first night because his father was gone. And both women sweet as honey. Sweet as poison, he thought, and took a gasping breath.

Oh lord, oh jeezum, it could be his last.

TWELVE

RUTH'S HEART was racing, it hadn't stopped since the battle with Bertha. And now the calls every hour from Pete, insisting he had nothing to do with the kidnapping—was he nuts, wanting the boy in New York City? For a visit, yeah, but to live? He was furious with Bertha, upset with his woman for not getting back to Ruth, for letting the boy run off. Well, Ruth had to believe him, didn't she? It was his guilt, she told herself, his guilt doing the talking.

And Colm talking, too, insisting she come with him now, to Marie's. He couldn't walk on the leg, he said, he needed support, more than his father's cane—he'd clutch her arm and hop. Besides, he argued, she knew Marie and Harold better than he did. Sharon could stay by the phone, he said, still talking. The police were on the job: New York Thruway, Northway, the Taconic, Route 22, all the towns west to east, Rhinebeck to Hoosick Falls, Manhattan to Vermont.

"You have to get your mind off things, Ruth," he insisted, "you'll have a coronary." She was alienating people, he told her: the press, the police, her family. "You'll alienate Marie, but I need you with me."

Though it wasn't really Marie, he explained, but Harold they were after. It might be a dead end, it might not. The intersection where Kurt supposedly dropped the man off was a half mile from Harold's house. And

Harold was a relative of Kosciusko's. They'd discovered that when they found that Esther Kosciusko Dolley was the fat man's sister, and Esther was a something removed of Harold's. And Colm had heard through a colleague that Harold had a job now, in Esther's new office. Though Colm said he couldn't imagine the man selling anybody anything.

"Something might be jelling on that end, Ruth. You never know. What can you do here today?"

"Build the barn back up," she said. "Help Tim and that guy he hired. I can handle a hammer, you know."

She wanted things right again, back on a routine. She had the cows out in the muddy pasture, they had to be hand-milked till the barn was rebuilt, new milking machines installed. There were insurance claims to complete—the inspector was crying "electrical" while she claimed "arson." There was the manure bunker to be cleaned out: there was a demand for composted manure, the papers said, you could market it as potting soil. She had to think of ways to diversify, stay alive, keep the farm.

She was going to keep the farm, she was, wasn't she?

But what was the farm without her son? She'd felt relieved at first to hear he was with Pete, he was safe. But now he was on his own, in that wilderness between New York and Vermont. He could have elected to stay with his father—was she glad that he'd run off? But worried sick.

"It's only a couple miles from here. We can have you back in minutes."

"Oh, all right," Ruth snapped, "all right. Just to

shut you up, Hanna." And began flinging orders at the girls. She'd make a terrific army sergeant, he told her.

She wasn't prepared for Marie's house, it had a complete new look. The walls were freshly painted, off-white, with an off-white carpet no farmer would have—a plop of manure and it was gone. Orange drapes and matching upholstery. It looked like a showroom from Sears.

It *was* Sears, Marie informed her, looking smart in black pants and a yellow silk blouse. "We made the down payment. Harold's got a job! He's in real estate now. When he sells a house we'll pay off the rug."

"Is he here?" Ruth asked. Marie shook her head. "Can we talk a minute? We know he got work with Esther Dolley—Colm's in the business, you know. She wants to buy my farm."

Marie said, "You'd be smart. Let Harold sell it, he'll get an exclusive. I got to convince Dad. We tell him, me and Harold, he's got to give up that farm, it don't pay, for Pete's sake. Say, you got that guy in jail, who killed Mom? He won't get off?" She looked scared, bit her lower lip.

Ruth said, "Over my dead body. Look, Marie, you were brought up here. Your mother used to say how she couldn't do without you. You filled a wheelbarrow full of stone once, proud as any farmer, you were ten years old. Belle told the whole neighborhood."

"That was then," said Marie, pulling on her curled hair.

"It's now. He needs you. It's all he's got, that farm." Ruth felt the anger building up again.

Colm was having a coughing fit—pretty obvious,

Ruth thought, but Marie just looked at him, offered water.

"Point out the kitchen, I can get it," he said. "Can I take a look at Harold's trains? I used to have some myself." And Marie said, "Sure. Just don't try to run 'em. Harold's particular."

When the phone rang Ruth jumped, though of course it wasn't hers. It was someone Marie wanted to talk to, she glanced at Ruth, shrugged. "Annette," she whispered into the receiver, "I got people here, I can only talk a minute. Help yourself to a soda," she told Ruth, waving at the kitchen.

The kitchen chairs had been freshly painted, orange. Ruth's spine hurt to look at the straight, stiff backs. The basement door was open, she heard Colm moving around down there. She got a Pepsi out of the refrigerator. She hated the stuff but needed the caffeine, Vic was always trying to sneak it into her cart at the Grand Union. Marie's voice droned on in the living room. A few minutes later Colm came stomping up. "Harold's got some setup," he said in a loud voice.

She made a face, but he wasn't looking at her, he was squinting down at a piece of paper. It was important, she saw, the way he was holding it close to his glassy eyes, he looked excited. If they could find that third assailant, she thought, she could get Vic back. An irrational thought, but it stuck in her head that all that had happened—murders, fires, kidnapping—were all connected. Like victims, thousands of them, all over the world.

Though Vic's disappearance was Bertha's doing,

she knew that for a fact, didn't she? Or was anything fact in this mad world?

Colm was waving the paper in her face, she saw it was a bank deposit. "Cash," Harold had scrawled on the pink slip. "Plattsburgh." Colm's lips formed the word, his eyes were exclamation points behind the thick lenses. She squinted at the date but couldn't seem to focus.

The living room was quiet now: she hurried back in, feeling nervous, met Marie in the doorway. "Marie, this isn't the time," she said, groping her way back to the old conversation, wanting to sound calm, feeling her heart scream. "It's too soon. I want you to tell Harold that. It's Harold pushing your dad to sell, right? And that broker he works for, his cousin?"

Marie looked coy now, suspicious. "Second cousin, that's all. He never even met her till a month ago, it's just a way to get a job. We gotta eat!" she said, looking put-upon. "He hated not having a job. He talked about killing himself, I was scared out of my gourd! He hated what it did to me and Michelle. I'm not going back to that. I'm not taking over any farm, if that's what you're getting at. It's a deadbeat farm, Jesus, look at it!"

Her eyes glazed over, like she could see the stony pasture juxtaposed on the new white carpet. "This is nothing new. I been telling 'em for years. You think I listen to everything Harold says, do you?"

She got up then, still pulling on her hair, went to the stairs, hollered, "Michelle! Time for Brownies, you hear me? Get on down here."

Michelle came down, dressed in a brown cotton uni-

form; it had been Emily's before she joined the Girl
Scouts and then quit. The girl halted on the third step
when she saw the visitors, nodded shyly.

Ruth held out her hand and Michelle came to her,
slowly. Her knees weakened: Belle used to bring the
child over to play with Vic. The girl was three or four
years younger, but they played well together. When
she slipped out of Ruth's grasp, Ruth felt her own head
hard on her shoulders, a mossy rock.

"Remember what I said," she told Marie. "Think
about it. Think about your mom."

Marie's face crumpled. "I'll talk to Harold," she
said, then looked back at the orange rayon drapes like
she wanted to take them down, she really did, but they
smelled so good, so fresh and new, and the color
cheered her up. She needed orange in her life.

"Where did you get that spot on the dress?" she
snapped at the girl. "Where's the scarf? You look like
a tramp."

BACK HOME, the phone rang just as Ruth was answering the door: a farm neighbor bearing a casserole,
like someone had died in this house. Wanting to sym-
pathize: about Vic, the burned barn. Ruth thanked her,
shut the door.

"Yes, we're building it back up, there wasn't so
much damage after all," she told the neighbor. "No,
I won't sell. She's been to see you, too, that broker,
Esther Dolley? No, Joan, I won't, believe me."

Did she mean that? Only an hour ago she'd told
Sharon she wanted to sell, go back to school, anyplace,
away from burnings, kidnappings, the Ku Klux

Klan—for that's what Bertha was, wasn't she? A Klanswoman? Burning barns and stealing children in the name of God?

She dashed back to answer the phone. Where was Sharon?

"Ruth? Where'n hell you been? I'm calling from the Plattsburgh bank. I've confirmed it, Harold's deposit. The seventh of April, day after the assault. And all in cash—barn money maybe, though nobody can tell me. His payoff, I suppose. And the police never checked over there, across the lake. Jeez. Though the whole thing was on Plattsburgh news. 'But this was a deposit,' the teller insisted. Incompetence?''

She couldn't think now about the implications. Harold mixed up in the assault—maybe Marie? It was impossible to think about, it was like incest. No, she couldn't imagine that. Not either of them, really.

Someone was banging on the door again, a policeman. She felt swept away, down Otter Creek like Willy, over the falls...

"Someone's at the door," she yelled, and dropped the phone while Colm's voice shouted something unintelligible.

The man was dragging a child with him, two, in fact, one in each hand. One in a blue parka; her heart leaped.

But it wasn't Vic.

The boys had been found, said the officer, lurking around the burned barn. He'd come himself, looking for clues. One boy had a canvas bag in his fist. "Tried to get away but I got 'em.''

The faces were familiar, she blinked. Under the dirt, one of them was Billy Marsh.

"It was just some old feed, some broken old bag," Billy said. "But you can have it." He dropped it on the porch, the feed spilled out in a round heap.

"Thank you," she said, "for returning what belongs to me."

"It was just sompin' to do," said the other, sticking up his pointed chin. "We didn't take anything important. You can't hold us for anything."

"You're in Vic's class, aren't you. What's your name?" she asked the second one, a lanky boy with hair hanging in his eyes like a poodle.

"Jimmy."

"Jimmy who?"

"Jimmy Southwick," he said, sticking up his chin a little.

"Your father's a lawyer? Hampton Southwick?" She'd seen the fancy sign up on Cherry Street. The name had struck her as something out of a romance novel.

The boy nodded, looked at her, arrogant, then glanced at Billy Marsh.

"That kid, that Joey, Willy's dumb friend," said Billy, standing there with his hands on his skinny hips, "said we can come, there'd be some old burnt stuff you wouldn't want. We're building something. We talked to him last night, down by the Alibi."

"The Alibi?" she said. "You go there? To a bar?"

"Not to the bar. Behind it!" Billy took a step back, nudged by his friend. "Mostly we fool around. That field down by the creek."

Something leaped in her head. But it wouldn't come together, some thought, some premise. Some second sight, Colm would call it, his dear old great-gran.

It was too late, anyway. The kids were running off, the policeman yelled, "Stop! Hey!" and ran after, but they were too sleek, too fast, they were gone before he could catch them. She saw them stop at the road, look back, then run again, jumping up and down, like they were boxing each other.

"It's all right," he said. "I know where one of 'em lives, that lawyer's kid. They're scared, I could see it." She nodded, distracted by the nagging thought.

"You have the bag back," he said, like the situation was resolved. "Don't think they took anything else."

"Yes, they did," she said, her brain still trying to tell her something. "Not anything you can see. Not anything material."

Back in the house Colm was still on the line, hollering at the top of his lungs. "Why'd you break off like that," he yelled. "I was worried, damn it!"

She pulled the window shade, and the room was flooded with light.

"I think I might know how Willy died," she said.

THEY WERE headed for Saratoga they said, north. Vic remembered the time he drove there with his father, it didn't take more than a couple hours. Why, he could walk from Saratoga! They were running out of beer now, there'd be another stop, already they were looking. He could breathe easier, even cough: the loud music, the laughing, the profanity. All the way up the thruway he'd prayed for a police car to stop them, he'd pop up—and wouldn't those guys be surprised! But only one came and sailed on past. He didn't dare show himself, they were too drunk.

"Man, by the time that guy knows his car gone we be in Canada," one of them said. And the other giggled and said, "Better ditch it there. Find us some fresh French meat, huh?"

Sure enough. It was a Getty station, some small town off the highway, it sold beer. They bowled in, one of them still singing. Vic spotted a phone booth, there was change, he didn't know how much, spilled on the car floor from the last beer stop. He swept it up, crawled out of the car, raced to the booth. He found a quarter, plunked it in, asked for the Vermont number.

"Fifty cents," said the operator. He threw in all the change he had. And the phone rang.

Sharon's voice answered, calm, then escalating when she heard him. "Where are you!" she shrieked. When he said, "I don't know," she screamed louder: "Mother's in a panic, and you don't know where you are?"

"In a phone booth!" he shouted. "They're coming out any minute. I left my knapsack inside."

He'd just realized. He had to get his knapsack, it had his important stuff: his books, some baseball cards he'd traded. His map of Australia—Ronsard would grade him down if he didn't turn it in.

"Who? Inside what? Coming out of where? Vic?"

"The ones who stole the car."

"God, Vic, what car? What are you near? What place?"

"New York," he said. That was all he knew.

He could hear one of them already out, yelling for the other. He'd have to hurry. He leaned into the phone, he had something important to say. "Tell Mother I found the glove by Wilder's puzzle box," he said. "It's Garth's, I seen it before."

"What? What glove? Mother's out by the barn, Vic, there was a fire, I'll call her. Vic, where are you?"

"A fire?" he said. But the operator interrupted. "Another fifty cents."

"But I don't—" He held up his empty palm, and the phone went dead.

He scooted low, back to the car, hung over the seat to reach for his knapsack. It was wedged in the rear, he had to dive for it. He'd get it and then he'd start walking north, then east. Or hitchhike maybe, back to Branbury. No, not hitchhike. They might take him back to his father in New York and he couldn't have that. He'd never go back there, with that woman.

The barn on fire? Jeezum! He had to get himself home, and soon. He gave a hard yank, and the knapsack came free.

But *he* wasn't. Something had him by the seat of his pants. He gasped.

"Hey, man, looka this. We got us a little buddy here," one of the men said, and giggled, like Vic was the funniest thing he'd ever seen, and clapped a hand over Vic's mouth. "You want a ride? You'll get one, kid."

And the car lurched forward, tires screaming.

RUTH GAVE Emily orders to phone the Unsworths if there was another call from Vic. But that stolen car.

Who was he with? Had he stolen a car himself? He'd driven the tractor, yes, but he couldn't drive a car. And where in New York? The police were alerted for a stolen car, somewhere in New York State. It was crazy—why couldn't he call back, collect? Or hadn't he thought of that? Didn't know how? She'd sheltered him, that was the trouble. He didn't know how to cope with the world!

But the glove—it was important to him. Important to her. He'd want her to do something about the glove, and she was going to. She pulled up to Unsworths': Carol smiled to see her and then looked alarmed when Ruth said, "There's a boxing glove. I want you to find it for me."

"What?" Carol said, "Why a boxing glove?" Her face was on alert, a panther with its young in the bushes.

"I'll explain. Now take me to Wilder's room."

Wilder was lying on his bed, reading a book. He looked so peaceful Ruth couldn't believe there was a boxing glove in his room that might have struck Willy. He smiled to see her.

"Glove? Sure, Garth has a pair. I mean they're mine. But I let him use them. Mom, it was your present."

Carol looked distraught, like she couldn't remember anything, even her son's name. The police had been there, she said, found barn money—Kurt hadn't spent it all. They'd see that Lucien got back the rest.

"I want you to find them. See if there's a pair," Ruth said. "Vic said he saw one in your room."

"You heard from Vic!" Carol squealed, wanting to be glad about something.

Ruth couldn't talk now, she had this mission, she had to get back home. To the telephone.

It seemed forever that Wilder looked. Finally he bent down to search under the bed. And there it was. A single boxing glove, for the right hand. Not big enough for Wilder now, only a young boy's hand would fit into it. Was it big enough to hurt Willy? The police had found a left-hand glove on the creek bank. She made him search: in his room, then in Garth's. Garth was gone and she was relieved: she didn't want to confront the boy. She didn't want to look at him now, he was part of that group, the Billy Marsh, Jimmy Southwick gang. They might be at the police station, those two, for all she knew, there'd been petty thefts at the other burned barns, the police had questions. Had fifth-grade boys set the fires?

But he couldn't find the matching glove.

"I don't understand." Carol's face was scarlet, tears were threatening. "Isn't it enough you have Kurt? Garth's only a baby."

Ruth embraced the quivering woman; Carol was stiff in her arms. "I'm sorry," she said. "I have to do this. It may not mean anything."

Afterward she couldn't remember leaving the house, getting into her car, stopping by the police station with the glove. She only remembered it matched the other. But somehow she got home.

And was met with two messages. The second, the most important one, Emily said, had come minutes before. Even so, Ruth scolded Emily for not calling her at Carol's.

"But I did. You'd already left!"

Emily relayed the messages in order. The first was from the insurance inspector. "He said it was definitely faulty wiring that started the fire. One of the milking machines. It wasn't arson at all."

"I don't believe it," said Ruth, "but go on. Go on. The second message? The one you said is most important?"

A state trooper had tracked down a stolen car. "By chance, actually, Mom, he'd seen it weaving along the Northway. Two guys inside who failed a breath test but swore they didn't have any boy in the car. But, Mom, the police found a knapsack in the back, olive-green, with kids' books inside—and a map of Australia."

"Vic's!" Ruth screamed, "that was Vic's! Why didn't you tell them that!"

"I did!" Emily shouted. "You never listen to me, Mom."

And Ruth still wasn't listening, she dialed Chief Fallon. "It was Vic's, Vic's knapsack," she shouted over the phone. "But where's Vic? What did they do with Vic!"

No one could tell her. They were grilling the thieves, that was all they could do, the chief would call back with any news—that was all *he* could do. The troopers were keeping the knapsack for now. The drunks claimed they'd found it in a rest area.

Now Ruth was bawling, for the first time maybe since Vic's disappearance. The tears poured out, like someone had dumped a pail of boiling water over her head.

The only thing for it was to scrub the kitchen floor.

"But you only just washed it, Mom, yesterday," Emily said. "It's hardly dirty."

"But not with a toothbrush. I didn't scrub it with a toothbrush."

It felt good, down on her hands and knees. Like she was scrubbing away the sins, the sorrows of the world.

CHIEF FALLON had Garth there already. Colm had left his father with a cadaver, hobbled down to the police station where Fallon was holding the gloves—they made a pair all right, he said, looking pleased. They were all there: three fifth-grade boys, looking insolent, scared, poking one another, their feet shuffling the floor. Fallon was leaning back in a chair, talking softly, like he was their uncle. He said Southwick and Marsh had denied seeing Willy that night by the creek—until Ruth brought in the boxing glove. After that they broke down. Marsh had just confessed.

"So let's have it out, kids, the whole story," said Fallon, sinking back into his chair, his eyes half shut.

Garth punched Marsh in the ribs, said, "Lenny Swaggart was there too, it was his idea to go down there and box."

"Yeah," said Jimmy Southwick, "he was there all right. He's in seventh grade," he told Fallon, like that excused the others—they were led on by a "big kid."

"We fooled around till it got dark," Garth said.

"Was that a crime?" said Southwick.

But they had nothing to do with Willy, Garth said,

his voice loud, though his feet were moving, up and down, like on a treadmill, his snub nose twitching. "We just teased him a little, like we always do, I mean, it was fun, that's all."

"Fun to tease a boy who can't fight back? Who doesn't understand?" Colm said. "Fun to rub manure on a kid and steal his telescope?" He was getting hot-headed now, carried away, and Fallon put a hand on his arm.

"Go on," the chief said to the boys. He sank lower into his chair, in a minute he'd disappear. "So what happened exactly? What did you do to, you know? Knock him around a little?"

The boys looked at Garth like they'd let him tell the story. Make up the story, Colm thought. But Garth looked innocent.

"Nothing, we did nothing," he said in his loud young voice, his legs jogging in place, like he'd be out of here in a minute, if he kept moving. "We just went home."

"Kids," said Fallon after the boys were released, though he agreed with Colm they were holding something back. "Could've hit Willy with the glove, knocked him into the creek. Then run, scared." But what else could he do but let them go? Book a bunch of fifth graders? "Three scared kids."

He knew how it was, he said, he had a nephew around that age, "He don't know his left foot from his right. That's kids for you."

"Willy's dead," Colm said. "That's 'kids for you'?"

COLM AND RUTH were in her kitchen: he with a whiskey, she with coffee, her fourth cup, she needed it. She was barely holding on. To take her mind off Vic, who could be lying hurt, or dead (her heart turned over) in a woods somewhere, she made him go back over the story of the boys a second time, in case he'd omitted something, she said.

Sighing, fiddling with his glasses that looked permanently crooked since the Michigan ordeal, he repeated the story of the interview, adding, yes, a detail he'd forgotten.

"I knew you'd forget something," she accused.

"It was that blue pickup parked in the lower lot, it had a dent in the passenger door. Southwick remembered that detail—he'll make a lawyer like his father. Harold has a blue pickup, remember? I've seen it parked at the fire station. Fallon will check out the dent. He's about to close in on Harold."

"Anything more?" she said. "Think!"

He shook his head.

"But there is. I know it and you know it." It was Vic. She felt they were all holding out on her: Colm, Chief Fallon, even Emily and Sharon.

But he just waggled his head again—he was infuriating!—and poured himself a Pepsi and Guckenheimer, his third, she reminded him.

There had been more reporters, more sightings of Vic—that was all he could tell her. He was seen in a Getty station in the town of Saugerties, forty miles south of Albany. In a 7-Eleven east of Rochester, New York; in a shoe store up in Malone. The police were checking everything out. As for Bertha and her driver, they were out on bail till the hearing. Esther Dolley was being interrogated, though she was "too, too smooth," Colm said. "Claims she knew nothing about anything."

"She could have set the fires," Ruth said. "She had the motive, she wanted the farms developed." And then, her mind leaping from one thing to the next these days, "Did Chief Fallon question those kids? They could have set the fires!"

But Colm just spread his hands. Was he giving a blessing?

Pete had gotten his sister a lawyer, Ruth told him, her mind jumping again. "You won't guess who." And when Colm shook his head: "Hampton Southwick, Jimmy's father. He'll get her a psychologist, too, Pete says, that's what she really needs, and for once he's right."

Pete was still calling every hour: on the fifth call she'd made him hang up; she needed the line clear for Vic.

Now it was ringing again, the phone.

But it wasn't Vic.

"Something new about Garth," she told Colm, and Colm sprang to her elbow, though he could sit in the attic and hear Chief Fallon's booming voice.

Garth had come back with his brother Wilder, he had more to tell about Willy. The boys had left him on the bank, he was "having a fit"—Garth "remembered" that after he got home (after Wilder jogged his memory, Ruth thought). The kids got scared and took off. Yeah, he could've rolled into the creek, Garth admitted. They hadn't meant to hurt Willy.

"Goddamn kids," Fallon roared, "they need a hiding. Was Willy bleeding? I ask 'em. And the kid remembers, 'Yeah, he was, bleeding, yeah, bruised some, he'd got in a fight.' Something had ripped his pants, something sharp."

"The boots," Colm said, nodding at Ruth. "The fat man's boots."

"So they told him to take a swim, the Unsworth kid says, clean off the, uh, blood. They left him then, on the bank. They never thought he'd go and, you know."

"They just left him there, just left him," Ruth repeated, "knowing he was hurt, was having a seizure, that anything could happen. And never reported it!"

Colm put an arm around her shoulder.

The kid was crying in the end, said the chief, his voice thundering over the wire, and so was the mother. "She come running down to the station. She was quite—you know. I see I got my hands full. But what can I do? Ten-year-old kids?"

"Are we losing our children?" Ruth asked Colm after she hung up, her hands still trembling.

"You can only hope they learned something," he said. "The parents have to teach what's right—or wrong. I think Carol Unsworth is trying, or will, when she calms down."

"I feel sorry for her."

"It's about time."

"What do you mean by that?"

But he just stuck a tongue in his cheek.

She wanted to kick him. "Then who set the fires?

We're back to that. Bertha? That broker? Harold? Those kids? Oh it's Bertha, I'm sure of it! Mine, too.''

"Ruth.'' He looked at her under his thick brows. "Yours was faulty wiring. You know that. You said it was old, that milking machine.''

"Then why were there three other fires?'' She glared at him.

"They think the Charlebois fire might have been matches, didn't I tell you that?'' She shook her head, furious. "You know, those 'strike anywhere' kitchen matches? Jeez, those things are dangerous. Police found two empty boxes outside. Mice carry them around, they like the smell of the sulfur. Matches contact a kerosene rag and—boom!''

"You're telling me mice set those fires? Come on. Then who left the matches there in the first place. Not the farmer!''

Well, he couldn't tell her that, but he did know about Rupert Sheldrake, that British biologist; he'd just heard him on PBS. "His talk about habits, about animals. Like why the tits ate the cream—''

"The 'whats'?'' she said.

"Tits, they're a kind of chickadee. Anyway, back before War World Two, some tits began pecking the tops of the glass milk bottles and eating the cream, and suddenly, tits all over Britain and Europe were sucking up the cream from milk bottles. Same thing with rats, Sheldrake says. If lab rats learn a new trick in America, rats everywhere pick it up, learn it faster. Like it's telepathy or something.''

"So what's in it for the barn mice? I mean, ridiculous. Mice, matches, and mental telepathy. Mad!''

"Sure," he said. "The world goes wacky now and then. Mad season."

"I don't care," she said stubbornly. "I think it was deliberate, those fires. Someone left those matches there. To see what fate would do with them, maybe. Colm, I'm on a roller coaster. I'm so dizzy I don't know where I am, what I think! Thank God I have the cows. They're my grounding point. Though Charlotte's gone," she added sadly.

He nodded, his cheek ballooned with ice. Was that all he could do? Drink and nod? He gave a lopsided smile.

"Get your glasses fixed," she said. "You look like a clown."

She had to stay rational. When Vic was found she'd have to think straight. She poured more coffee.

"It's funny," she said, thinking of Brontë's novel. "After Bertha, Rochester's mad wife, burned the house down, herself with it, Rochester was blinded. And Jane found she was his equal, because he was maimed, he'd lost his power. They lived in a woods, on the 'outside.' Like this farm, maybe, once the heart of things, now on the 'outside,' right?"

"How do I fit into that?" he said, blinking through his crooked glasses, wanting to be part of her life, she saw that. "Am I Rochester? Or is he Pete?"

"Oh, Pete will always keep his power. Some men are like that. Besides, he's a city man now. He never did like farming—it's not all his fault. He'll come to see because of Bertha, and the kids. Of course he loves his children, I know that, he's not a bad man. He's offered me the whole farm if I won't prosecute Bertha.''

She was suddenly indignant. ''Won't prosecute? After that crazy woman took my child!''

''The whole farm? You'd like that.''

''I'd like my child more. A farm's nothing to a son.''

''I know.''

They sat in silence for a time. When she poured a sixth cup, he put his hand on the pot. She stuck hers over his glass, too, told him it worked both ways.

He said, ''You'll be too wound up to listen if Vic calls. Look, Ruth, I need to say something. About the farm. When Vic comes back—he will, you know. He probably escaped, out of that car. He could walk in here any minute. The second sight, my great-gran—''

''Oh, hell,'' she said, about the great-gran. ''If he escaped,'' she argued, ''if he's alive, if he's not hurt, he'd get to the police somehow.''

''He'd be afraid they might ship him back to his father. Kids' minds work that way.''

''But why would it take so long, all this time since they found the knapsack? Why wouldn't those men admit they'd given him a ride—if they hadn't hurt him?''

He had no answer for that.

She felt like a child, she needed consoling. She saw a spot of dirt she'd missed on the floor and went over to wipe it up.

Still on her knees, she said, ''He's alive. I have to cling to that. I have to believe that.''

He nodded. "As I was saying about the farm, when Vic comes home—"

"When Vic comes home, yes?"

"Jeez, am I talking to a scrublady?"

She got up, her knees were killing her anyway.

"Well, Tim's a help around the place," he said, "and Joey, the kids. But they have their own lives. What I'm saying is, you can't run the place alone."

"Not you too," she cried. "Not you wanting me to sell! You real estate pirate!"

"Down, woman! You've a mean temper, you know that? I've seen a side of you lately I never—"

"Finish your sentence, you sound like Fallon."

He smiled. "I mean, I'm thinking of leaving the body business. I've had it down to the bones. I'll find someone else to help Dad. I'm wondering if you'd take me on, just part-time, couple of hours a day, a second hired man. Out in the pasture—That barn manure, I might be allergic."

"You?" she said, incredulous. "You don't know one thing about farming."

"I could learn. I can pick stone good as anybody. And I know something about fathering. I mean, I've fathered my own dad. That's what it's been, really."

"I see. You've something more in mind than farming."

He looked at her winningly (he seemed to think). "Just consider, that's all, okay?"

"Okay."

But she couldn't really, not now. She couldn't concentrate on anything else, nothing in the world—because outside a small boy was trudging up the walk, she saw him through the window. He was dressed in a dirty T-shirt and raggedy blue shorts; his bleeding, dirt-streaked arms were pumping up and down.

At the last he broke into a run, crashed up the steps, fell, got up again, and burst through the door. She was out of her chair in a shot, to meet him.

"Vic!"

"Mom!"

He sobbed in her arms, clung to her like he'd break in a million pieces if she didn't hold on to him.

And she did, she did!

WHEN THE PHONE rang again, Marie this time, about Harold, found "slumped over his electric trains," Marie screamed—he'd shot himself in the head, Colm didn't call for Ruth. He couldn't keep a mother from her son, could he? They were out in the pasture, Vic wanted to see his pet calf, he'd neglected it, he felt bad, he'd worried it might have got burned. "From now on—" he promised, and they moved out of earshot.

"Hang on," Colm told Marie, "I'll be over," and hung up on her screaming. He called Fallon, the ambulance, and jumped in his car.

"Divine retribution?" he said, and thought of Bertha.

THIRTEEN

OVER HER DEAD BODY that woman would get off! Ruth beat a tattoo on the refrigerator door. Bertha was out on bail, thanks to Pete, but wouldn't come out of her house. She refused even to speak to the counselor Pete had hired, and tomorrow was the hearing. Pete was worried, he'd said on the phone, that his sister would do something desperate, shoot herself maybe, like poor Harold, though Ruth felt she wouldn't. Bertha might be crazy, but she was a survivor.

And not wholly crazy either, Ruth told Colm on the phone. Just "calculatingly" crazy. Ruth's mission was to see that the woman didn't get off on any plea of insanity.

And so she was planning to storm the place, see that Bertha got to the hearing. Did Colm want to come along?

He guessed so, he said. "Bertha? Jeez, Ruth. Not again." But had to sign off—a body had just arrived on the funeral home doorstep.

She didn't ask whose.

She got Vic off to school with his telescope, repaired now. He was something of a hero, telling and retelling the story of how he got away from the car thieves. And an amazing tale it was: she ached to hear it, shuddering to think what *might* have happened— denying the thought. They'd stopped at a Burger King, locked him in the car, his hands tied with shoelaces. He was able to break the laces, smash a rear window with a jack he found in the rear compartment, and climb out. Then hide in a Burger King trash barrel until the thieves gave up and left.

Each time he told the story there was another more colorful—scary!—detail, a bit of profanity the thieves had used, and Ruth, smiling in spite of herself, had to ask him to tone it down.

Of course in his panic he'd left his knapsack in the car, but old Ronsard wasn't mad at all, Vic said, she even asked him to give a demonstration of his telescope, though Ruth worried about Garth and the others, back in school. A boxing glove left on a creek bank couldn't prove they'd hurt Willy, was proof only of irresponsibility.

"I'm afraid they'll take it out on Vic," she told Emily.

The girl was making an elaborate hummus and sprouts sandwich to take for lunch; she and Wilder were turning vegetarian. They couldn't eat animal meat anymore, Emily said, it was like "being a cannibal."

"I don't think so," Emily said. "Wilder doesn't think so. It was Kurt made Garth confess—did you know that? Kurt said he'd knock Garth over the head if he didn't. He said, did Garth want to be like him, Kurt? And Kurt made Wilder take him down to the station. And Mom, remember, Garth told on the others. So if anybody's in trouble in school, it's Garth. Wilder says he's one scared kid."

Ruth guessed she was right.

Anyway, that fat man was just as responsible for Willy's death, Emily reminded her mother, waving a spoonful of yogurt. "The police know that, Mom."

"More responsible. He's a grown man!" Ruth cried.

Her nails dug into her palms to think of Kosciusko, to think of Belle. To think of Harold, even, too weak, too much the victim—of the fat man, of Marie with her new carpet, her orange drapes. Marie had moved in with Lucien now, that was a move in the right direction. At least Ruth hoped so. Only yesterday, when she'd gone over with baked ziti, Marie had a fit of hysteria: she yanked the ice out of the old Kelvinator, flung the watery cubes in the sink, said she couldn't "look at that thing one more christly minute," then collapsed in a pink heap on the floor. "Well, you have the insurance, you can get a new fridge," Ruth had said by way of consolation and promised to help her shop for it.

Probably Harold had thought of that insurance when he picked up his hunting rifle, shot himself through the brains. The note said Marie could sell his trains, they were antiques, would help pay off the new white carpet. Though Marie didn't know if she wanted to live in that house anymore. "He helped kill my mother!" she'd wailed.

"Vic's going to Unsworths' after school," Emily said, shoving her lunch into a paper bag. "Garth invited him. And Vic wants to go."

Ruth felt a sudden alarm. Was it Garth who'd invited him, or Carol?

Then squared her shoulders, she had to quit this.

Vic had stepped over some magical line now, as though the kidnapping, his running away, had aged him, emotionally if not physically. If he wanted to go he'd go. Carol would be there, at least.

Carol had called again last week, about renting the north pasture, and Sharon and Emily advised Ruth to let her. For one thing, the insurance wouldn't pay for two new milking machines. Extra income might even buy that plate cooler she'd read about, one that could save hundreds of dollars in energy costs. It was like getting a month's power for free, the papers said; the payoff time would be a year and a half at most.

She had dreams for the place now, as if the fire had been a cleansing, a chance to start over. She was trying to look at it that way.

But the thought of the other fires still nagged at her. "Mice, huh!" she said aloud, remembering Colm's crazy solution, the "strike anywhere" matches. Maybe Charlebois used those matches in the kitchen, thought he *might, possibly,* have left some in the barn, but the Ashers *definitely* didn't, they said, and their barn burned. She'd heard they were thinking of simply selling out. And the police were interrogating everyone—kids, Marie (about Harold), Esther Dolley—and no one would admit it. Of course they couldn't even get to Bertha to ask her. She was locked up in her house.

Well, Ruth determined, she'd get a confession out of that one.

The anger spit up again, like undigested milk, into her throat.

SHE PICKED Colm up at the funeral home, his Horizon was "down" again. At least he'd had his glasses straightened, he looked human now, more or less. He was pushing a corpse into a back room, a glimpse told her it was an old woman, her face was the color of sour milk. She didn't look closely in case it was someone she knew. Bertha?

He winked, he was so cavalier about death. She was glad when he wheeled the body out of sight, went to clean up. She waited in a shabby parlor, on the edge of a horsehair sofa that scratched her legs; the wallpaper wept with a hundred willow trees. Appropriate, she thought, for a mortuary. She could smell the formaldehyde. Why hadn't she waited in the car?

"I've got a battering ram in the garage," he said, emerging in royal blue corduroys and a kelly green sweater. "We can knock her door in." And she had to laugh, though she worried. What if Bertha *had* killed herself, lay dead even now, in the house? If that was why she wouldn't answer the door, the phone?

"I mean, her car's still in the driveway, she hasn't pulled a single dandelion in her yard."

She nodded at Colm's father, emerging from an inner sanctum in a gray jacket and wide blue tie, slightly askew. His hair stuck straight up in the back, like he'd been hit by lightning. A middle-aged couple was tiptoeing up on the porch, to pick out a box, she supposed. She wondered if Marie had chosen the oak, with Harold's train money. Only immediate family: Marie, Harold's relatives (Esther with the acrylic fingernails?) had been at the burial. Michelle stayed home with Lucien (poor Michelle, her daddy dead).

Kosciusko—who'd finally implicated Harold, but not his sister, Esther—was in custody.

The bereaved woman's sleeve brushed hers; the woman looked in her eyes, as if for sympathy. But Ruth couldn't relate. With Vic back, there was life in the house again, the daffodils were in bud. She nodded and plunged down the steps.

"And I'm glad," she told Colm, coming back to the present, to spring. "Bertha has a war on dandelions, you know. Even pulls mine up, and I like them. All that furry yellow stuff springing up in the grass! We'll have to make wine. Vitamin C for the cows."

"Won't they get drunk?" And then, when she tried to help him down the steps: "I can do it myself. See?" He jumped a step—then flailed his arms and banged into the side of her pickup.

"But I'm worried about what we'll find in the house."

"You're getting paranoid, Ruthie. We'll have to commit you and Bertha together. You'd give those nurses the runaround."

"I would."

She watched him ease his body into the pickup, groan, and rearrange his legs. "You could have helped," he accused.

Bertha's doors were locked, front and back. The house was shut up like a tomb, the shades were drawn on the windows. She feasted her eyes, though, on the dandelions, popping up everywhere on the greening lawn.

"What good will it do to break in?" Colm squinted

at the shut-up house. "The woman is loony, we know that."

"I'm convinced some of this is an act. She was in a couple of plays in school, remember?"

"Sure. She played Grandma in *The Sandbox*. Threw sand in people's eyes."

"In Community Players," she went on. "She did one show, small part, she has trouble memorizing lines. But she likes the limelight. Like I said, this could be an act. I've known her a long time."

"I knew her too. The way she hunted me down, she was loony back then. Add a megadose of religion—"

"Enough," said Ruth, and hushed him.

Bertha was inside, she was watching them, Ruth was sure of it. They had to get to her, make her talk to her lawyer, appear at the hearing. Pete would arrive at the last minute, he had an overnight sales meeting across the lake in Malone.

She didn't care what Colm thought. Bertha had to account for her actions, admit she was in the wrong. Harold had, hadn't he? By his suicide? But she didn't want that for Bertha.

Colm had found an opening: the cellar doors had no lock; they were warped, like their owner. Together they yanked, and the doors screeched open. She followed him down into the basement that smelled of dry rot and mildew. It was crammed with junk: a rusted iron bedpost, boxes and boxes of damp discolored cardboard, a warped pair of cross-country skis, three worn snow tires, a plastic tray of apples, wrapped, rotting. The chaos was unlike Bertha, whose house was usually immaculate, like she was determined to meet her maker with a scrubbed floor, a starched blouse, clean underwear.

Ruth wanted to run back out in the fresh air. Why had she come here? What was she thinking of, anyway?

Colm was on the narrow steps that climbed to the kitchen. He turned at the top. "Locked," his lips read.

She looked again at the cellar doors, at the apple tree at its entrance; already there were pale rosy buds that would break into the sweetest of spring scents. That very day Carol was to plant apple trees on the edge of her rented meadow. Would sheep eat apple trees? Nibble a bit, maybe.

Overhead the floorboards cracked, a voice squeaked through. "I know you're there. But you can't come in my house. I already have a visitor. He won't want to see you."

Colm said, "Who won't? Who's this visitor?"

"God," said Bertha. "God's here."

"Bertha, let us up," said Ruth, feeling the old alarm in her chest—was God here to take Bertha away? "We need to talk to you, Bertha. There are things you have to do. Do them for Pete—he's coming tomorrow. Now let us up."

There was no answer.

Ruth made a kissing sound in Colm's ear. He grimaced. But caught on.

"Bertha, it's me, Colm. I want to talk to you, Bertha. I'm sorry for, for a lot of things. I want to help you now, Bertha. You can let me up." He glanced back at Ruth. "Just me, Bertha? You said you wanted to see me?"

The silence upstairs was total. Not even a board creaking. Bertha was thinking it over. Ruth held her breath. They had to get the woman out of here, whatever it took.

Colm said, "Unlatch the door, Bertha."

Bertha said, "All right. But Ruth can't come. Only you, Colm. God doesn't want Ruth in here."

Ruth lifted her arms in surrender. Did Colm look smug? Well, she didn't want to be here either, she thought. She didn't want Bertha's god, a god that stole young boys from their mothers! Her own god was, well, out in the pasture with the cows, wasn't she?

But when the door opened, and then slammed again after Colm squeezed through, she panicked. It was like the walls were closing in on her, any minute they'd crush her into a mash of blood and dust.

Behind her something moved in a pile of old newspapers. A rat?

She hammered on the door, she wouldn't be left behind. "Colm! Bertha! Let me up, dammit! Let me in!"

The bolt slammed.

COLM WAS face to face with a woman he'd never seen. The outer trappings maybe, the short pearlike body, the dyed orangy hair, though it was hardly groomed now. He could see the gray where the dye had worn away with washing.

But it was the face he was least prepared for, something out of myth—Medusa came to mind, her snaky hair. Would she turn him to stone? She grabbed his lapels, a cigarette in her fingers; any minute he'd be on fire.

"I know you," she said. "I know your kind. Love them and then stamp on them."

"Bertha, I never—"

"Don't tell me. I have eyes. I have ears. I know how you all laughed at me in school, I know what you and that woman—"

"Ruth?" he said, he had to particularize, keep this dialogue grounded.

"Ruth," she said, crushing the cigarette into a saucer. "You've been scheming against me, you two. Trying to prove I set fires."

"Ruth's was electrical, Bertha. Nobody set it. We know it wasn't you. Elder's was set, though. Asher's, maybe Charlebois." He watched her closely. He was serious about those "strike anywhere" matches. But who put them there?

That stopped her a minute, she stumbled back against a chair; it tipped, he righted it, then moved off. For one thing, Bertha smelled—not of scent, but unwashed body. He could think of several figures of comparison.

"Charlebois," she said. "That French Canadian."

He was almost relieved to hear it, the old prejudice, she was sounding like Bertha again. He tried to make small talk, told about Marie moving back with her father.

She looked up at him, coy. "How do you know it wasn't Harold took Victor?" she said. "He's a Polack, you know that!" She corrected herself. "Was."

"Come on, Bertha, we know it was you. Ruth talked to Pete. He confirmed it, his lady friend. We have to face things. They'll go light on you if you own up."

"Anyone could say she was me! It could've been Marie." Her eyes narrowed at him, sly: the schoolgirl who'd followed into the locker room to borrow a quarter for a soda, hoping he'd have one with her. And never gave up when he wouldn't.

"Bertha." He looked in her eyes. She looked away, hurt. "When Vic got away from those guys—and he was damn lucky—he walked half the way. Hitchhiked the rest. He was desperate to get here. Anything could have happened to him, Bertha, a young kid like that. Did you think it through, what you did? Stealing him away? Leaving Ruth with that worry?"

He was leaning into her, never mind the smell. She had to realize something, Ruth was right.

Bertha was right, too, so she thought. She gazed down at her fingernails, buffed them, an old habit. Then she got up slowly, walked into the dining room. He followed her there. Last night's supper was still on the table, something half eaten, spilled on the lace tablecloth. A nub of a candle was smoldering in a centerpiece of paper roses. He went to blow it out, and she shoved him back.

Whoa! He was unprepared for that. The woman had muscle!

"Don't come near me," she said, her back hunched against a window. "I know what you are. You're a hypocrite."

"Bertha," he said, dropping into a highback chair. "Let's talk a minute. About you. About what will happen to you. Ruth is concerned about you, Bertha."

Bertha laughed.

"It's true, believe me. Now that Vic's back, she's trying to understand what made you do it." He'd be patient, try to be. He wanted to be done with this. "You were concerned, weren't you, about Vic's safety? That's why you did it?"

Bertha's tongue licked her upper lip, slowly came to rest in the corner of her mouth. "Yes. Why else do you think I did it?"

He noted the "I." "You have to be at that hearing tomorrow, Bertha. If you don't come, they'll think you're not sorry."

She got up, he could see the vertebrae stiffen, straighten, one by one. "I'm not sorry," she said, pacing her words. "What am I sorry about? I tried to save him! I almost did. You have to understand, Colm," she said, sounding reasonable now. "He was in danger, he'd be the next victim. If you hadn't interfered, he'd be safe now with Peter. It was that woman Pete took up with he ran away from."

"Safe from what, Bertha? We know who killed Belle Larocque. Safe from whom? People who can't face themselves, accept others as they are? Use God as a scapegoat?"

She was hunched over like she had a bellyache. There was something in the curve of her shoulder that looked vulnerable, soft. He got up, put his hand there.

For a minute she was still, crying softly now.

"I'll pick you up tomorrow," he said. "You can tell your story straight. You have a counselor, but you have to let him see you. Go to the hearing."

"I can't!" She jerked away from him, dashed out of the room and up the stairs. He saw there were holes in the backs of her purple socks.

He leaned his elbows on the banister. "Bertha, come down this goddamn minute. Quit this charade."

It was getting to be too much. He thought of Ruth waiting, probably pissed, in the basement. "Bertha? Be reasonable, Bertha!"

There was no answer, though he stood for ten minutes, and he decided to give up. So she didn't come to the hearing. They'd get her one way or another, wouldn't they? If the police couldn't do it, Pete would come get her, she was his sister. In a way Pete was implicated, wasn't he? It was still possible he had planted the idea in her head.

He went back to the kitchen, saw a mound of cookies there, dozens and dozens of cookies he hadn't noticed when he first walked in. That's what she'd been doing since she'd locked herself in here—baking cookies. Pretty soon she'd run out of ingredients, then she'd have to come out of the house. He took a bite of one, spit it out. What if it was laced with arsenic?

Stupid thought. The woman wasn't a murderer, not overtly, anyway. But he threw it in the trash, unlocked the cellar door, and Ruth literally fell in. He grabbed an elbow.

"She's upstairs," he told her. "I'm not going up after her. Suppose she gets me on a bed."

"It'd serve you right," she said. "Okay, it's my turn now. I've got an idea." She headed back down the cellar steps.

"Jeez, Ruth, where you going? It's no use, she's probably locked herself in."

But she was running around back to the bedroom window. "There's a big maple there. If we could surprise her..."

He followed, what else could he do? She was squinting at a maple, one of its limbs reached within a foot of an upstairs window, open on the crack. "I practically lived in trees as a kid," she said. "I could make this one, easy."

He'd like to offer, but he had this bad ankle. And there was his acrophobia. Heights made him want to throw up, dash himself into whatever lay below.

Anyway, she was already heaving herself up in the tree. She looked like a nymph, a bunch of new leaves in her tangled hair, her blue-jeaned legs kicking toward a higher limb. Even watching her made him woozy, so he focused on the window. Something was happening up there, he wasn't sure what. He watched, ready to warn her. It was like the window was misting with rain, turning darker, clouding up. Was Bertha coming out? Ready to knock Ruth down with a chair?

Then he saw what it was. "For chrissake, Ruth, I see smoke!"

"What?"

"Her window. It's smoke coming out of there. Look."

"Oh," she said, and swung up on the next limb.

"Come down, Ruth, you dumbbell!" he shouted. "You want to kill yourself?"

He went back in the house to call the fire shed, he was taking no chances. Twisted his one good ankle on a root but, oh hell. When he hung up he looked through the kitchen window for Ruth. She wasn't in the tree. He stumbled back around the house, Bertha's window was wide open, Ruth was inside. Jeez!

There was no way out now but to climb up himself. That damned Ruth! What had got into her, anyway? She used to have sense. He heaved himself up, he was so lightheaded he forgot to be sick. He crawled out on the branch by the window. He was dragging a dead limb with him, or was it the bum ankle?

And froze. "Ruth," he called. "They're coming. I can hear the sirens. Get out of there, Ruth. Ruth, I can't—"

He'd lost his footing: hung, helpless, his hands ripped. He imagined what it was like, the Chinese tortures, hanging by one's hands. Chinese, hell, he thought, the IRA did it, he'd heard of that, his own people. He measured the ground with his eyes—two stories down. The branch could crack and he'd be in the hospital for a month, a year. He could be paralyzed for life.

"Ruth!" he cried.

The beeper went off in his ear. "Answer me, Ruth!"

SHE'D SET the curtain on fire with a cigarette, she was still waving it in her hand. "Idiot," Ruth shouted. She wrenched down the curtains while Bertha babbled on about the Day of Judgment.

"You'd better get to yours," Ruth warned, raced into the bathroom, flung the smoldering curtain in the tub, turned on the shower. She stuck her arm under, she'd singed one wrist, it stung like a hundred bees.

"Bertha, you madwoman," she yelled and ran back in the bedroom with a glass of water.

Bertha was heaving pillows at the window, then a nightgown, a pair of pink slippers. The woman was bonkers, obsessed with her heaving, her eyes were red moons. Ruth tried to pull her out, toward the stairs, wrestled with her. Bertha flung herself at the window, then stopped, like she'd seen a stranger trying to get in. Smoke was coming out her ears.

Ruth grabbed a quilt, threw it over Bertha, dragged her to the shower, shoved her under and turned it on full blast. Her sister-in-law stood there, docile now, she wasn't about to burn up—her hair singed, stinking; stoic, her lips in a half grin. She held up a burned sleeve, watched, seemingly fascinated, as the flames sizzled out from the rush of water.

"It's not enough to put Vic's life in danger, you're trying to burn the house down. Us in it."

Bertha just stood there, looking like Frankenstein's mate.

Ruth ran back to the bedroom, threw the charred pillows out on the grass, heard Colm yell—what was he doing upside down on that branch? She heard sirens shrieking into the driveway, dashed back to the bathroom.

And realized what a fool she'd been, leaving the woman in there, alone.

Bertha had locked the door.

HOURS—WELL, maybe minutes—later, Colm saw Ruth standing under him, with Ed Swider and a ladder. "You were a big help," she complained, and he groaned.

"Where's Bertha?" he said. The men had the hose aimed at the upstairs window. "Hey, wait for me, Ruthie. Ruth?" But Ruth was running around the house after Ed. They had more urgent business than Colm Hanna, stuck, like a scared kitten, in a tree.

It was her fault, though, that he'd hurt the ankle, he was going to tell her so. If he could catch up with her.

He followed, limping, up the stairs. The leg was killing him—both legs, to tell the truth: he thought he'd sprained the other one. Upstairs the men were busting through the bathroom door.

And there was Bertha, wrapped in a bathrobe full of holes. Holy Robe, Colm thought, and swallowed the pun. Her hair was in a glittery hairnet, her cheeks rouged, her mouth a bow of red lipstick. There were burns on her neck and ankles, but she stepped out through the men, chin up, like they were her suitors, come to take her to a dance.

"I did nothing wrong," she told the ceiling. "I'll tell them that tomorrow, at the hearing. I don't need any lawyer. I have a higher judge."

And she moved past and down the stairs, went into the living room, lit a cigarette.

"I'm sorry the house is such a mess," she announced, waving the cigarette. "I've had things on my mind."

THEY WERE IN Ruth's kitchen that afternoon, she was making popovers, they outsmelled a dozen vases of jonquils. Outside the mud was drying up with the wind, the apple trees were in rosy bud, a dozen more going in where Carol was planting, with Wilder and Joey's help. Tim was supervising, his feed cap on backward (Colm admired it, a red rooster on green cloth—maybe Tim would swap for one of his). Joey did a somersault, kicked over the water pail, and Carol smiled, the first time he'd seen her smile maybe, she was still knocked out by her boys' involvement. The old man couldn't buy Kurt's way out of that one, though he'd probably appeal. Wilder had withheld evidence; so had Garth.

Carol Unsworth was taking over more than just a meadow: she'd share a life now with a Vermont farmwoman. Or vice versa, Colm thought: the Vermont farmer would share it with the city woman. Whether Ruth realized it or not, they needed each other.

Ruth hadn't mentioned *his* helping out in the pasture. And just as well, maybe. He could break both legs, sliding around on those cow patties. As for any inside help, well, he'd just have to wait and see.

"She's sticking with him, though," Ruth said, following his eyes. "That macho husband of hers. Because of the boys, they need family, she says. I only hope it works."

"Sticking together for the 'united front' doesn't always work." He was thinking of Pete, due at the house tomorrow for breakfast. Who was Ruth making the popovers for, anyway?

But she didn't really want to, she'd hinted, stick with Pete. Still, he worried. The girlfriend was back in New York. What if—?

He decided to intervene, a man had to show his colors, didn't he? Ruth was slow at taking hints. She was bent over the stove, he put a hand on her back, let it slide, slowly, down. Took a long breath, felt his bones give; waited for her to kick, like one of her bovines.

But she turned around. She was smiling, her nose was shiny with steam, she smelled a little of barn, she was beautiful.

Her lips tasted buttery, like popovers.

And just as they were drawing apart the door

banged open, people pounding into the kitchen for something to drink: Wilder and Emily—that smug look when he jumped back, like the girl had caught her mother going through her drawers. Tim joking with Joey: "You're gonna learn how to swim, man, I mean it—you want to go and drown on me, do ya?"

And Joey yelling, "I can, I can so swim, I swimmed in the beaver pond yestidday, down back the meadow."

And Tim had news: he'd just heard it at the local diner. "They searched that woman developer's car, found a caseload of Ohio Blue Tip matches in the trunk, at least eight boxes missing. What'd they call 'em? 'Strike—'?"

"Strike Anywhere," Colm said, looking at Ruth. "The mice love them. Leave the box open in the barn, and the mice'll carry them around, ripe for combustion."

"It was still arson," said Ruth. "You have to admit that. She obviously scattered them around. Maybe left a kerosene rag nearby. Leave it to 'chance' and keep her hands 'clean.' More than chance! Esther Dolley, that murderer!" she cried, thinking of the cows the Ashers, in particular, hadn't been able to get out of the barn.

"She'll be sorry. They'll give her the works," said Vic, coming into the house with a baby rabbit—while his mother protested, pink-cheeked, confused, talking too loud, too fast, too many things happening at once:

"Well at least get a box for the damn thing, Vic, before it drops all over the floor!"

"You can help me set up my telescope if you want," Vic told Wilder, worlds older now, ignoring his mother, carrying the rabbit upstairs in his arms. "Saturn's out tonight, in the southeast, under the moon. You can see the rings. You want to take a look?"

Everyone was talking at once, then, Sharon thumped down with the baby. "Mother, you can't let Vic have that rabbit upstairs!"

Ruth was running around like a madwoman (delete that word, Colm thought), stirring up a pitcher of lemonade, yanking out popovers. "They'll cool in a minute," she said (they weren't for Pete's breakfast after all). It was nice to see the way her hands worked: quick, deft, like they were independent of her thoughts. Like if they didn't keep moving, she might fall down.

But the hands kept moving. She smiled across the room at him—was she upset that he'd kissed her, with Pete coming tomorrow? She didn't look it. Sharon came over and dropped the baby in his lap. Whoa.

"Hold him, Colm, would you? While I get something to drink?"

He squinted down at a bare bottom, a tiny plump penis. Ruth, laughing: "Get him a diaper, Sharon!"

But it was too late. The yellowy liquid was spreading across his lap, seeping into his new blue corduroys.

"It's all right, love, it's all right, little fellow," Ruth murmured to the child, like Colm was the one who made him pee.

She scooped him up out of Colm's lap and looked closely into the child's chubby face, as though for the first time she was seeing what he really looked like.

Prove The Nameless
An Owen Keane Mystery

Obstructed View

Working for an Atlantic City newspaper, Owen Keane is intrigued by the unsolved murder of a local prominent family—even more so when the sole survivor asks him: why was *she* spared?

With his talent for uncovering murky pasts, Owen, ex-seminarian turned seeker of lost souls, starts digging. But to confront a killer, Owen must also face himself—and the myriad fears locked in the hearts of those trying to prove the nameless....

Terence Faherty

MYSTERY **WORLDWIDE LIBRARY** ®
™

WTF269

Take 3 books and a surprise gift FREE

SPECIAL LIMITED-TIME OFFER

Mail to: The Mystery Library™
3010 Walden Ave.
P.O. Box 1867
Buffalo, N.Y. 14240-1867

YES! Please send me 3 free books from the Mystery Library™ and my free surprise gift. Then send me 3 mystery books, first time in paperback, every month. Bill me only $4.19 per book plus 25¢ delivery and applicable sales tax, if any*. There is no minimum number of books I must purchase. I can always return a shipment at your expense and cancel my subscription. Even if I never buy another book from the Mystery Library™, the 3 free books and surprise gift are mine to keep forever.

415 BPY A3US

Name	(PLEASE PRINT)	
Address		Apt. No.
City	State	Zip

* Terms and prices subject to change without notice. N.Y. residents add applicable sales tax. This offer is limited to one order per household and not valid to present subscribers.

© 1990 Worldwide Library.

MYS-796

UNTIL IT HURTS
AN IKE AND ABBY MYSTERY

WHO'S GOT THE SHOOTER?

When a shotgun blast drops basketball superstar the Big Chill at Madison Square Garden, it's another murder for Ike and Abby, co-workers at TV's "Morning Watch." As the bickering exspouses dive into the world of New York's biggest hoop gods and into their strange rivalries on and off the court, a trigger-happy killer nearly cancels Ike and Abby permanently.

One thing is for certain: the divorced duo must keep moving because this killer is playing a game of sudden death.

Polly Whitney

MYSTERY WORLDWIDE LIBRARY®
TM

WPW272

The Drowning Pool

A WILLOW KING MYSTERY

Hard Labor

Willow King, civil servant, romance writer, amateur sleuth and wife of Scotland Yard detective, has a new baby daughter, plus all the worries that come with it. And then some. Not long after her child is delivered, Willow's doctor, Alexander Ringstead, is murdered.

Few women deal with postpartum depression by tracking a murderer, but Willow fears the danger is far from over. Digging into Ringstead's past, she comes to the disturbing conclusion that the killer is very close indeed....

Natasha Cooper

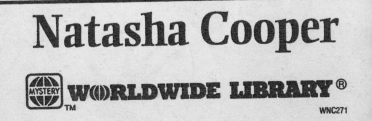
WORLDWIDE LIBRARY ®

WNC271